FORBIDDEN SECRETS

Payback Mountain– Book Five

Diane Benefiel

www.BOROUGHSPUBLISHINGGROUP.com

FORBIDDEN SECRETS
Copyright © 2025 Diane Benefiel

ISBN 978-1-957295-94-7

AI TRAINING IS NOT ALLOWED

TRIGGER NOTICE

Forbidden Secrets contains themes that may be difficult for some readers. While the story focuses on healing, love, and justice, it includes references to past sexual assault (off-page) and domestic abuse (discussed but not depicted in real time). These elements are integral to the characters' emotional journeys and are handled with care and respect.

If these topics are sensitive for you, please take care as you read. Your well-being always comes first.

To Grace, Sam, and Rose
You make the world brighter with your curiosity,
your sense of adventure, and your wide-open hearts.
Never stop exploring.

ACKNOWLEDGMENTS

Heartfelt thanks to child protection specialist Lae, who generously shared his professional expertise on child abuse investigations. His dedication to protecting children and making the world safer is truly inspiring.

I'm also deeply grateful to Officer Sandy, whose insights into law enforcement procedures continue to enrich my writing. She's always quick to remind me when I stray too far from reality in the name of creative license. I appreciate her keeping me honest.

Their contributions lend authenticity to my stories, and I am thankful for their guidance. All mistakes, of course, are entirely my own.

A special thank you to Michelle at Boroughs Publishing Group, who has been a sounding board, a champion of this series, and a source of unending patience during my slower-than-ideal writing process. My work is stronger because of her belief in it, and in me.

FORBIDDEN SECRETS

Some Secrets Refuse To Stay Buried

Melanie Brennan's world revolves around her daughter, and she's worked hard to build a life rooted in safety and love. But when a disturbing incident shakes their quiet town, Melanie turns to former FBI agent Gage Landry, the one man she shouldn't trust but can't ignore.

He's intense, protective, and far too perceptive for Melanie's comfort. Yet Gage sees through the walls she's built, and he refuses to back down from either the mystery at hand or the connection growing between them. But uncovering the truth may demand more than she's ready to give.

As long-buried secrets surface and danger looms closer, Melanie and Gage must learn to trust each other if they want to protect what matters most.

Set against the rugged backdrop of Sisters, California, *Forbidden Secrets* delivers emotional depth, pulse-pounding suspense, and the unforgettable power of found family.

CHAPTER ONE

"Where do you want this desk, Mel?" Paul asked.

"Office." Lugging the box with her printer, Melanie followed her mom, Donna, and stepdad, each holding an end of her desk, into the room that would be her writing space. She set the printer in a corner. A small room in a small house but a space specifically for writing. The thrill had yet to wane.

Added bonus? A French door that opened to a wide patio with a table and umbrella and incredible views of the jagged peaks of the Sierras that dominated the eastern sky. In the spring she and her little girl would fill terra-cotta pots with geraniums and petunias, or whatever pretty plants they fancied.

Melanie had bought the small house on the big piece of property at the end of Bluebell Lane, which sounded cute but was an unpaved road with nary a bluebell in sight. Maybe they'd see some in the spring.

Her house-purchasing timeline had been shortened significantly with the unexpected success of her book series. That success had also bought her time to see if she could make a living as a full-time author. Her stomach clenched at the thought. If she stuck to her budget and could finish her current manuscript and build on the success of her last release, then maybe she wouldn't have to find a day job.

Paul and Donna followed her outside, Donna brushing her hands on her jeans. "That's the last of the furniture. If we want to get the U-Haul back in time, we need to go."

"Thank you," Melanie told her parents. "I couldn't have done this without you."

Donna put her hands on her hips and scanned the area. "I know what's done is done, but I still don't like you being so far from town."

"I know, Mom. But we're not all that far, and this is what I want." Donna had been her rock for so many years, which made it doubly hard to withstand her disapproval of the house and property Mel had chosen.

Addy came tearing across the spotty grass of the yard as fast as her six-year-old legs could carry her. "Mom, Mom, Mom." "Mom" times three was Adelyn's new thing when she was excited. She skidded to a stop, dirt clinging to the knees of her jeans.

Grabbing Melanie's hand, she tugged. "Mom, there's a *pumpkin* in the garden. A real one. It's connected to a vine. Can I pick it? Can we make a jack-o'-lantern? Or a pie? I think there's a tomato plant too, and it has tomatoes on it. They're all shriveled up. Yuck. Tomatoes are gross."

"Hang on, Addy. Nana and Grandad have to leave."

Addy let go of Mel's hand to fling her arms around Donna. "Bye, Nana. Love you."

Paul crouched for his hug and Addy wrapped her arms around his neck. "Thank you for the new bed you got me."

Melanie moved in for her hugs. "Love you."

Donna hugged her back. "I'm glad you found what you wanted, my girl," she murmured. "We'll come back in the morning and help you get settled."

Once Donna and Paul had driven away, Addy took Melanie's hand. "C'mon, Mom. You *have* to come see the pumpkin."

Melanie allowed herself to be tugged across the yard. "Show me this pumpkin, then we're making tacos to celebrate our first dinner in our new house."

"I love tacos." Addy'd be happy with tacos for dinner seven days a week.

Melanie shivered, glad for the heavy flannel she wore. "It's getting cold."

"I'm not cold." How many times had Melanie heard that when she wanted to bundle her girl up?

The high wire fence bordering the garden probably meant deer were a problem. The gate hung open, and Addy pulled her across the uneven soil. A sad-looking tomato plant with a couple of sickly tomatoes, which did indeed look gross, grew at the end of one long row. Along the back fence that bordered the creek, a leafy vine had twined itself through the wire.

Addy pulled back a large leaf. "See? It's a pumpkin." Her gummy grin highlighted the recent loss of her top front baby teeth.

Melanie crouched to examine the bright orange pumpkin about the size of a soccer ball. "That's a terrific pumpkin. I wonder if there are more."

Addy began searching through leaves already turning brown with fall. "Do you think the person we bought the house from planted this pumpkin and forgot to take it with them?"

"The house was vacant for a year, so I think anything growing came up volunteer."

"What's volun– " Addy stilled, and Melanie followed her line of vision.

"*Mom*. It's a *dog* and it has a ball in its mouth."

A beautiful golden retriever stood at the open gate with a tennis ball clamped in its jaws, tail wagging. Knowing her daughter, Melanie laid a hand on her shoulder.

"What are the rules, Adelyn?"

"Don't get too close, let the dog come to you. Let it smell your hand. If there's an owner, ask permission." She glanced up. "Mom, I think it's a stray and needs a home. It found us because it wants to be part of our family."

Addy showed no subtlety in her campaign to get a dog. Maybe now that they were in their new house, who knew?

"Do you think a stray walks around with a ball in its mouth?"

"Maybe?"

They retraced their steps across the garden, the pumpkin forgotten. Addy approached the dog, talking to it in a soft voice. She stopped with her hand outstretched. The dog was having nothing to do with rules. Tail wagging its entire body, it gave Addy a quick sniff then shoved its head under her hand.

Addy went down on her knees and stroked the dog's head. "It's friendly, Mom. Do you think it's a girl or a boy? I wonder what its name is. I think it's a stray and needs a home." Still holding the ball, the dog dropped to the ground and rolled onto its back. Melanie could have sworn the dog sighed when Addy rubbed her belly.

"She's a girl and she's got a collar," Melanie pointed out. "I bet her people live on our road."

Melanie glanced at the house closest to them. Their place had uninspired architecture from the eighties with a basic stucco exterior while their nearest neighbor's home was gorgeous and made of wood with stone cladding and lots of windows. A creek ran between their properties.

The dog rolled to her feet and dropped the ball in front of Addy. Her gaze went from Addy to the ball, then back again.

"She wants me to throw it." Addy picked up the ball and tossed it high in the air.

The dog pounced on it and dropped it on her sneaker. This time when Addy threw the ball, it sailed over the wire fence. Dog and girl ran for the gate.

A sharp whistle pierced the air and the dog skidded to a stop. Her head whipped between where the ball had landed and the direction of the whistle. Seemingly unable to decide what to do, she collapsed on the ground.

Addy dropped next to the dog, who rolled so her big head lay in Addy's lap. Another whistle and the dog closed her eyes. Addy buried her hands in the dog's golden fur. They both looked in the direction of approaching footsteps.

A man stepped from the pine trees lining the creek.

Melanie blinked to clear her vision, convinced her imagination was playing tricks on her. The man looked exactly how she'd written Alaric, the brooding warrior hero of her romantasy series. If Hollywood ever came calling, this guy would land the role without an audition.

Long dark hair swept back from a high forehead. High cheekbones and a jaw that might have been carved from stone. Dark brows slashed over eyes that seemed to assess her like she was a threat, or an inconvenience. He looked to be in his mid-thirties, tall and lean with the kind of presence that made the air around him feel ten degrees cooler.

And he was scowling.

Great.

"C'mon, Pancake." His voice held a rough edge.

"Her name's Pancake? Why's her name Pancake?" Addy turned her face up to the man. Pancake opened one eye, then closed it, and gave a blissful groan when Addy stroked her neck.

His long pause had Melanie worried he was going to ignore Addy's question. When he finally spoke, it was like he had to force the words past his lips.

"Yeah, her name's Pancake. I'll let you guess why."

"I bet she likes to eat pancakes." Addy grinned. "She's not a very good listener."

"Right on both counts."

Telling herself firmly there was no way Alaric had come to life and lived next door, and deciding one of them had to demonstrate good manners, Melanie cleared her throat. "I'm Melanie, this is my daughter Adelyn." She gestured to the house across the gully. "We, ah, I guess we're neighbors."

There was a long searching look that made Melanie think he could read every thought in her head before his expression returned to neutral. "Gage."

He switched his attention to his now snoring dog.

"Aw, she's sleeping on my lap." Addy gently rubbed Pancake's nose with her finger.

"She's faking it. Pancake, get up." He nudged the dog with a booted toe.

"She can stay with us if she wants. I'm six and responsible. I'll take care of her." Addy must've realized inviting the dog to stay required parental approval because she asked, "Mom, can Pancake stay with us? Please?" Did every kid in America make "please" into a long drawn-out entreaty?

"Ah, no. Pancake belongs to Mister Gage and he wants to take her home. Why don't you find her ball and maybe we can coax her to her feet."

Addy scooted out from under the dog's massive head and trotted after the ball.

Gage jammed his hands in his pockets. His serious expression, which had barely eased when talking to Addy, returned. "Pancake likes kids and has trouble with boundaries. She bothers you, chase her off. She'll eventually get the message."

"You met my daughter. You're more at risk of her appropriating your dog than Pancake being shooed away."

Addy returned. "Here, Pancake, here. Here's your ball."

Pancake sprang to her feet and stood quivering, proving she had indeed been faking it. With the dog's attention laser-focused on the ball, Addy tossed it in the air and Pancake leaped to catch it.

Gage produced a leash from his pocket and snapped it onto the dog's collar. Pancake immediately dropped her head and stared at the ground, the ball in her mouth.

Gage tugged on the leash. "C'mon, Pancake." He raised his gaze to Mel's. "Now that she knows there's a kid here, it'll be a battle to keep her away."

"We like dogs. Pancake can visit us any time, right, Mom?"

Addy's utter confidence that Mel would back her up meant there wasn't a chance she'd disagree. "Yeah, we like dogs. Pancake is welcome."

Gage shook his head. "You say that now. You've been warned."

With the reluctant Pancake plodding after him, occasionally turning her head to gaze woefully at Addy, man and dog disappeared into the trees.

***

Wearing only sweatpants, Gage wandered into the kitchen, Pancake following him, her nails tapping on the tiles. He scrubbed a hand over his face. He'd thought he'd broken the cycle of night terrors, yet here he was with the groggy hangover from the nasty dream clouding his brain. At two in the morning he'd lunged up in bed, breath jammed in his throat, heart racing. He'd been back in that black hellhole, Tino standing over Rafe, fingers smeared red. Blood dripping from the long-bladed hunting knife forming a puddle in the dirt.

Tino, a cartel enforcer out of Mexico, was a sadistic motherfucker. The nightmare brought back horrific memories and made Gage queasy. Shackled to the wall, chains cutting into his skin. Straining with all his might to break free. Knowing escape from the compound was impossible. Tino had become the focus of his rage. Gage could only hope to somehow kill the evil bastard and take out as many of the others as he could before they ended him.

But he hadn't been able to do a goddamned thing to stop the twisted fuck from using that knife on his partner. The worst part had been the utter helplessness of watching Rafe die as the life drained out of him.

Head bent, Gage rubbed a hand across the back of his neck. The night terrors had left him alone for the past couple months. Maybe the bureau-mandated therapy had helped. But last night he'd been slammed back into the memories, and the aftereffect felt like his soul had been ripped from his body.

He dropped his hand and punched the start button on his coffeemaker and stared at it until the smell of fresh brew began to permeate the air.

Pancake headbutted the back of his leg.

"You're not subtle, you know that?" In the mudroom adjacent to the kitchen, he scooped dog food into her dish. She stared at the kibble, then at Gage. "It's your own damn fault. Vet says the canned shit makes your farts into toxic gas clouds. Now you get straight-up kibble." He could have sworn his dog sighed before giving up on the guilt trip and digging in.

Gage grabbed socks and a heavy shirt from a basket of clean clothes. He hated folding clothes. He also hated grocery shopping, but he liked to eat so that was another chore on the list for today. Socks on, he buttoned the shirt against the chill. Having inhaled her breakfast, Pancake nosed her way through the dog door. He didn't have a fenced yard, but his dog generally stayed close and did her business out in the trees, same spot every day so it was easy to clean up.

He returned to the kitchen and grabbed a mug from the cupboard. It had a heart around the sappy words "Best Brother Ever." It'd been a gift from Emery at Christmas.

Gage wasn't anyone's brother anymore, but he couldn't bring himself to toss it. His best friend's wife refused to leave him to his solitude and generally bullied him into attending family events. When he'd pointed out they weren't his family, her wounded look had stung. Which had been exactly her intent. Now the mug was somehow the one he reached for first. He filled it with coffee, blowing across the top before taking that first hit while standing at the sink and looking out the window.

The view never failed to center him. He figured living in the mountains helped him heal more than the therapy. There was Payback Mountain towering mightily behind the ridge that rose like a shelf about a quarter mile behind Bluebell Lane. The mountain sky was a deeper blue than any place he'd ever been, and the tall, shaggy pines swept up the slopes like an advancing army.

He often saw deer, and had even seen bear a couple times. When he and Rafael had been in that hole in the ground, he'd thought he wouldn't live long enough to see anything like that again. Rafe hadn't.

Gage took nothing in his life for granted.

He shifted his gaze to the house across the way. Meeting his neighbor had been like a sucker punch to the face. He didn't like having that kind of reaction to a woman. And the kid? Little Addy was a firecracker. She'd grinned up at him with twin dimples, her top teeth missing, and a light shining in her eyes that had him rubbing a hand over his heart. That's how kids should be. Happy and free, not worrying whether the electricity would stay on, or if your sister would survive her diagnosis.

Addy was a dead ringer for her mom, minus twenty-odd years. Same dark hair that was nearly black but not quite, same deep brown eyes with glints of gold, same pointed chin. Melanie hadn't smiled so he didn't know if the kid's dimples came down that side of the gene pool. And while Addy's hair went down her back, the mom's was cut short, a thick cap that left the long curve of her neck exposed.

It wasn't even eight and the older couple who'd been there the day before were coming up the driveway from where they'd parked a pickup truck. The woman carried a caddy of drinks and the old guy a white paper bag Gage would bet had the Three Sisters Bakery logo printed on it. He had a sudden craving for their blueberry lemon muffins. He didn't go to the bakery often because invariably there'd be some old geezer looking for someone to shoot the shit with. There wasn't much Gage disliked more than making idle conversation.

The kid ran out, her mom following her. The flash of a smile lit up Melanie's face. It packed a punch but was too far away to confirm dimples.

He turned over the thought that had occurred to him after meeting her the day before. After being rescued from the cartel, Gage had arrived in Sisters following a weeks-long hospital stay. He'd been in bad shape, lost too much blood. But he'd been alive. At the time, he'd wanted nothing more than to find somewhere dark to lick his wounds.

When he'd healed enough, at least physically, to be discharged, Shane had stepped in. His best friend from college, a brother in every way that mattered (hence the mug), Shane Keller had shown up at the hospital and informed Gage he was coming home with him to recover.

He'd loaded Gage in his pickup and taken him to Lone Pine Ranch near Sisters. Gage had been too beat down to put up much resistance. His mother had wanted him home, but she'd recently gotten married and didn't need to be worrying about him. Beyond that, he'd needed space, and the ranch had a helluva lot of space.

Gage's natural inclination was to keep people at a distance. Superficial relationships kept his life simple, and he liked simple. But staying at the ranch had meant Shane's friends showing up to hang out or help with a project. Somehow, he still wasn't sure how it'd happened, they'd made him part of what was essentially a family. And they hadn't let go.

The core of that group were the women, the three half-sisters, Delaney, Emery, and Cam. Over the past couple years they'd paired off. Emery and Shane had gotten hitched, while the other two had married the McGrath brothers, Delaney with Walker and Cam with Sawyer. The most recent wedding meant two others in their group, Owen and Keeley, had tied the knot. And now they were all having babies.

It was like none of them realized how precarious life could be. Anyone could be living in a normal family, safe and secure one moment, and the next the rug was pulled right out from under them, leaving them scrambling to survive.

He shook his head to clear it and focus on the thought that'd occurred to him. A few weeks before, Gage had been at the McGrath clan's Cider Mill Farm and Delaney'd mentioned a friend from high school was moving back to Sisters and had bought a house. The friend's name? Melanie Brennan. He hadn't gotten his neighbor's last name, and the name Melanie wasn't uncommon. But add in that she was about the right age and Delaney'd said she had a daughter, and Gage had a feeling he knew more about his neighbor than she might be comfortable with.

Over a decade ago, Delaney's Melanie had been at the heart of an atrocity that had rocked the community and sent Walker to prison, framed for a crime he hadn't committed. The crime? Sexual assault against Melanie.

Gage took a deep pull of his coffee, feeling the warmth spread through his chest. Because he had a background with federal law enforcement, he'd gone over the details of the case with Walker and his cop brother, Sawyer. Walker's conviction had eventually been overturned, but the perpetrator had never been caught. The injustice against Walker was bad enough, but that Gage's neighbor might've been the victim? Fucking infuriating.

Movement at her house snagged his attention. "Shit."

There were two doors that opened to his neighbor's patio, a French door at the far end and a slider that led to the kitchen at the other. His dog had planted her butt outside the kitchen, tail swishing, peering through the glass like a nosy neighbor. The door slid open and Addy kneeled on the threshold to embrace Pancake in what looked like a lovefest. When the mutual adoration was over, Addy rose and Pancake bounded inside like she'd been invited for a sleepover.

"Dammit." Pancake didn't only like pancakes. She would consume the entire contents of that bakery bag if given a chance.

He pulled on his running shoes and grabbed a leash. With a last hit of coffee, he left the house and followed the trail that wound through the trees and over the footbridge spanning the creek. He approached the back patio and the slider opened again.

Melanie stood, arm pointing. "Out, Pancake."

Addy's voice carried from inside. "But Mom, she can't help it if she's hungry."

"Adelyn, she just ate a whole croissant."

"Maybe she didn't have breakfast. Hey, she has my stuffie."

Pancake bolted through the door with a brightly colored toy in her mouth. He couldn't really blame the dog since the kid toy looked like a dog toy. Addy raced after her, which meant a fun game of chase to Pancake.

Before she could take off, Gage gave a sharp command. "Pancake, sit." Pancake skidded to a stop, and to her credit, sat with what looked to be a stuffed penguin clamped in her jaws. "Drop it."

Pancake shook her head.

Addy's peal of laughter rang through the morning air. "She understood you, Mister Gage. But she's still not a good listener."

Melanie had gone back in the house and returned with a pink coat. Addy pulled it on, her attention on Gage. She scrunched her nose. "Is your wife Mrs. Gage?"

"Addy, don't be rude."

"But I want to know."

"She's fine," Gage said, then addressed Addy. "Just Gage, no 'mister,' and there's no Mrs. Gage. Sorry about Pancake. She has a hard time overcoming her baser instincts." He motioned to the dog. "Drop it, Pancake."

"What are baser instincts?"

"Pancake's baser instinct is her desire for mayhem."

"Oh."

"And mayhem is a good word for what Pancake stirs up."

Melanie gave him a quick look. Her cardigan had slipped off one smooth shoulder to reveal the strap of a tank top. No bra strap made him wonder if she was wearing one. And he should definitely stop those thoughts. Any idea the hard punch of attraction the day before had been a one-off was definitively proven wrong. *Fuck.*

She cast an amused glance in his direction. Gage took it as a plus she didn't appear pissed about the croissant. "You're right that Pancake knows no boundaries. Has she had obedience training?"

"Several classes. She uses her manners only when she wants to."

Pancake dropped to the ground and began tugging at the penguin's wings.

"Hey, Pancake, give me my stuffie." Addy reached for it and Pancake was ready to play tug. Gage made a grab for her, but she evaded him and pulled the penguin from Addy's grip. Addy grabbed it again and in seconds the penguin was ripped open, and bits of fluff littered the patio pavers.

Gage expected tears, but Addy turned to him, eyes wide. "Is this mayhem?"

The kid killed him. "This is exactly mayhem."

He grabbed Pancake by the collar and snapped on her leash, saying in a firm voice, "No, Pancake."

"Yeah, Pancake," Addy said. "That's not nice."

Pancake didn't give a shit about Gage's admonishment, but ducked her head when Addy spoke.

The older couple came to the door to watch the drama. Great, an audience.

"Sorry, kid. It looks like I owe you a stuffed penguin."

"It's okay. Mom's good at fixing things. Maybe she can fix Puffy the Penguin."

Melanie was wearing black leggings, the deep green cardigan hanging below her hips. She bent down to gather the fluff. Gage liked a curvy woman and Melanie had good ones. He forced himself to look away from her perfect heart-shaped ass. Nope. Not going there. He didn't want to be attracted. He hadn't seen a husband or boyfriend, but that didn't mean there wasn't one. Even if she wasn't attached, Gage wasn't relationship material. He was finally feeling like he had his shit together and didn't need any more complications than those already dogging him.

Melanie rested her hands on her knees. "I don't think Puffy can be saved, Addy. We'll have to give him a proper burial."

"It's okay. Pancake thought we were playing." Addy looped an arm around Pancake's neck, ducking her head as she whispered in the dog's ear.

The older woman came out onto the patio, eyes narrowed at Gage. He knew a protective parent when he saw one. He handed Addy the leash. "Hold on to this a minute."

He crossed to the woman and held out his hand. "Gage Landry. Pancake and I live next door."

She shook his hand. "Donna Bukowski. I'm Melanie's mom. This is her stepdad, Paul."

Gage shook Paul's hand.

"We live in Sisters proper," Paul said. The guy looked to be about seventy and had an erect posture and a shrewd gaze. Gage pegged him as ex-military. "Mel or Addy need anything, they've got us."

"Got it. Sorry about Pancake. She's a thief and likes kids. I'll work on keeping her from bothering your daughter and granddaughter."

"I like dogs and can deal with Pancake." Melanie telegraphed a warning glance to her mom, then turned back to Gage. "Addy'd be heartbroken if she couldn't visit with her new bff."

"Yeah, I'd be heartbroken."

The two of them turning big brown eyes on him? He was positive there wasn't a man alive who could withstand their pull and he didn't like it.

"That doesn't mean she can come to your house and be a pain in the…butt." Melanie's raised brow said clearly he was on shaky ground.

He took the leash from Addy and Pancake did her best prisoner-facing-the-executioner walk. "C'mon, mooch. And don't even think about slow walking it." He gave a general wave and tugged Pancake to follow him.

CHAPTER TWO

"Bye, Mom. Bye, Pancake."

Melanie watched her little girl climb the steps to the bus with her green and pink backpack. Thursday had been move-in day, then Friday afternoon she and Addy had gone to Mill Creek Elementary, where they'd met her new teacher, Mrs. Delgado, who had shown them her classroom with its small-scale furniture and cheery bulletin boards.

It was hard being the new kid. Melanie could only hope the first graders weren't cliquish and would accept Addy for the terrific kid she was. For her first day, Melanie had wanted to drive her to school, but Addy'd been excited to ride the bus and then delighted when Pancake had joined them on their walk up the lane.

The kids from the house at the top of the road had been at the bus stop. The little girl was Olivia and her brother, Jordy. "He's nine and I'm six," Olivia told Addy.

Melanie'd been as thrilled as Addy when they'd learned Olivia was also in Mrs. Delgado's class.

The bus pulled away and Melanie waved while Pancake let out an unhappy howl. She dropped her hand on the dog's head. "You and me both, friend."

Melanie trudged up the driveway and around to the back patio. She paused to soak up the moment. She'd done it. She had a place where Addy could have the childhood she deserved. A place where her daughter could run wild and do kid things.

There was a barn with a run-down chicken coop. No chickens now, and to avoid being asked about them twenty times a day, she was waiting to tell Addy, but they'd get chicks once the weather warmed in the spring. Which would give her the time to work on repairs.

Then there was the fenced garden. She had so many plans for that. Add in the creek and the big oak tree in the yard with the tire swing, and there was so much for her little girl to explore and do.

Sure, they were a bit out of town and cell coverage was iffy and the house needed work. Lots of work. Runs to the grocery store would take longer. Addy would be taking the bus to school. But Melanie was determined this place would be good for them and worth every penny she'd scrimped and saved for years to afford.

In the house with a cup of tea, she considered the pile of carefully labeled boxes stacked in a corner of the living room. As much as she wanted to unpack, she resisted the temptation. Answering emails and fulfilling her social media obligations were the priority. Those chores were aspects of being a writer she didn't hate but didn't exactly love either.

At ten o'clock Melanie closed the lid to her laptop, tipping her head to stretch her neck. Posts were scheduled for the week, she'd responded to messages from readers, and sent an email to her editor. A half hour later, showered and with jeans replacing joggers for a trip to town, she was ready to go. Post office, hardware store, bank, then grocery store. If she could complete all her errands and be back by lunchtime, she'd have a couple hours to work on her manuscript before the bus brought Addy home. Maybe there'd be time to tackle unpacking a couple boxes before dinner.

She drove her smallish SUV along the winding road that connected Bluebell Lane to the town of Sisters and wondered again if she'd made the right choice in returning to her hometown. She'd been seventeen when she left Sisters. She and her mom had moved to Portland after her world had imploded.

She'd worked with her therapist to process and manage the memories—the hood thrown over her head, the sexual assault—but that didn't mean they didn't sometimes show up like a movie reel playing on repeat in her head.

Queen's "You're My Best Friend" blared from her phone, a welcome break from her tortured thoughts. Esmeralda Padilla was her go-to for getting out of her head.

Melanie tapped the accept button on her steering wheel. "Hey, friend."

"Mel, guess what? I have a *date*. A real date that's not a sympathy date."

Melanie smiled as her friend's voice filled the car. "A non-sympathy date is awesome." Sweet and kind and radiating girl-next-door charm, Esme never had trouble attracting attention. The problem was her inability to say no. She hated hurting anyone's feelings, which had led to too many dates completely lacking in sparkage.

"That's the best part. It was totally organic," Esme gushed. "Isla and I were at the park and he was there with his daughter. His name is Andres and he's a single dad. He works from home doing tech work. We met up at the park a few more times and yesterday he asked me out. We still have to work out what day, but I'm excited."

"I can tell you like him."

"I do. But I'm shutting up about him until I give you the post-date analysis because I don't want to jinx it." Esme took a breath. "Tell me all about you and my Addy and how you're surviving up in the mountains."

She made it sound like moving to Sisters meant leaving civilization behind.

"Sisters is not the wilderness, Esme, as you'll see when you visit."

"You don't exactly live in town, right? So it's really the wilderness."

"Not in town, but I'm not out in the middle of the woods, either. Promise."

"Have you seen a bear? Remember that reel I shared with you? That bear got into someone's car and made a stinking mess. I read up on it and bears break into cars because they're looking for food. Make sure you don't leave snacks in the car."

"Got it, no snacks. There's really nothing to worry about." Esme was convinced living in the mountains was a constant battle of human versus nature. She regularly forwarded Mel videos of wild animals doing all sorts of crazy things, usually because the people involved were being stupid.

"We're settling in. Mom and Paul have helped a lot. Our closest neighbor has a goofy golden retriever who visits. Addy adores her." Melanie shared Pancake's antics with the penguin and had Esme giggling over the phone. "And all that was after Addy had let her in the house and she wolfed down a croissant."

"I want to meet this dog. What are her owners like?"

For having only spoken to Gage on two occasions, he'd certainly taken up a lot of space in her head the past couple days.

"As far as I know, only one owner. Male. I'd guess the younger side of mid-thirties. Addy asked him straight out if he was married. He's not.

"Hmm. Single man with a dog. What's he like?" Esme had a sparkly-hearts-and-rainbows romantic streak and Melanie already knew where this was heading.

"TBD. I only just met him, and interactions have been centered around Pancake. That's the dog."

"He named his dog Pancake? I like him already."

"He doesn't really seem like a golden retriever kind of guy who'd name his dog Pancake. I'd peg him more of a German shepherd named Brutus type."

"Maybe he's alpha with a good heart under a rough exterior. Tell me what this neighbor looks like and then I'll need updates on his personality so I can decide if he's a good match for you."

"Esmeralda Alondra Padilla, I am not looking for a boyfriend."

"The best time to find one is when you're not looking. Is he hot?"

"Way hot."

"Details, please."

Melanie briefly debated sharing her original impression of Gage. It somehow made her feel vulnerable, but Esme was her bestie. "Okay, this will sound crazy, but he's Alaric."

"What do you mean, he's Alaric? How can he be Alaric?"

"I swear it's true. Gage is exactly how I imagined my main character. Same tall, rangy build. Same cheekbones. Even his hair is the same. Not long down his back like Alaric, but with a wave and combed back from a high forehead. The cover model on my books is good, but my neighbor beats him, hands down."

"Are you freaking kidding me? That cover model is all green-eyed and smoldery. I want a magic wand to turn him into a real dude. And you're telling me your neighbor is hotter?"

"Oh yeah. I didn't see what color his eyes are, though. But he has this look that says 'fuck around and find out' that makes me want to do exactly that."

"Ooh, that gave me a shiver." Esme's voice dropped. "I can't believe you've moved next door to your hero."

"*I know*. I'm playing it cool around him because I don't want to start babbling and make a fool of myself. Plus, he seems to like Addy, but he barely speaks to me."

Melanie arrived at the first stoplight on Main Street. The old buildings from the town's gold rush past gave her a pang. She'd missed her hometown.

"Now I'm even more excited we're coming for Halloween and I can meet Alaric in person."

"Ha. You have no subtlety, Esme, but we're looking forward to your visit. Addy will be thrilled having Isla for an entire weekend."

"Isla and I are looking forward to it, too. But now for the serious stuff. Have you contacted Delaney?"

Mel's emotions concerning Delaney and Walker were a jumbled mess.

As kids, she and Delaney Bryant had been friends, and Melanie had sometimes hung out with Delaney and her bestie Keeley while they explored the creek and orchards at Cider Mill Farm.

For one birthday party they'd camped overnight in a big tent in the grassy meadow. The farm belonged to Delaney's family and Melanie'd heard that her grandmother Clara, the matriarch, had passed ownership to Delaney and her two sisters.

Melanie was curious to hear the story of the sisters because when they'd been kids, Delaney'd lived at the farm with her grandmother and there hadn't been any sisters.

"I haven't yet, but I will. I need to apologize to Walker."

"You have nothing to apologize for, Mel."

"I feel like I do. He lost two years of his life behind bars. I should have been able to convince the jury it wasn't him."

With evidence from a DNA match, Walker McGrath was put on trial and convicted.

Nobody would listen when she'd insisted Walker wasn't her attacker. She hadn't had solid evidence to support his innocence, only the knowledge he was a decent man and a firm conviction the man who'd assaulted her lacked Walker's height and muscled frame. Melanie'd returned to Sisters for the trial and even though she'd defended Walker, he'd been convicted and sentenced to prison.

With no alibi, the DNA match had been all the jury had needed to decide Walker's guilt.

"Walker being sent to prison wasn't your fault, and if he's as upright as you claim, he'll say the same. It's the other thing I'm more worried about."

"You don't need to worry about me."

"Telling me not to worry doesn't make me not worry. I know I've said this before, but I need to say it again." Esme paused and Melanie thought she was gathering a full head of steam. "You want to find the fucking bastard who raped you. I get that. I do. He shouldn't be free to live his life and not be held accountable. If he still lives in Sisters and hasn't died a violent and painful death like he deserves, preferably with his dick chopped off and fed to wild dogs, he'll be supremely anxious when he learns you're back. You could uncover who he is and out him and jeopardize whatever life he's built for himself. He's used violence before, so what's to stop him from using it again if he thinks you're a threat? What all that means is I want you to promise me you'll be careful."

"I will, Es. Promise. I've got Addy to think about too. I'll be careful."

"You better. There are only a few people I love, but you're one of them and I want you safe."

"I love you too. Best of luck on your date. You should wear that blue sweater that makes your boobs look fantastic. I'll expect a full recap."

"I was debating between the blue sweater and the red one, and now you've decided for me, so thanks for that. Bye, friend."

Melanie disconnected the call. Steering toward the post office, she considered what Esme had said. Was it dangerous to try to identify the man who'd assaulted her? She didn't think so, and the injustice of what had happened ate at her. She had to do something.

She hated that like so many women, she'd felt shame after being assaulted. Then there were those who'd insinuated the blame was somehow hers. Sheriff Grafton had commented on the low-cut top she wore that night, as if a hint of cleavage excused a man's violence. She'd thought the outfit was cute, maybe a little sexy. But if you followed his logic, men weren't responsible for their actions and it was up to women to stop them.

That twisted thinking had nearly drowned her. Back then, the shame, anger, and self-doubt had come in relentless waves. She'd felt like she was drowning, constantly struggling to keep her head above water. Therapy, at her mother's insistence, had helped Melanie find her footing again. Running off to Portland had been a survival move. Now, she was done running.

The blame belonged solely to the man who'd assaulted her. He was the one who should feel ashamed. He should live with the humiliation of being exposed for exactly what he was—a rapist.

Walker had finally been exonerated. Sheriff Neil Grafton, the man who'd swapped DNA results and let an innocent young man stand trial, had been convicted of tampering with evidence. The disgraced former sheriff had never revealed whose name had actually matched the rape kit and was currently rotting in a state prison.

Maybe she should pay him a visit.

Melanie tried to bring her thoughts back to the present. She turned into the little lot beside the post office and parked.

After waiting through the short line, she turned in a change-of-address form and set up a PO Box for her writing business. Next stop was Sisters Hardware. Paul would fix the toilet if she asked him. She knew he would. But she was a homeowner now, and if her toilet wouldn't stop running, it was up to her to fix it. She'd watched a video explaining the process step by step and it looked doable.

Wandering the aisles of the hardware store felt different now that she owned her home. Every display sparked an idea for how to spruce up the plain little house and make it more theirs. Her gaze lingered on a wall of cheerful paint chips. That lotus yellow would be perfect for Addy's room. Bright and sunny. Maybe they could add some stenciled stars or hearts in a contrasting color.

Turning a corner, she spotted a kid's wooden desk with a hutch and a matching chair. Simple, sturdy. The kind of space where a little girl could draw or do homework. She liked that the top was hinged and lifted for storage. Perfect for crayons and treasures. They could paint the desk together and maybe do some stenciling there too.

She wrestled the desk set into her cart and made herself walk past the paint section without stopping. Addy deserved to help choose the colors for her room and the desk. They'd assemble the desk, then pick out the colors together.

Melanie had almost escaped the home improvement area until a bathroom display sucked her in with ideas for sprucing up the dingy bathrooms. Twenty minutes later she forced herself to hit the brakes. She'd add the pretty mint green with white trim to her idea board for the house, but there were other things that needed to take priority over the bathroom. Like painting the outside and replacing the roof.

Paint was peeling on the window trim and eaves, and she'd known the roof was old when she bought the house. That's how she'd gotten such a good deal on the price. She hadn't seen any signs of leaks so fingers crossed it would stay that way until she could get to it.

She finally made it to the plumbing aisle, which wasn't nearly as interesting as choosing paint colors. Melanie studied the information on the back packaging for a toilet flapper.

"Hey."

Holy hotness. Gage Landry stood with his hands in his pockets, looking all ruggedly handsome in his faded blue jeans, his jacket open over a shirt of charcoal gray, dark hair combed back from his forehead. And dammit, this close she could see his eyes were green, a deep forest green fringed with spiky eyelashes.

She was beginning to wonder if she'd somehow imagined her character into being. Put a longbow over his shoulder and a broadsword at his side, and he was Alaric, warrior defender of Vaelora, queen of Balendon.

Dark brows winged up in question because, yes, she was staring.

"Hi, neighbor," she said, fighting a blush.

"Problem with your toilet?"

Toilet. Focus on the toilet. "Yep. It keeps running."

His fingers brushed hers as he reached for the package. A jolt zipped up her arm like a live electrical current.

Good lord. She'd written the "electrifying touch" trope a dozen times in her novels. But she never believed it happened in real life. But here she was, living proof, with the tingles still skittering through her system. Her pulse kicked and awareness flooded through her, more intense than anything she'd ever put on the page.

Gage, however, appeared oblivious. He studied the contents before handing back the package. "You don't need this."

She frowned, taking it carefully so as not to touch him again. Her heart couldn't take another bolt of lightning. "A plumber guy on YouTube says I should replace the flapper. But this kit has a fill valve as well as the flapper and now I'm wondering if I need to replace that too."

"You only need the flapper."

Even his voice was yummy—low and gravelly. She cleared her throat. "But what if that doesn't fix the problem? What if there's something else going on?"

Gage shook his head. "It's the flapper. Replace it and you're good."

She turned over the package to again scrutinize the back information. "It doesn't say what tools I'll need."

"You don't need tools." His brows came down in a scowl. "Want me to replace it?"

"No." Her refusal was abrupt. "But thank you. I can do it myself."

"Yeah, you can."

Was he offended? He didn't look like the type to be easily offended, but you never knew. Some men thought a Y chromosome was required to do household repairs, but she could learn like any guy. It was her house and she'd figure out how to take care of it.

Gage glanced at the desk set in her cart, then leaned closer to read the label. "You will need tools for this."

"What tools?"

He tapped the sticker. "The ones listed here."

"Oh." She scrutinized the list. Screw gun, wood glue, clamps. The desk project was more involved than she'd anticipated. "I'll have to borrow these things from Paul, but when I ask him, he'll want to put it together for me." She cast a hasty glance at the man at her elbow. "Not that that's a bad thing. I love him to bits, but he can be super insistent that his way is best."

Gage looked at her thoughtfully. "I have the tools listed. Let me know if you want to borrow them. No offers of help included."

"Oh, thanks. That would be nice."

He raised his hand in a brief wave and walked away toward the lumber section. She rolled her eyes when she realized she'd been staring at his butt.

CHAPTER THREE

Melanie pushed her cart to the checkout. An employee helped her wrangle the bulky box with the desk into the trunk of her car. She tossed the flapper kit next to it – no fill valve, just the flapper, thank you very much, hot neighbor. Deciding to walk the couple blocks to Sierra Valley Bank, she circled the building to the covered boardwalk that ran the length of Main Street.

Sisters was in full-on fall mode. Driving into town, she'd been talking with Esme and the scenery hadn't registered. But now? Wow. The sky was a deep mountain blue, and a light breeze stirred the trees cloaked in oranges and reds brought out by the cool October temperatures.

Along Main Street, shops were decorated with pumpkins, some ghost white, some dusky green, and others bright traditional orange. Half barrels planted with marigolds and chrysanthemums carried the theme with colors ranging from yellow to rust. The faint whiff of woodsmoke made her think of a cozy fireplace and hot chocolate. Pumpkin spice season was in full swing.

She stopped to study a flyer taped inside a shop window. Cider Mill Farm encouraged visitors to enjoy autumn by spending a day at the farm. The photos of the rustic cider mill and packing shed brought back memories from her childhood.

Open to the public Friday through Sunday, visitors could pick their own apples and pears, enjoy hard cider tasting, and listen to live music. According to the flyer, there was a gift shop, a hard cider operation, and the café bakery was stocked with pastries and pies made from fruit grown on the farm.

Delaney had reached out by email a while back, but at the time, Melanie hadn't been ready. She hadn't been in a place to face the emotional fallout so she'd suggested they meet up once she got settled.

Well, here she was, and it was time. Delaney and Walker deserved a real conversation. They were looking for closure, as Melanie was. That meant offering Walker an overdue apology.

And beyond that, she wanted to understand. How had he finally been exonerated? What had brought the truth to light after all these years?

She continued her walk. A man with dark skin and a halo of white hair stood next to a ladder, hands on his hips. He gave her a considering look, then pointed. "What d'ya think?"

She tipped her head back and gave a startled yelp. "What the heck are those? Are they alive?" Black, lumpy forms hung from the rafters above the boardwalk. One blinked beady red eyes, and another extended its wings. Bats. Ugh.

The man's face split with a grin as he cackled and slapped his hands together. "That's exactly what I want. Scare the bejesus out of folks. Not real, by the way."

"Scared the bejesus out of me so I guess they work."

"You betchya. Gonna hang a vampire from the post next."

"Well, good luck." She edged past and left him to his efforts to scare shoppers into heart attacks.

She wasn't the only one out enjoying the day. Touristy types strolled by, checking out window displays and wandering into shops.

Melanie pushed open the bank's double glass doors and stepped into the lobby. After talking with the receptionist, she was directed to a seating area and asked to wait for a customer service representative.

She nearly walked out the door when she saw the woman calling her name. Rhonda Sherman stood with a fake smile and fake eyelashes and the same snooty look she'd had in high school. Melanie had known running into unpleasant people from her past was a risk of moving back to Sisters. But she was stronger now and could deal with whatever came her way. At least that's what she told herself.

Now she had the opportunity to test that theory.

She rose to her feet. "Hello, Rhonda." She saw from her nametag that Rhonda's last name was now Lockwood, which meant she'd married her high school sweetheart. Rhonda had been cute in high school with sandy brown hair and a compact, curvy body. She'd been one of a clique of mean girls that had included Rhonda's best friend Josie Whitlock. Those girls had made life miserable for so many others.

Rhonda's hair was artfully arranged with blonde highlights and tawny lowlights, and her makeup was beautifully done. Melanie felt like a female lumberjack in her jeans, ankle boots, and flannel shirt, and didn't have on a speck of makeup. But she was here to open a bank account, not revisit insecurities from high school.

"Hello, Melanie. Right this way." Rhonda led the way to a desk and motioned to a chair. "Have a seat. I've helped your mother set up an investment account. I was surprised when she said you were moving back after so many years."

A framed photo sat next to a computer monitor, Rhonda, smiling next to Joshua Lockwood, a teenage boy standing between them. Melanie guessed the boy was thirteen or fourteen, probably their son.

Rhonda tapped on her phone without looking up, then set it aside. Melanie drummed her fingers against her knee. She hadn't come back to Sisters to sit quietly. Rhonda had been at the bootlegger that night—the night everything changed.

No time like the present.

"Rhonda," she began, voice steady, "you were at the bootlegger the night I was attacked. I remember you and Josie hanging out with Chase Bradford and Greg Delano. I'd like to know what you remember."

Rhonda looked up slowly, her expression unreadable.

Rhonda and Greg had done more than hang out. Even though Rhonda had recently gotten back together with Josh, she'd cuddled up on Greg's lap, making out next to the fire. Melanie pressed on. "I need your help to understand what happened that night. What you saw. What you know."

Rhonda's hands were frozen, hovering over the keys. Melanie didn't understand the flash of alarm on her face.

"You're mistaken. I wasn't hanging out with Chase and Greg."

"I could swear you were." Melanie frowned. "One reason I came back to Sisters is to identify who assaulted me. I want to talk with the people who were at the bootlegger that night. I'm looking for clues. Maybe I can uncover details the detectives missed."

"There's nothing I can tell you." Eyes flashing, she bent forward and hissed, "You already did enough damage to this town, you'd best leave that alone."

Melenie narrowed her eyes. There it was, blaming the victim of an assault for how it played out in a small town. She already regretted putting value in the idea of having her money in a local institution.

Rhonda's hands fisted, knuckles white. She took a deep breath and Melanie thought she was searching for calm. "Now, what kind of account are you interested in, Melanie? Is it still Brennan? I heard you have a daughter, but not everyone takes their husband's name."

"It's still Brennan. I want to open checking and savings accounts and start the process of transferring funds from my current bank."

"Is there anyone you want to add to the account?"

"Nope." Melanie wasn't about to satisfy Rhonda's curiosity about her marital status.

She filled in forms and signed documents, then dug in her purse for her driver's license.

Rhonda finished setting up her accounts and gave Melanie a forced smile. "Be sure to let me know if you need any of the other services our bank can offer you."

She squared her shoulders and reminded herself of her goal. "Would you like to get lunch sometime?"

Rhonda reared back like Melanie had slapped her. "No, no." Her face flamed red and her voice was stiff. "I can't meet for lunch today. I mean ever. I'm too busy for that."

"Okay. Let me know if you change your mind." What had flustered Rhonda? And why lie about who she'd hung with at the bootlegger?

Melanie made her way to the door, pondering Rhonda's reaction. "Melanie, wait." A tall man she immediately recognized approached. Chase Bradford.

First Rhonda, now Chase. The ghosts from her past were making an appearance.

Chase Bradford still looked like the golden boy quarterback who'd taken Sierra High to the state championships. Broad shoulders, a firm jaw with conventionally handsome features. He'd filled out, and a bump on the bridge of his nose suggested it had been broken somewhere along the way.

Back then, he'd always had a calculating edge with watchful eyes that seemed to size people up, probing for weakness. No doubt that had been an asset on the football field, but it had made her uneasy, especially when he'd been interested in her.

"Hello, Chase."

She kept her tone even, though her pulse jumped. Afterward the bootlegger, he and the others—Greg Delano, Mateo Reynoso, and Walker McGrath among them—had all given cheek swabs for DNA testing. She recalled some had been reluctant, but there'd been peer pressure in the form of *what do you have to hide?*

She still wondered who had truly wanted justice, and who had something to lose.

"I couldn't believe it when I saw you in the lobby. I see your mom every now and then when she comes in. Are you visiting?" His smile oozed charm and confidence, but she suppressed a shiver. Something about him suggested darkness under the surface.

"Not visiting. I moved back to town last week."

"No kidding?" Why did she get the feeling he wasn't actually surprised? "If that's the case, I'm happy to welcome you home. Did you choose our fine establishment for your banking needs?"

"I opened checking and savings accounts. Do you work here?"

He gave a self-deprecating laugh. "I'm bank president."

She must have looked surprised because he shrugged. "I know it's hard to believe when I wasn't the best student in high school. I certainly wasn't brainy like you. But I want to serve my community, and I find banking one of the best ways to do that."

A memory surfaced of Chase during senior year boasting that his dad was bank president and on the city council. Hadn't George Bradford also served as mayor of Sisters at some point?

Chase looked at her expectantly.

"Um, good for you."

Another customer approached the door. Melanie moved to the side to let her by, and Chase opened the door. "Good to see you, Mrs. Martinez. Have a nice day."

Melanie wanted to follow the woman out of the bank. Chase was pleasant, charming even, and so different from how he'd been in high school when she'd found him self-absorbed, even mean on occasion. But if she and Addy wanted to belong to the community, she needed to put in the effort to make friends.

"What brings you back to Sisters?" Chase asked. "You're probably used to the big city, and as much as I love my hometown, there's not much to do here."

"I have a daughter. We wanted to live near my mom and stepdad."

Chase's gaze sharpened. "Are you married?"

He was certainly more direct than Rhonda.

"No. Adelyn's dad and I aren't together." She gave herself a mental push. She knew how to be social. "What about you, Chase? What's been going on in your life besides earning the impressive job title of bank president?"

"How much time you got?" He gave an aw-shucks laugh that seemed forced. "Just kidding. Why don't you come to my office and we can catch up. I'll even spring for a cup of coffee." He gave her a wink.

In high school, Chase had run with the jock crowd. She'd found his behavior erratic. On one occasion, Greg and another football player had been mocking Thad Stimson, a boy with a stutter, and Chase intervened to shut them down. Then days later she turned into a nearly empty hall to see him body check Thad into a wall of lockers and walk away.

Maybe he'd matured. Most people weren't the best version of themselves in high school and worked to be better as adults.

"Sure, that sounds nice."

She followed him to his office where he stood aside for her to enter.

He started to close the door.

"Leave the door open, please."

Something flashed in his eyes, but then he smiled and it was gone. His tone was laced with concern. "I'm sorry, did, ah, what happened make you nervous around men? Perfectly understandable, if that's the case."

Maybe it had, but no way was that something she'd discuss with Chase. "I prefer the door open. Thanks."

He motioned her to a chair while he walked around his desk to sit. His gaze traveled over her, and she shifted in her seat.

"Sorry. If you don't mind me saying, you really are beautiful. Other pretty girls from high school? Most of them lost their looks by the time they hit thirty. But not you. You're as gorgeous as ever."

She kept her expression neutral even as she cringed internally. "Your comment makes me uncomfortable. Maybe this is a mistake."

He pinched the bridge of his nose. "Damn, you're right. I need a filter. How about we start over?"

She nodded slowly when he looked at her expectantly. "Would you like coffee? I can ask Doris to put on a fresh pot. I can also offer soda, if you prefer."

"No, but thank you. I can only stay a few minutes."

He folded his hands over his flat stomach. "You asked what was going on in my life. I won't bore you with college. My time there mostly revolved around football and classes. I did public service with my fraternity. Chased girls." He gave a boys-will-be-boys shrug. "Typical college life."

"College can be an exciting time," she said noncommittedly. Melanie's experience included working as a night clerk at a motel and commuting from home to minimize student loan debt.

"True. I graduated with a degree in finance and then was fortunate to be hired right here at Sierra Valley Bank. As vice president I oversaw our expansion. We've got four branches now serving our corner of the Sierras. I was fortunate. When Dad retired a year ago, the bank's search committee recommended hiring me to replace him." He shrugged "So, like you, I've come back to my roots. Folks must like what I'm doing here because there's a local group encouraging me to run for public office."

"Is that something you're interested in?

"I am," Chase said smoothly. "Filed papers last week to run for county supervisor in the March election. I'm always looking for new ways to serve my community."

He leaned back in his chair, all ease and confidence with his tailored suit and expensive watch. His gaze swept over her, slow and assessing, and Melanie felt her shoulders tense.

"If I win, some folks suggested with a few years' experience, I'll make a good candidate for Congress."

"Congress?" she echoed. "That's a big step."

He smiled faintly. "We need leaders who've worked their tails off, who value integrity and understand what it takes to succeed. Voters want to know that their elected representatives will work for them. Having a good head for finance doesn't hurt."

A flicker of something harder entered his eyes. "Of course, there are always obstacles. But I've never been afraid to play rough when I need to."

There it was, the gleam of steel beneath the gloss.

She had to hand it to him, Chase sounded like a politician, on the one hand polished and unabashed about singing his own praises, and on the other, ruthless and determined. She guessed the best politicians believed whatever narrative they'd created about themselves, and Chase's would probably present well to the voting public.

He also benefitted from the privilege of wealth and the social standing of his family. Odds were, he'd been hired as bank president because of his father, and George Bradford would likely bankroll his son's political campaign. Chase hadn't climbed the ladder of success. He'd started at the top.

She spoke carefully. "Serving in public office can be a noble endeavor. I hope it works out for you. You never married?" He wasn't wearing a ring.

A muscle ticked in his jaw. "Divorced. It gutted me, splitting up with my wife. Things don't always work out. Wife got the kids. Better that way. They need to be with their mother." Anger wound through the clipped phrases.

A gray-haired woman poked her head into the office. "Mr. Herrada is here for his meeting, Mr. Bradford."

Chase gave a nod of acknowledgment. "Thank you, Doris."

Melanie rose to her feet. "You're busy and I still need to stop at the grocery store. It's been nice catching up, Chase."

He stood, his sharp gaze feeling too personal as it traveled over her face.

"I'd like to see you socially, Melanie. We only talked about me. I want to hear what's happened with Melanie Brennan since she moved away all those years ago."

Her instinctive response was to decline. But even though the entire conversation made her wary, he might have useful information. "Oh, sure. I'd like that." She smiled in an effort to sell it.

"How about Friday? If you're free, we could go to Easy Money. It's small-town but has a decent ambience and the food's reasonably good."

"That sounds fine, though I'll need to check with my mom and stepdad to see if they're up for babysitting before I can give you a firm commitment." Did her upbeat tone sound forced?

"Great. Let's exchange contact information. I'll pick you up."

"It's better if I meet you there since I'll have to drop my daughter off. I'll text you if there's a problem with childcare."

"Okay." After swapping numbers, he said, "I'm looking forward to it."

Stepping out of the bank and onto the sun-warmed boardwalk, Melanie reminded herself people could change. Fifteen years had passed, and Chase wasn't the same person he'd been in high school, and neither was she.

Maybe he deserved the benefit of the doubt.

But the truth was, she wanted to uncover anything he knew and had only agreed to meet him as a first step into her investigation.

CHAPTER FOUR

Melanie and Addy had reestablished their morning routine and it had run well all week. Except Friday morning. Addy insisted only her purple and pink striped socks would work with her outfit, and while Mel was pretty sure two purple and pink socks had gone into the washer, only one had made it out of the dryer. In the laundry room, she pawed through the basket of clean clothes.

"You need to be flexible, Addy." She held up matching socks. "I don't know where the other striped sock is, but you have two purple ones right here that match, and if we don't hurry, you'll miss the bus."

"I want my striped socks and if I miss the bus, you can take me."

"I'm wearing flannel pants and a sweatshirt with a bleach stain. I haven't had caffeine. And the bus driver takes you to school so I don't have to."

Addy glared at her mutinously. "Nobody cares what moms wear and you're grumpy."

"Nobody cares if your socks are pink and purple either, and I'm not grumpy." Was she? Waking that morning with the realization that this evening she was meeting Chase could lead to a case of the grumps.

Did he think it was a date? She'd text him and suggest a time before the "date zone" she pegged at from six to nine. Maybe she could get away with only having a glass of wine.

But her immediate challenge was getting Addy out the door and on the bus.

Melanie pushed aside the laundry basket and studied her daughter. Addy was not a difficult child and could usually be reasoned with, but she'd been out of sorts since she'd gotten home the previous afternoon.

"What's going on, Addy? Did something happen at school that upset you?"

Addy hung her head and shrugged her thin shoulders.

"Adelyn?"

Another shrug, then she mumbled, "This kid called me gummy because my top teeth came out."

Mel sat next to Addy on the floor where they leaned with their backs against the washer.

"Who called you gummy?"

"A boy on the playground. He's in the other first grade class. His name is Liam. Liam's a dumb name and he's mean."

"You know everyone loses their teeth and the new ones grow back. Yours will come in soon. But Liam calling you gummy is unkind. People say hurtful things for all sorts of reasons, but it doesn't make it right."

"He pushed me when we were in line."

"He pushed you?" Oh hell no. "Tell me what happened." She wrapped an arm around Addy's shoulders and brought her into her side.

"We were lining up to go to the library and he pushed me and took cuts." Addy's tone was indignant. "But Olivia told him he's a pathetic little worm and I told him not to push me again."

Mel wanted to do more than call Liam a pathetic little worm, but being an adult meant she couldn't hunt the kid down. "I'm glad you're sticking up for yourself and that Olivia backed you up. Though calling him a name back probably doesn't help.

But Addy? I want you to tell your teacher if he keeps it up. He's being a bully, and is *not* allowed to touch you." The kid needed to have that drilled into his head.

"Okay." Addy's sigh was heavy for a six-year-old. "I guess I'll wear the purple socks."

Melanie kissed her daughter on the top of her head and held her close for another moment.

They made the bus, but only by hoofing it down Bluebell Lane. Olivia grabbed Addy's hand and they clambered up the steps together. Melanie watched the bus pull away, taking her baby with it.

Maybe she should've waited until summer to move so Addy would start with the new school year, but that would've been months from now and they might not have found a house that suited at that time. She burrowed her hands into the pockets of the denim jacket she'd thrown on over her sweatshirt.

Did all parents worry this much about their child fitting in at school?

She retraced her steps along the dirt road. Maybe she should contact Mrs. Delgado herself and let her know this boy was bothering Addy. She was trying to raise a resilient, independent child, and part of that was giving Addy support while encouraging her to solve problems on her own. But if that kid put his hands on her daughter again, for damn sure she'd be talking to the teacher and the principal.

She walked back along Bluebell Lane, a light breeze stirring the pine-scented air. Melanie wasn't sure what made her look. Maybe it was the prick of unease. The feeling of being watched.

She and Addy had passed a truck parked on the other side of the road on their way to the bus stop. Now she realized a man was sitting in the driver's seat. He held a phone in front of him and the way it was angled made her think he was taking pictures or video. Of her.

She marched across the road. The guy saw her coming and fumbled his phone. She rapped sharply on the passenger side window.

"Hey." She raised her voice to be heard through the glass. "Are you taking pictures of me?" Were there laws against taking pictures of people without their permission? She didn't think so.

The guy turned his face away and the engine roared to life. She barely had time to jump back before the truck sped away.

She stared after the truck as it turned onto the road that led to town and disappeared.

Well, that was past strange. She filed away details: dark-haired white guy driving an older metallic gray Tundra with temporary paper plates. There was a dent in the tailgate like the driver had backed into something.

Her mind sifted through possible explanations for the guy's behavior. She could probably chalk it up to weirdos being weird, but she'd keep an eye out. Experience had taught her to be wary.

A happy bark had her looking toward Gage's house. Pancake stood at the top of the driveway, her gaze riveted on the tall man beside her holding a ball. Gage hurled the ball in a long arc worthy of a center fielder, sending it sailing into the open space behind his garage and out of Melanie's view. Pancake streaked after it in a golden blur.

Gage spotted Melanie. He shoved his hands in his pockets, clearly hesitating before strolling down the slope of his driveway.

He did the guy chin-lift thing, which she guessed was kind of a greeting.

He looked vital and fit in his athletic pants and slim-fit shirt with a beanie covering his longish hair. Worn running shoes and the ruddy color in cheeks bristly with dark stubble made her think he'd just returned from a run.

She didn't want to speculate on how she looked in her not-for-public-view clothing. She hadn't had time to do anything with her bedhead, which meant her hair was likely sticking up in all directions.

With an internal *oh well*, she decided to ignore the hotness imbalance. "Hi."

"Get your toilet fixed?"

"Yeah. You gave good advice. I only needed the flapper, no tools were necessary, and my toilet is no longer running."

He gave what might have been a miniscule nod of acknowledgment.

His lack of communication wasn't exactly encouraging, but joining her on the road had to mean something, right? It was enough for her to press on.

"Speaking of tools, can I borrow what's needed to put Addy's desk together? She's excited about it and we'd like to work on it this weekend."

"Yeah. I'll bring them over." His dark eyes glinted.

"Thanks." She turned to gaze up at the mountains. The feeling that he could see more than she wanted made her uncomfortable. Not that he said a lot. Pancake trotted back with the ball and dropped it at his feet. Gage scooped it up and rocketed it back up the driveway between his house and garage with Pancake again in hot pursuit.

"That's quite an arm you've got."

"Get a lot of practice." He cocked his head, that all-seeing gaze back on her. "You good?"

"Of course."

His attention didn't waver.

"Addy good?"

He'd managed to pick up on her worry and was questioning her much like she'd done with Addy that morning, though she used a lot more words to communicate.

Melanie shrugged. "Mostly. It's tough being the new kid in school."

"She rides the bus with Jordy and Olivia. They're good kids." Growly Gage Landry knew the neighbor kids. Why did that surprise her?

"They are. Kids make friends amazingly fast. Addy and Olivia have already declared that they're besties. When a boy pushed Addy, Olivia called him a pathetic little worm. That's good backup."

His gaze locked on hers. Receiving the full force of his attention felt almost like a physical touch. "What the fuck? A kid pushed Addy?"

"Yeah. And took cuts in line." Melanie laughed when Gage scowled. "You and me, we could take him."

48

"Don't tempt me." He didn't exactly crack a smile, but his tension eased, and the corner of his mouth lifted infinitesimally. She really liked that hint of humor, the feeling like he got her on some unspoken level.

Remembering what she'd seen earlier, she asked, "Did you see the guy in a gray Tundra parked on our road?"

"No. Why?"

Wow, that was quick. Razor-sharp intensity replaced any trace of humor. "There was a truck parked down the road near that tree." She pointed. "I noticed it when I walked Addy to the bus stop. When I came back, I saw there was a guy inside." She shrugged. "I thought it was odd."

He waited a beat, then said, "There's more."

She crossed her arms over her chest. How did he do that? How did he know she hadn't told him everything? She huffed out a breath. "Okay, I know it sounds weird, but I thought he was watching me. He had his phone up and it looked like he was taking my picture or maybe recording me."

"You do anything?"

"Hell yeah, I did. I knocked on his window and asked what he was up to. He got all flustered and sped off up the road. I had to jump out of his way."

He unzipped a side pocket on his pants and pulled out his phone. "Give me the vehicle information and the man's physical description." No-nonsense, direct, clipped delivery. Maybe he was a cop.

She rattled off what she remembered. He stared at her hard, then asked, "License plate?"

"He had a temporary paper plate. I didn't get the number. The tailgate had a dent on the left side."

Gage stared into the distance before growling, "I saw him earlier, probably forty minutes ago."

"Where? Here?"

He shook his head. "When I was running."

He tapped on his phone and held it to his ear, then spoke when it was picked up on the other end. "Sawyer, take this information." He repeated what she'd told him about the man and the truck, then said, "My neighbor Melanie Brennan says he was taking pictures of her before she chased him off." He listened for a second, then said, "Yeah, that's her."

His gaze zeroed in on Melanie as he continued speaking. "I clocked him earlier. I was running the ridge trail, came around a bend and he was sitting on a rock. Had binoculars and said he was bird-watching. He wasn't. Dress and demeanor didn't track. Physical description matches what Melanie gave me. From where he was sitting, he'd have a view of the back of both my house and hers." He listened, then said, "I told him to move on and followed him to the trailhead. Truck description matches what Melanie got, down to the dent in the tailgate. I took a picture and will send that to you. The paper plates are fake." He listened, then said, "Got it. I'll look on my security feed and see if he shows up." He disconnected the call.

"The guy is watching me." Melanie hated the cold feeling in the pit of her stomach.

"Maybe. Or he could be watching me."

"He was taking pictures of me, not you."

"True." Gage opened his phone, then held it up for her to see the image of a Tundra with paper plates and dented tailgate.

"That's the truck." She'd felt safe in her house, but that sense of security was now fractured. She pulled her jacket more tightly around her as a shiver snaked down her spine.

He tapped on the screen, sending the photo.

"Was that Sawyer McGrath you were talking to? Is he a cop now?"

"Yeah, that's him."

"I knew the McGraths when I was a kid."

"Sawyer's a lieutenant with the sheriff's department. He'll have patrol deputies keep an eye out for the truck." He crossed his arms over his chest, his expression all kinds of serious. "Why didn't you get me as soon as you saw the guy?"

"I chased him off, and I don't think taking pictures of someone on a public street is a crime."

"Next time come get me. Immediately."

She gave an abrupt laugh. "You're kidding, right? I'm not bothering my neighbor because someone sitting in their car is looking my way. Maybe I was a little creeped out, but that's just me."

The idea of running to Gage for help ran smack into her need to be responsible for herself and Addy. After the assault, her mom had become over-the-top protective and nearly smothered Melanie with care and concern. She'd been fighting for her independence ever since.

"Don't dismiss what your gut tells you, especially now that we know the guy was also watching from the ridge."

She didn't want to dismiss her gut, she of all people should know better, but she also didn't want to rely on others for protection.

Pancake returned, panting heavily, and flopped down beside them on the driveway. Ball in mouth, she rolled onto her back, closed her eyes, and groaned with her paws hanging in the air.

"Your dog is blissed out."

"She does this in town and won't budge when it's time to leave. Then it's a pain in the ass."

He tapped the screen on his phone, then handed it to her. "Put in your contact info and give me your phone. I'll do the same." He must have caught her look because he said, "Looking out for one another is what neighbors do."

He was right. That her feelings about him were a little more than neighborly was her problem. She unlocked her phone and handed it over, then input her information into his.

After giving back her phone, he said, "Anything makes you nervous, and I mean anything, tell me. If it's safe, take pictures."

She sighed. "Okay." Having a way to get in touch with her neighbors made sense. She might prefer not relying on others, but she needed to be smart, especially where Addy was concerned. She knelt to give Pancake a belly rub. Squinting against the morning sun, she tipped her head back to look up at Gage. "If it's something serious, I'll call. But I can take care of myself. I'm not bothering my neighbor every time something goes bump in the night."

"Wrong way to think about it. You have a problem, call me."

He strode back up the driveway while Pancake remained motionless.

"You're not taking your dog?" she called after him.

"She'll come when she's ready."

Well, alrighty then. Melanie stood. "C'mon, Pancake. You can come with me."

Not even a twitch. With a sigh, Melanie left Pancake splayed out on the driveway, looking like she was at the beach getting a suntan.

***

Even with the evening looming before her, Melanie had a productive day. She'd wrestled a difficult scene into shape for her manuscript and that felt like a win. More times than she wanted to admit, she'd picked up her phone, ready to text Chase and cancel. But that felt cowardly. She needed to grow a spine.

Her biggest hang-up was his comment about wanting to see her socially. She'd only agreed to go out with him to gather information, and now she couldn't shake the feeling that she was using him.

She'd be honest and make it clear she wasn't interested in anything romantic.

She'd say it kindly, of course, but she'd still make sure he got the message.

As sincere as Chase seemed at the bank, the memory of him slamming that boy into the lockers remained stuck in her head.

She wondered if he remembered she'd turned him down when he'd asked her to prom junior year. She'd declined, nicely, she thought, but remembered the flash of fury on his face. That afternoon he'd been in a fight and broken another boy's nose. After that she'd steered clear of him even though their social circles overlapped, as they had at the bootlegger.

Those memories made her even less enthusiastic about the evening ahead. But it was too late to cancel without being rude, and she'd committed herself to learning what she could about the night she'd been assaulted. Talking to the people who'd been at the bootlegger was the obvious place to start.

Addy'd finished her mac and cheese and was leaning on the miniscule bathroom counter watching Melanie in the mirror as she used a brush to apply eye shadow.

"You're putting makeup on. Are you going on a date?"

"Not a date. I'm meeting with someone I knew in high school."

"A man someone?"

"Yeah, a man someone." She studied Addy's reflection. "Does that bother you?"

Addy shook her head. "Is he like Gage? Does he have a dog like Pancake? Are you going to marry him?"

Melanie laughed at the barrage of questions. "No, he's not like Gage." Chase didn't spark a fire in her belly simply by looking at her. "I'm definitely not marrying him, and I have no idea if he has a dog."

"You can't marry someone unless they have a dog. Dog people are good people."

Who knew a six-year-old could be so wise?

"Why the question about marriage?" Melanie asked while Addy examined the palette of eye shadow shades.

"Lots of kids have parents who are married." Addy cocked her head to the side. "Did you know girls can marry girls? Lucy in my class has two moms. Can boys marry boys?"

"They can. Since I don't plan on getting married anytime soon, we can set marriage aside for now. Are you okay with it being just you and me?"

Addy gave her gap-toothed smile. "Dad hardly ever visits, but that's okay. You and me are the best together."

"We absolutely are."

If there was a solution to Phil's inconsistency regarding his daughter, Melanie would grab onto it and make it happen. He paid child support but seemed to think that's where his obligation ended. He was satisfied with a few visits a year and didn't care to actually know his daughter. All of which made Mel question her judgment in men.

She and Phil had been together for almost five months when she'd found out she was pregnant. In all that time, why hadn't she recognized how self-absorbed he was?

Not that she was blameless. She didn't need Esme telling her to know she'd kept her few boyfriends at a distance emotionally, and, unsurprisingly, when they eventually broke up there was barely a dent in her heart.

Addy picked up a sponge applicator. "Can I try?"

"Of course. We'll need to wash it off before we leave. I think Grandad would have me arrested if you showed up with makeup on your pretty face."

Addy giggled. "Makeup's not against the law."

"We'll have to ask him to make sure. Do you have your overnight things in your backpack?"

Addy nodded as she smeared blue shadow on her eyelids. "Nana said she has a project to make *real* soap that we can use in the bath. We can even put flowers in it. And Grandad said he has a movie picked out for tonight that comes from a really long time ago. He said the nineties. When were the nineties?"

"Not that long ago and now you're making me feel ancient."

"Well, even though it's real old he says it's still good. We're making popcorn. And Grandad says he's cooking up pancakes with chocolate chips for breakfast because they're my favorite, and you're invited, but you need to bring strawberries because strawberries are the best with chocolate chip pancakes."

"I can do that."

And what did it say about her that Addy's plans sounded a lot more fun than hers?

CHAPTER FIVE

After dropping off an excited Addy—minus the blue eye shadow—with Paul and Donna at their comfortable ranch-style home, Melanie parked on Main Street and walked through the front doors of Easy Money. She hung her coat on a row of hooks by the door and turned to take in the comfortable and inviting space with its open beams, warm colors, and twinkling lights.

Upholstered barstools stood in front of a long bar made of reddish-brown wood that gleamed under the low lights. Booths lined the walls with tables in between and a three-quarter wall separated the bar from a small area for restaurant dining. The welcoming tone complemented the glowing recommendation Paul and Donna had given the place.

Not seeing Chase, she took a stool at the bar. Besides actually using makeup, she'd made her bangs a little spikey and for her outfit had decided on a V-necked sweater in deep burgundy with slim-fitting black pants and dangly earrings. With some people in jeans and hoodies and others in suits, she figured her outfit hit the sweet spot—dressy, but not too much.

Donna had passed on the news that Keeley Montaigne, a friend from high school and Delaney's bff, had married Easy Money's owner. Melanie spotted Keeley behind the bar squaring off with a hunky guy who stood with his hands on his hips. They were glaring at each other. That might've been concerning except for the sizzling vibes and the possessive expression on the man's face suggesting what he'd really like to do was haul Keeley somewhere private to get his hands on her.

Keeley's tone was crisp. "You said you'd teach me, Owen. So teach me."

"I said I'd teach you, but not when you're four months pregnant." Mel shifted to peek over the bar and sure enough, baby bump. The guy—Owen—rumbled, "I want you sitting, princess, not standing all night behind a bar. Take a booth and work on the lesson plans you said you have to do this weekend."

She took a fistful of his shirt and pulled him down until they were nose to nose. "You can ask but not order, and I don't want to do school stuff right now. I'm four months pregnant not nine. I feel fine. And I want to learn bartending." She gave him a peck on the lips and when she would have stepped back, Owen reeled her back for a kiss that was a hundred degrees hotter.

Yay, Keeley. She'd gotten herself a sexy one.

A man in a Sisters FD sweatshirt came in from the back door holding hands with a curly-haired redhead. "You two get a room."

Melanie's couldn't stop the smile. "Mateo?"

Another pal from high school. Nothing like ripping off the Band-Aid on all the worry she had about meeting up with the old group. In addition to being a friend, Mateo was another person to talk with about the night of the assault.

But for the moment, she wanted to enjoy seeing him after so many years. Mateo Reynoso had been hands down one of the nicest boys at Sierra High. And the cutest.

The wide grin that flashed across his face made the nerves jumping under her skin settle, and when he gave her a warm, one-armed hug, they disappeared completely. "Hey, Mel. Welcome home."

"Thanks, Matty."

He tugged the redhead closer. "This is my fiancée, Juliette."

"Oh, you're getting married. That's wonderful. You've got a good guy, Juliette."

Juliette smiled. "Thank you. I think so too."

The couple took seats at the bar.

"Melanie, you're really here." Keeley skirted around the bar to give Melanie a hug. Owen dipped his head when Keeley introduced them.

"Congratulations to you both on the baby."

"We're excited. I heard you made the move back to Sisters with your little girl," Keeley said. "This is your home, and I'm glad you've brought your daughter here."

Melanie hadn't realized how much she needed to hear that. Her school friends could have blamed her for Walker being sent to prison. That they didn't appear to helped ease her anxiety about returning to Sisters.

Keeley moved back around the bar, and, with a haughty look at Owen, turned to those seated on barstools. "I'll be your bartender this evening even if my overprotective husband thinks he's the boss of me. What can I get for you all?"

Melanie had fun watching the couple who clearly enjoyed simply being near each other. "I'm waiting for someone."

Mateo ordered a Coke and Juliette a glass of wine. While Keeley was getting their order, Owen dropped ice in a glass and filled it with water, adding a twist of lemon before setting it on a coaster in front of Melanie.

He braced his arms on the bar, gaze direct. Mel figured that intense look had sucked Keeley right in. "Welcome home. My wife shared what happened with you. Anyone bothers you or makes you uncomfortable, let me know."

A lump rose in her throat. "Oh, thanks. I can take care of myself."

Owen shook his head and grabbed a pen from behind the counter. He used it to scrawl across a paper napkin that he slid in front of her. "That's my number. Put it in your phone. We look out for each other around here." Which was much the same as what Gage had said.

She swallowed down the stupid lump, and not trusting her voice, nodded. "Thank you," she whispered.

Her neighborhood in Stockton had been fine, but there hadn't been the sense of community she was finding in Sisters. She'd had that as a teenager until all sense of safety had been shattered. Maybe she could find it again.

Owen moved down the bar and Melanie checked her phone. Chase was ten minutes late. She entered Owen's number. She wouldn't call him, but it wouldn't hurt to have the number just in case.

Someone slid onto the stool on her other side and she turned, expecting Chase, and instead her heart gave a kick when she recognized her neighbor.

"Mateo, Juliette." Gage gave the couple on her other side a nod, then shifted his attention to her. "Melanie."

Okay, it was totally unfair for a man to look that good. The black sweater Gage wore with jeans encased broad shoulders and gave a hint of the lean muscle underneath. Then there was all that dark hair swept back from a high forehead and the slash of dark brows that gave him a barely tamed look. Add the way he said her name with his growly voice and she was getting decidedly hot and bothered.

"Gage." She hoped he couldn't see the warmth creeping up her neck.

Keeley wagged a finger between them, eyes gleaming. "Gage is your date, Mel? Nice."

Gage gave her a considering look while Melanie tried to mentally force the flush from her cheeks. "No, he's not my date. We're neighbors."

"Oops, sorry. Bartenders should be more careful about that kind of thing. Though, if you ask me, you two look good together."

"Jesus, Keeley," Gage muttered.

Owen tugged on Keeley's ponytail and said to Gage, "Sorry, pal. She has no filter."

"That's not true. I simply like the idea of Melanie and Gage. They're both good people." Her smile brightened. "What can I get you, Gage?"

"How about a draft beer and mind your own business?"

She grinned. "Fair enough."

Keeley tilted a glass under the tap to fill it with dark amber liquid then set it with a head of foam in front of Gage.

"Thanks." He turned to Melanie, sharp green eyes glinting under the bar lights. "You're here for a date?"

"No, not a date. I'm meeting someone."

"A male someone?"

"You and Addy should team up for your inquisition. She asked me the same question. And yes, a male someone."

"She has good instincts. Where is he?" Gage sipped his beer.

"Not here." She shrugged. "He's late."

"He didn't pick you up and then he's late? Not cool."

What had happened to taciturn Gage who spoke in one- or two-word sentences? He was suddenly all up in her business.

"Maybe if it was a date it wouldn't be cool, but since it's not, it's not a big deal. It was more practical for me to drive myself."

"He text you?"

She didn't allow herself to roll her eyes at his persistence. But she wanted to. She pulled up her phone to confirm. "No, and I'll agree that part's not cool."

Keeley began assembling an order for cocktails under Owen's watchful eye. A group of people came through the door to the back and the noise level in the bar rose. Gage drummed his fingers on the bar, then leaned closer to be heard. "Addy with your folks?"

Melanie nodded. "She gets to do soapmaking with Mom, and Paul's got a movie picked out that's from the nineties. Addy made it sound like ancient history."

"Ouch."

"Right? And to prove she's the princess and her grandparents are merely subjects to do her bidding, her grandad is making chocolate chip pancakes for breakfast. Life is good for Adelyn Brennan."

"Life should be good for a six-year-old. She have a better day at school?"

Points for Gage asking about her girl. "She did. She said the kid Liam made a dumb face, but she ignored him and had a good day otherwise. She was excited because today she got to pick out a book at the book fair. She loves books and is reading well above grade level."

"She's a smart kid. Pancake would slay dragons for her."

She liked the imagery. Before she could respond, a hand gripped her shoulder. "Melanie. I don't like to keep my date waiting, but something came up I had to deal with."

She turned in her seat, shifting uncomfortably under his hold.

Chase looked worn-down, the charming demeanor from the bank absent. He wore a sport coat over a button-down shirt open at the collar, his hair slightly mussed.

She gave him a quizzical look. That hadn't been an apology.

It occurred to her that neither Mateo nor Keeley had greeted Chase even though they'd all been at Sierra High at the same time.

Chase wasn't looking at Melanie, his flat stare instead focused on Gage. Gage tracked Chase's grip on her shoulder. He rose to his feet, forcing the other man to step back and release her.

Gage's calm exterior was deceptive. She had no idea how she knew, but his long, lean body was primed and ready for a fight. Melanie looked from one man to the other. The undercurrents swirling between them felt deep enough to drown in.

"Landry."

"Bradford."

"I heard you're leaving the FBI. A high-pressure job like that isn't for everyone. At least it'll no longer be your job to harass people for a living."

Her gaze flew to Gage. He was with the FBI? Why was she not surprised? His response over the guy in the truck now made sense. But what did Chase mean about him harassing people?

Gage flicked his glance at her before returning his attention to Chase. "We try to limit our harassment to criminals."

There was an unmistakable flash of anger before Chase's mouth twisted into a sneer. "Guess it's a step up from playing ranch hand. Gives you more money to burn drinking at a bar."

"At least having a beer doesn't make me a mean drunk. What's your excuse?"

Chase's cheeks reddened. "I don't need a fucking excuse. Come on, Mel," he said abruptly. "We'll get a booth."

Trying to make sense of the exchange, she slipped off the stool. That the two men detested each other was clear. "I'll see you later, Gage."

"Yeah."

She moved across the floor with Chase, and Melanie felt Gage's gaze on her back as surely as a touch. And his wouldn't be unwelcome.

***

Gage sipped his beer. It irritated the shit out of him that Melanie was with Chase Bradford.

Their rivalry had started not long after Gage arrived at Lone Pine Ranch. He and Shane had been at Easy Money the night Bradford—drunk and loud—exploded at his then-wife. When the asshole backhanded her and split her lip, Gage and Shane had stepped in. Bradford took a swing at Gage. He'd easily dodged it and hit back, catching the other man with a solid punch that had broken his nose.

Bradford had hated him ever since.

The man was an asshole, plain and simple. Especially with women. Too bad being a jackass wasn't a crime. But bank fraud was.

True to form, Bradford had assumed Gage was a ranch hand, and adopted that smug, condescending air he reserved for anyone he thought beneath him.

Gage would be lying if he said it hadn't been satisfying to show up at the bank earlier that week, badge visible on his belt and Glock in his shoulder holster, and hand Bradford a target letter from the FBI.

62

The guy had gone beet red, sputtering with outrage as he demanded Gage's credentials—because apparently anyone could flash a fake badge. Gage produced his ID without so much as a smirk, then calmly informed Bradford he was now the subject in an active investigation and was required to preserve all evidence.

The weapon at Gage's side might've been the only thing that kept Chase from taking another swing. Or maybe it was the memory of that broken nose.

From there, Gage had gone straight to the Bradford estate. George Bradford opened the door mid-phone call—probably talking to his son—and took the envelope without a word, then shut the door in Gage's face.

Gage moved to a booth across from where Melanie and Chase were seated. It kept her in his line of sight.

Gage sipped his beer, watching Melanie try to look interested. The waiter took their drinks order and left bar menus on the table. Bradford had spread himself across the seat with his arm along the back and his legs spread wide. It was a dick move to show dominance and authority.

He was talking effusively with big hand gestures. Probably thought Melanie was hanging on his every word. The waiter brought their drinks, white wine for Melanie and, since Bradford had made sure everyone could hear him order, top-shelf scotch for the asshole.

Watching Chase wine and dine Melanie like he didn't have federal heat bearing down on him, Gage couldn't help but wonder. Maybe Bradford was trying to distract himself with a beautiful woman. Or maybe he had another motive entirely.

His phone vibrated. He glanced down. A text from his mother.

LifeGiver: *Hi, my boy.* ♥□♥□♥□ *Stu and I are planning a cross-country road trip in his RV as soon as the weather warms in the spring. First leg is the Pacific Northwest. Would you and Pancake join us for a few days? The RV sleeps six, so there's room. I miss you.*

His mom deserved to be happy. God knew she'd had enough years when she wasn't.

Gage had been a kid when his dad died in a head-on collision with an asshole who'd been taking the edge off his day with a few nips of vodka. In the twisted way fate worked, the drunk had walked away. Steven Landry hadn't.

A decade later, grief had come for them again. His sister Janie, funny and brave, lost her fight with cancer. Gage had been afraid his mom would simply fade away from heartache until she completely disappeared.

But Judy Landry had clawed her way back. Bit by bit.

She bought her little house in Oakland, planted flowers she fussed over, had even gotten an orange kitten she named Samson. And then a year ago, she met Stuart. A retired lineman for the electric company, he was a solid guy and treated her right.

Gage liked him well enough. Even if he'd pulled a background check first. The DUI from thirty years back had pissed him off. But Stuart owned it. Said he told Judy up front and swore he hadn't touched a drink since. Gage believed him.

They'd had a small courthouse wedding. Now they acted like they'd won the damn lottery.

Judy even got along with Stu's daughter, and now had grandkids who called her "Mimi."

Gage was glad she was happy. Truly. Still, it was strange. His mom with a whole new family that didn't include him. She tried to make space for him. But he couldn't help feeling like the odd man out.

He typed a reply:

Gage: *Let me know when you're leaving and I'll arrange my schedule.*

A moment later:

LifeGiver: *Good! Do you remember I told you about Stacy who does my hair and how her cousin's daughter lives in Sisters?*

Gage: *No.*

LifeGiver: *Stacy told her about you and that you're single. She wants to meet you.*

Gage: *No way in hell.*

LifeGiver: *You might like her. She's a yoga instructor. I hear they're very bendy.*

Gage: *STOP. Don't say things like that.*

LifeGiver: *Don't be a prude. She thinks your little town has vortexes or swirling centers of energy or something equally woo-woo. I know that's not your thing, but Stacy says she's sweet as can be.*

Gage: *That's horrifying. For the love of god, don't try to set me up with a woo-woo yoga teacher. Or anyone. Ever.*

LifeGiver: *You need someone who makes you happy like Stuart makes me happy.*

Across the room, Melanie sipped her wine while Bradford talked nonstop. Didn't take a psych degree to see she was bored.

He could tell his mom he was interested in someone.

It might not even be a lie.

He dismissed the idea almost as soon as it formed. Even protection from woo-woo yoga teachers wasn't worth the fallout that would follow.

Gage: *I'm fine. Glad you're happy.*

LifeGiver: *Gotta go. My show's on. It's a reality show about cousins who marry. Love you!* ♥☐♥☐♥☐

Gage: *Love you back.*

He chuckled softly and shook his head, then opened his email app. He deleted a few spam messages before tapping on one from Imani Bentil, his boss at the bureau. Reading the email, he could hear the West African cadence of her voice in his head.

She thanked him again for delivering the target letters and said she'd enjoyed working with him. Wished him well in his new chapter.

This morning, with his separation paperwork finalized, his time with the Bureau was officially over. He wasn't sure how he felt about it. Maybe a little regret. He'd liked the people. Liked fighting for something that mattered.

But the bureaucracy? That he wouldn't miss. He still planned to chase justice, but with fewer layers of red tape in the way.

Gage contemplated what was bugging him about Bradford. His interest in Melanie set off something in his gut. A trigger warning, loud and insistent. Something was off.

Maybe Melanie didn't think of it as a date, but Bradford sure as hell did. And it wasn't only that.

It wasn't hard to see why he'd be interested. She had spine, a face that intrigued, and then there were those curves. Tonight she'd done something to make her eyes look mysterious that boosted her from knockout to sexy siren. Add the red lipstick and Gage was wrecked. Call him weak, but that shade short-circuited his brain.

And it wasn't only about looks.

When they were together, something between them sparked. Then there was the way she lit up around Addy that showed her utter delight with her child. Melanie possessed an inherent goodness that set all his protective instincts humming.

What the hell was she doing with Bradford? She didn't seem the kind to be impressed by a bank president or political candidate. At least Gage hoped not. But if it wasn't a date, why meet him at a bar on a Friday night?

He didn't have the answer. And that unsettled him more than he wanted to admit.

Gage settled in, nursing his beer to make it last. He'd hang out and make sure there were no problems.

Not that it was any hardship, especially when Shane came in with his wife. That his best friend was not only married but had a kid was a kick in the ass.

Emery spotted him and grabbed Shane's hand to pull him with her to the bench seat across from Gage.

"Hey, pal, I'm so glad to see you. We didn't expect you here."

Emery wasn't subtle in her efforts to get him out more. Everyone having babies had changed how their people got together, though. With the vast quantity of paraphernalia needed when going out with the tiny humans, it was easier for the group to get together at the ranch or Cider Mill Farm.

"What'd you do with the short one?"

"Harding's got Violet tonight." Emery sent her husband a worried look. "Do you think we should call to check if everything's all right?"

"Darlin', she's fine. Harding's got your number, my number, Delaney and Cam's numbers. He's got a dozen numbers to call if he needs help. You know he likes nothing better than to sit in the rocking chair and rock our girl to sleep."

"Right. She's fine. I know she's fine, but what if she wants me and I'm not there?" Emery held up a hand. "Don't answer that. I know I'm being crazy. She's a well-loved child, and with my parents coming tomorrow morning for a visit, between them and Harding we'll be lucky to even get to hold her."

Shane dropped an arm around her shoulders and whispered something in her ear that had her smiling.

While they chatted, Gage kept tabs on the couple across the room. The waiter arrived, and Melanie shook her head. Chase leaned in, clearly pressing the issue, but she held her ground. Hands up, firm.

Accept it, pal. She doesn't want dinner with you.

The waiter left and Melanie leaned forward. She emphasized with her hands as she talked. Bradford's posture changed. Arms crossed. Chin down. Closed off.

"You're keeping a close eye on your new neighbor," Shane noted, grinning.

"Bradford's an asshole."

"Agreed. That the only reason you've got your eye on Mel?"

"It's enough of one."

"Oh," Emery chimed in. "Shane told me what happened to Melanie. It's brave of her to move back to Sisters. I can't wait to meet her."

The waiter circled to their table. Gage ordered sliders and fries with a Coke. He raised a brow at Shane and Emery. "It won't hurt my feelings if you two want to get your own table for date night."

"Trying to get rid of us?" Emery teased. "Harding is so besotted with Violet we have to fight him for time with her. He makes sure we get plenty of date nights." She gave a wry grin. "He's scheming for more babies so he's making sure we have time to do the deed."

"Are you kidding me? That's why he's always taking her?" Shane looked vaguely horrified.

Emery shrugged. "Pretty sure. I mean, he loves her, but he'd be happy if we had a half dozen babies."

Gage laughed when Shane paled.

"Anyway," Emery added, "you're one of our people. I'm happy we ran into you."

Funny thing was, he knew she meant it.

He leaned back as Emery launched into a story involving baby vomit and Shane's poor choice to hold Violet overhead.

"How can that tiny kid hold that much milk?" Shane grumbled.

"I'd warned you not to hold her like that. That was top-quality breast milk. All wasted." Emery sent Gage a grin. "Let me know if it's TMI. After giving birth, the guardrails are down. I have zero modesty and everything's open for discussion."

"I'm good," Gage said, laughing.

The food arrived and everyone dug in.

As he dipped fries into ketchup, Gage glanced back across the room. Melanie was talking and Bradford was on edge. He'd shut down, legs crossed, arms tight, jaw clenched.

Whatever she'd said had rattled Bradford's smug façade.

Good, Gage thought. *She can handle herself.*

But the restlessness inside him kept humming.

Mateo and Juliette wandered over.

"Hey, Gage," Juliette said, nudging him with her hip. "We need dog advice."

"What's up?"

"Pancake is such a cool dog. Would you recommend a golden?"

Gage shot a look at Emery, who didn't look even a little guilty. She and her sisters had cooked up the idea and ambushed him at Christmas with the one-year-old goofy pup. Then they named her Pancake after she stole breakfast off the table.

He rolled his eyes. Emery just batted her lashes.

He cocked his head to look at Juliette and Mateo. "You two thinking of getting a dog?"

Juliette nodded. "We want one, but I'm concerned about leaving a dog home alone with both of us working long shifts."

"I think I've got it worked out," Mateo said. "Davey at the station mentioned a woman who's opened a doggie daycare and boarding business out at the edge of town. We should check it out. If it looks good, the dog goes to daycare when we're both on shift. She does training too."

Gage nodded. "Good idea. You don't want to leave a golden on its own, especially if it's young. It'll get bored and tear your house apart. You'll need to find a way for it to run and burn off energy. But Pancake? She's all heart. They're great dogs."

Chase and Melanie rose from the booth. They talked a minute longer, then Chase tossed bills on the table and stalked through the bar to the back door.

He was pissed and barely keeping a lid on it.

Melanie got her coat and headed for the front. Gage pushed his empty plate back. "Mateo, you and Juliette have a seat." He nodded to Shane. "Tell Owen I'll come back to settle up."

He ignored Shane's low whistle. Grabbing his coat, he headed for the door.

CHAPTER SIX

Bradford's behavior confirmed what Gage knew: Bradford was an asshole. Even if it wasn't a date, dude should have walked Melanie to her car.

Gage pushed through the double doors.

Melanie paced across the covered boardwalk in front of the bar. A late-model truck roared up the alley from the parking lot. Gage recognized it as Bradford's. He floored it, tires squealing as he sped onto Main Street.

Melanie spotted Gage, her arms crossed under her breasts, face reflecting anger and misery. The glint of tears infuriated him.

Her long look reached him—unspoken but raw—and something clutched in his chest. He didn't want this. Didn't want what she stirred up inside him. He was finally starting to get his footing again.

But instead of walking away, he crossed to her.

"What the hell did he say to make you cry?"

"Nothing."

She took a breath and held it for a second, the kind you took when you were trying to stop crying. "Dammit. I hate crying. It's stupid and weak."

He didn't agree but let it pass. "I've learned that when women say 'nothing,' it usually means something."

"I guess 'nothing' means I don't want to talk about it."

"Fair enough. Take a walk with me."

Her gaze flew to his and gave him a glimpse of swirling emotions. He wanted her to agree more than he should.

"I'd like that," she said, and the tightness around his heart eased.

They strolled along the covered boardwalk that was part of the town's charm. There were only a few other couples out, probably because it was so damn cold. Their breath puffed in front of them before being whipped away in the stiff breeze. They passed closed shops, their glass windows reflecting lights that twinkled like stars under the overhead rafters.

They passed the hobby shop and Melanie jumped, grabbing his arm. A leering vampire hung from a post, bony fingers extended.

"Holy shit, that scared me. The old guy from this shop freaked me out the other day with the demon bats." She motioned up and Gage tipped his head back to look.

"Cool decorations."

"Not cool. I like fun Halloween, not creepy Halloween." She shivered but released his arm.

"I dig the community buy-in." He shrugged when she glanced at him. "This town goes all in to celebrate holidays."

"I see that now. I didn't appreciate Sisters when I was younger."

"You were a kid. Kids take their hometown for granted."

"True. But I value it now. Downtown is charming, and I like how the shopkeepers coordinate the seasonal decorations."

They stopped before the lighted window display for Retro Days featuring vintage Halloween costumes. "Oh my gosh. I wore a Velma costume from Scooby-Doo like that one when I was in fourth grade. It's the second time tonight I'm feeling ancient. I swear fourth grade wasn't that long ago."

"Mateo's mom owns this place."

"Antonia? Really? She was so fun when we were kids." Melanie looked wistful. "Matty, Delaney, Keeley, me—we were all in the same class through elementary school. Mrs. Reynoso was always one of the room moms. She had a way of making every kid feel special. I'll need to stop in to say hi when she's open."

She blew on her hands and rubbed them together. Gage took her hand in his and tucked it into his pocket.

She gave him a side-eye look but didn't pull back. He didn't want to examine too carefully why her fingers twined with his felt exactly right. They reached the end of the commercial district and crossed the street to the other side. The wind was picking up, cold enough to cut through you.

Holding hands, even for warmth, took this thing between them a big step past simply being neighbors. He didn't want to be attracted, but that didn't seem to matter because everything about Melanie appealed to him in a way that made her impossible to ignore.

Another issue? Gage needed to come clean and tell her what he knew about her past. He withdrew their clasped hands from his pocket and drew her into a sheltered alcove. They were standing close enough that if he wanted to kiss her, he'd only need to tip down his head.

Who was he kidding? He'd wanted her mouth from the first time he'd met her. She must have read his mind because her big brown eyes went wide and more than a little wary. But she didn't step back.

"Look, Melanie, I need to give full disclosure." He forced himself to let go of her hand.

"About what?"

"Shane Keller and I have been friends since college. Through him I'm friends with Walker and Sawyer and their wives."

"What does—" Her tone cooled. "Oh, I see. With you being FBI, they told you what happened to me and about Walker being sent to prison."

"Yeah, they did. I wasn't positive that Melanie was you until Sawyer confirmed it." He shrugged. "It didn't seem fair that you didn't know I knew what happened."

"Thank you for telling me." The warmth had disappeared from her face.

He should have let it go, stepped back from his attraction, kept their relationship superficial.

But he couldn't. "It doesn't change anything."

"You mean knowing I was raped during my senior year of high school? Or that Walker went to prison because I couldn't convince a jury it wasn't him? That doesn't change what you think of me?"

"Why the hell would it? The sheriff framed him, and it was his lawyer's job to prove he was innocent, not yours."

She lifted her chin even as pain flashed across her face. "Walker lost over two years of his life behind bars. The predator who assaulted me was free to terrorize others. I should have tried harder, done more. Something."

"Jesus Christ, Mel. You were a traumatized kid. The victim of a horrific crime. That wasn't on you. Not the sheriff, not the jury, none of it. You did what you could to survive. You and Walker were both victims."

She stayed stubbornly silent. He shook his head. "There are assholes out there who deserve blame, but not you."

They'd drawn closer, breaths mingling. Her red lips tantalizing. Gage wondered if she felt the same surge of warmth around her heart he did.

There were a lot of reasons he should keep his distance. She had a kid who didn't deserve to be hurt if a relationship didn't work out. The most recent nightmares notwithstanding, he was only now feeling like he'd recovered from the operation against the cartel, mentally and physically, to the point where he was fully functioning.

But lately, he'd been watching his friends fall in love, raise babies, build lives that didn't feel temporary. And for the first time, he wondered what it would be like to want that again.

Want *her*.

The fear was still there, lodged like a bullet under his ribs—fear of losing, of failing, of loving someone too much.

But standing here, her eyes searching his, none of that seemed to matter. Melanie lit something bright inside him, something he'd never experienced before that pushed back the darkness. Something hopeful. The feeling was intoxicating and made it impossible to step away.

He tilted his head. "You want to tell me why you were crying?"

"No. You want to tell me why you and Chase hate each other?"

"No." He thrust his hands back in his pockets to combat the urge to touch her again. "How about I beat the shit out of him for being a dick?" The tears he'd seen earlier still pissed him off.

"I think you'd like that, so I'm sorry, but no. Chase didn't make me cry."

He watched her steadily, not saying a word. The tactic usually worked. People had a compulsion to fill the silence.

Her gorgeous eyes narrowed. "I'm on to you, Special Agent Landry, but you win this one. I'm not a crier. I hate crying. But being in Sisters, talking with Chase earlier this week and then tonight, it brought what happened closer to the surface than it had been.

"Addy's the center of my world and focusing on her has helped me move on from that time in a way that's healthy for me." She lifted her shoulders. "I knew coming back would be difficult, especially seeing people from when I was growing up. Talking about the night I was assaulted hit me hard."

"He brought it up? Maybe I'll beat the shit out of him anyway."

She smiled at him for the first time and revealed twin dimples. God dammit. Since when did he have a thing for dimples? He had a set of his own and had been gratified when they'd morphed into creases as an adult. On Addy they were adorable. On Melanie? They were sexy as sin.

"Don't beat the shit out of him. I brought it up, not Chase.

"Why did you?"

"Because he was one of the guys there that night, at the bootlegger."

"What the hell's a bootlegger?"

"Didn't Walker and Delaney tell you we'd been at a bootlegger the night I was assaulted?"

"They said there'd been a party."

She shrugged. "A bootlegger is a party, but not at someone's house. Kids would get together in the hills away from adult supervision. We'd have a campfire, play music. There was definitely underage drinking. That's a bootlegger. Didn't you do that kind of thing when you were a teenager?"

He shook his head. He'd been too busy doing what he could to keep his sister alive and working to pay bills to do typical teenager things.

"There were a lot of kids there because it was going to be the last bootlegger of the year. It was October and getting too cold to be outdoors like that at night. We had a big fire going. I'd had to beg my mom to borrow the car so I could meet my friends there. She made me swear on everything holy not to drink or smoke weed or anything. She didn't want me driving under the influence. A bunch of upperclassmen from the high school were there, along with some like Walker who'd graduated in the few years ahead of us. It was fun, until it all came crashing down."

She swallowed. "That night marked a thick black line through my life, separating before and after the assault, childhood and adulthood." She shook herself, he thought, like maybe she was trying to shake off the emotions that undoubtedly still echoed. "Anyway, that's why I agreed when Chase asked me out. I want to know what he remembers about that night and the people who were there. Meeting him in public seemed safe. I didn't expect the memories to hit me so hard."

Gage frowned. "Why do you want to know what he remembers?"

"Not only him. I've made a spreadsheet and listed every person I remember being there. I plan to talk with as many of them as I can get a hold of." Her brows lowered as she spoke. "Rhonda Lockwood was there that night. She acted weird when I asked her about it. She'd been dating Josh Lockwood, but when Chase and his friend Greg Delano showed up, I recall her and Greg being *very* friendly. She denied being with him."

Melanie looked thoughtful. "Then I ran into Chase and he asked me out. I thought I could find out what he remembers about the bootlegger and see if he recalls Greg making out with Rhonda." She shrugged. "I doubt what Rhonda was doing that night is all that important, but it's a piece of the puzzle I'm trying to put together. But Chase wasn't any help either."

"Wait a minute. They weren't help with what? What do you want to know?" The target letter was confidential so he couldn't tell her Chase was the subject of an FBI investigation, but what she was telling him added another layer of complexity.

"The person who assaulted me was probably at the bootlegger. I know that's what the detectives were thinking because they got DNA samples from the guys who were there. One of the men on my list could be the assailant."

"What exactly are you planning, Melanie?" He was getting an idea where she was going with this, and it set off internal alarm bells.

"To figure out who it was. The person who attacked me got away with it. I want him arrested, put on trial, and sent to prison." She squared her shoulders. "Because I was a minor, the statute of limitations hasn't run out. I want it all over social media. I want it in the newspaper. I want him publicly humiliated for what he did. I want everyone to see him for the contemptible human being he is." Her voice was fierce. "It haunts me that he was never held accountable and may have gone on to assault others."

He studied her face in the shadows. "Fuck."

She crossed her arms over her chest. "That's not the response I expected."

"Okay, let's try this. It's your right to seek justice, and for this asshole to be exposed and held accountable. I want that too. But it could be risky. Putting yourself in danger to expose him? Hell no."

"I'm not putting myself in danger. I'm simply acquiring information."

"If the assailant is still around, he'd likely have a lot to lose if you out him. That makes him dangerous."

"My friend Esme said the same thing, but too bad. He's been a monster in my nightmares for too long. I don't like the power that gives him over me. The person who assaulted me was weak and used sexual violence to exert dominance and control. I want to take away his power to scare me. And when I get new evidence, I'll ask the sheriff's department to reopen the case."

"Fair enough." He could admire her grit but still worry about her safety. "But realize that anything could've happened to him. He might not live in the area. He might be in jail. He might be dead."

"True. Or he might be living here in town hiding his depravity behind a socially acceptable façade. I need to know. *People* need to know. He shouldn't be free to live in the open while practicing evil in the shadows. I'm going to talk to everyone I can."

"Bradford was irritated. What did he say?" Now Gage knew why his body language had turned defensive.

Her dimples had disappeared. "He was affronted I'd brought it up, like it's not something to be mentioned in polite society. After it happened, I was so ashamed, and I put a lot of pressure on my mom to leave town. My aunt encouraged us to move to Portland where she lived. I was all for it at the time, but I'm done with that. I won't be ashamed because I was raped. It's the person who attacked me who should be ashamed. I'll ask Chase about it again some other time. He can get over his delicate feelings."

Gage tipped his head back, looking out to the street as a truck went by with a noisy muffler. The details he knew about Chase Bradford made him want to keep Melanie well away from the bastard.

He wanted to tell Melanie to leave it alone. Not that she had any reason to listen to him. He wanted her safe, but she had a right to justice.

"I'll look into it for you."

"As an FBI agent?"

"No. As of today, I no longer work for the FBI. I started my own company, a private investigation and security firm."

"So, what, I'd be your client?"

"Not a client. My neighbor. I'd be helping out a neighbor. No charge." What the fuck was he doing? There were so many reasons to keep away from her, and yet here he was getting involved. It was more than her intriguing face sucking him in.

She gave him a skeptical look. "That's not a good business model, giving away your services for free."

"I'm not saying I'll do a full investigation. Send me your spreadsheet. I'll do initial background checks on the people listed there. See what they've been up to." He studied her face. There might have been a few tears, but she was strong. "You and I need to talk more so I have a clearer picture of what happened. If that's more than you want to get into, I can go with what I know."

She stared at him with big eyes. "I'm fine. We can talk. I promise not to cry like a baby."

"Give yourself a break, Mel."

Her expression turned pensive. "I have a lot of guilt about what happened to Walker and feel like I owe him an apology. I've been procrastinating getting together with him and Delaney, but I need to do it."

"What happened to Walker's not on you. The sheriff framed him. Grafton's at fault, not you."

She shrugged. "I should have tried harder. About Grafton, though? I've thought about his involvement. I want to visit him at the prison. He never revealed whose name was originally on the sample, and I want to ask him about it face-to-face."

"No. No way, Mel."

The perfectly arched brow over her right eye said *what the fuck, pal?* as clearly as if she'd spoken the words.

"It may have escaped your notice, but you can't tell me what to do. To use Keeley's phrase, you're not the boss of me."

"I don't want to be the boss of you, but you don't belong anywhere near a state prison. Regardless, Grafton would have to agree to a visit and then the warden would still have to approve it."

"Then I'll go through the approval process and hope Grafton agrees. If it's possible to email him, I'll do that. If not, I'll write him a letter. Maybe I can persuade him. He's the key, Gage. He knows who did it and could have pled to reduced charges if he'd given up the name. He didn't do that. He's protecting someone."

"What makes you think he'll talk to you?"

"He probably won't, but the first step is asking."

"I don't like you going there, but if I can't stop that, I don't want you going alone." He held up his hand as soon as the words left his mouth. "Don't even say it. Let me rephrase. I'd like to go with you."

Dimples flashed when she gave the briefest of smiles and he felt like the sun had come out from behind the clouds.

"Okay."

"Good." He didn't want to analyze why he felt so relieved.

"I'm taking Addy to Cicer Mill Farm on Sunday. I'll try to find Delaney and see if I can set up a time we can get together next week when Addy is at school." She tilted her head. "You said you wanted to know more about what happened. You could join us if you want."

He didn't even have to think about it. "I do. Tell me when and where and I'll be there."

She nodded. They were back in front of Easy Money. She turned to face him. "Here's my car."

She gripped his open coat and leaned forward so he caught her scent that reminded him of fresh rain. Up on tiptoes she brushed a brief kiss to his lips. "I enjoyed the walk."

His hands tightened on her hips, and he fought the urge to pull her fully against him and make his own move. Not the time, but that little taste wasn't going to be enough.

He stood at the driver's door as she slipped behind the wheel and clicked her seatbelt into place.

"I'll text my email address. Send me that spreadsheet."

"Yes, sir, Special Agent Landry."

"Smart-ass," he muttered.

He moved to the sidewalk, watching as she backed out of the angled parking space. Dimples winked as she grinned at him and waved before driving off.

He rubbed a fist slowly over his chest.

He felt like he's taken an arrow to the heart.
What the hell was he supposed to do with that?
Shaking his head, he headed inside to settle his bill.

CHAPTER SEVEN

Melanie glanced in the rearview mirror at the two girls in the backseat. Addy had invited Olivia along for their Sunday outing, and the girls hadn't stopped chattering since getting in the car. It'd given her the opportunity to meet Olivia's parents. Nick and Ashley had a good vibe with each other and their kids—Olivia, Jordy, and four-year-old Emmy. To Addy's delight, the family had two goats and a flock of chickens. Ashley had issued an invitation to come over sometime so they could have tea and get to know one another.

Addy's excitement helped distract Melanie from *The Kiss*. Not that it was a big deal. A friendly peck was all.

So why couldn't she stop dwelling on that brief meeting of lips?

Because no matter how casual she'd pretended to be, that kiss had lit something inside her that still hadn't faded.

Had she shocked Gage? Freaked him out? He hadn't acted shocked or freaked.

She wondered what he'd do if she marched over to his house to try it again. Just to test the results. That's what scientists did, right?

Beyond the electrical pulse thing, there'd been something between them she had trouble defining, a connection that made her yearn.

Melanie drove along Mill Creek Road where a welcome sign with a smiling red apple pointed to the entrance of Cider Mill Farm. Gravel crunched under her tires as she followed arrows to a dirt lot and parked at the end of a row of cars.

Fall foliage and puffy clouds on an otherwise crystal-clear sky made the scene perfect. Given the cool temps and light breeze, they wore heavy sweatshirts and jeans.

"Come on, girls. Let's go see what there is to see."

They walked along the road with its split rail fence, apple trees heavy with fruit on the other side. A descriptive sign identified the grove as Honey Crisp, a variety with a crisp, juicy texture and sweet-tart flavor.

"Look!" Olivia looked up, craning her neck. "There's apples."

"We can climb up on the fence to pick some." That was her girl, always ready to dive in.

"Hold on," Melanie said before the girls could start climbing. "We'll come back later. We need to pay first."

Across the road stretched an open area that sloped down to Mill Creek. A section was planted in trellised berry vines, their leaves withering with the fall weather. Picnic tables dotted a wide expanse of brittle grass, and huge chestnut trees in fall colors of yellow and brown provided shade. At the far end of the meadow a crew was setting up equipment on a stage.

The girls ran ahead as they neared the old farm buildings repurposed for a store and the bakery café. "Cider Mill Farm" was painted in big block letters on a tall barn-like structure. A sign by the door invited visitors inside to learn about cider production.

"Can we go in, Mom?"

"Sure, lead the way."

They filed into the building with a wide plank floor. The girls stood behind a large viewing window to watch workers operate the apple press.

"Look, the machine is squishing apples," Olivia said.

Addy had her face pressed to the glass. "And that big tube is sucking them up." The tube carried the mashed apples to what a sign identified as the press.

The production room looked clean, and workers wore white overcoats and blue bonnets over their hair. There were stainless steel vats and troughs, and lots of tubing. The air was fragrant with the tang of fresh apples.

"Can we get some cider to take home?" Addy asked.

"Sure we can, but let's wait until the end of our visit so we don't have to carry it around."

Olivia grinned up at Melanie. "My mom gave me some money so I can get some cider too." With her blonde hair and blue eyes, the little girl was the opposite of Addy's nearly black hair and brown eyes, but they matched each other in enthusiasm.

"We should look around before we decide what to spend our money on. And we'll want to pick apples."

They wandered outside and through sliding barn doors into the charming country store. Melanie paused inside the door to take it in. The operation had grown to be much bigger than she remembered.

After admonishing the girls to look but not touch, Melanie strolled through rustic displays of jars and bottles filled with anything that could be made from apples and boysenberries: jam, jelly, butter, syrup, pie filling.

There were bottles of golden honey harvested from hives located on the farm.

She'd have to follow the same advice she'd given the kids. It would be too easy to spend her budget for the day in the gift store.

That said, Melanie couldn't resist dishtowels printed with the Cider Mill Farm logo and the smiling apple from the welcome sign and ended up buying a cookbook with recipes from the café. Her stepfather liked to bake so it'd make a great Christmas gift for him.

She found the girls at a display of old-fashioned toys. "C'mon, girls, let's get our buckets so we can pick apples."

Behind the checkout counter, wooden pails were stacked high on a bench and a sign listing u-pick prices in chalk hung on the wall. And at the register was Delaney McGrath.

A flood of emotions had Melanie taking a minute to get her balance. One night had changed the trajectory of so many lives. She and her mom had left their hometown and only recently returned. But Delaney? The young man she'd loved had been sent to prison. Melanie didn't know the full story, other than that when his conviction had finally been overturned, Walker had left the area for a number of years before returning home.

When she'd run into Delaney the previous year, she'd acted friendly and not like she hated her. That didn't alleviate the weight of guilt Melanie felt over Walker's conviction.

She waited while a large family purchased pails. Delaney told the parents, "Pay attention to the signs in the orchards. They identify the variety of apples with their flavor and texture characteristics so you can decide which you want to pick. Feel free to mix and match."

The family trooped out and Delaney spotted her. She skirted the counter and surprised Melanie with a warm hug she wasn't sure she deserved.

"Welcome home, Mel. I'm so glad you're back."

She swallowed against the sudden tightness in her throat. "Thanks, Delaney." She set her hand on Addy's shoulder. "This is my daughter Addy, and this is her friend Olivia."

Delaney beamed at them. "Hello, girls, welcome to Cider Mill Farm." The girls said their hellos, then crowded around a display of jars holding old-fashioned stick candy in a rainbow of colors.

Delaney said, "If it's okay with Melanie, you can each choose a stick candy, my treat."

"Sure, go ahead, girls," she said when two sets of pleading eyes turned on her.

Delaney looked good. No, more than good. Her childhood friend looked truly happy. "Mom said you and Walker have a baby girl. Congratulations."

Delaney's smile was warm and easy. "We do. Harper is almost eleven months old and is a champion crawler." She whipped out her phone and pulled up a picture. "Here are my two favorite people."

Melanie's heart melted at the photo of Walker cradling a round-cheeked little girl whose green eyes matched his. "Oh my gosh. She's adorable. Walker looks like a man who knows he's struck gold."

"We're in a good place. Only a few years ago, neither one of us would have guessed we'd be married and have Harper. We don't take it for granted."

"Can we see?" Addy asked.

Delaney turned the phone to show Addy and Olivia.

"I'm happy for you, Delaney."

The girls picked out their candies, and Melanie said, "We're excited to pick apples."

"Today is a great day for it. And if you get hungry for more than apples, my sister Cameron manages the bakery café next door. Our apple cider donuts are very popular, and if donuts don't do it for you, she was baking apple pie cinnamon rolls this morning. You won't want to miss them."

Addy's eyes grew wide. "Mom, Mom, Mom. *Apple cider donuts.* Can we get some?"

"They do sound amazing. We'll have to check out the bakery after filling our buckets." Melanie pointed out the door. "Addy, why don't you and Olivia go outside and sit on that bench by the door while I get our pails." Addy didn't question the request and the kids trotted off, holding hands.

"I'd like pails for each of the girls." Melanie looked into the eyes of the friend from so many years ago. She took a breath to calm her nerves. "You emailed me last year and said you and Walker wanted to talk about, well, everything. If that's still the case, I'd like to set up a time when we can do that."

Delaney nodded. "I do. Walker and I both want to have a better understanding of what happened that night and with the trial, if you're comfortable talking about it. We feel like there's a lot we don't know."

"I want that too." The tension in Melanie's shoulders eased. "I bought a house east of town. I'm still unpacking, but I'd be happy to host if you and Walker want to come over one day this week."

"Let's exchange contact information. I'll talk with Walker and check our schedules. Would you mind coming here? It'll be easier with Harper's nap schedule."

"Sure, that's fine. I'd prefer a time when Addy's at school."

"Okay, then I'll text you so we can set it up."

With numbers exchanged, Delaney asked, "What street is your house on?"

"Bluebell Lane. The house needs work, but Addy and I are excited about having a couple acres. We're already planning our garden for next spring."

"Oh, that's fun. I can't wait until Harper is old enough to do things like that. You must be neighbors with Gage Landry, he bought a house on Bluebell Lane last year."

"We're next-door neighbors and kind of friends." Were they friends? What was between them was hard to define. "Gage asked to be included when we meet. He seems to think he should keep an eye on me."

Delaney raised her brows. "Ooh, that's interesting."

Melanie shook her head. "Oh no. It's not that kind of interesting."

That didn't stop Delaney from grinning. "Gage is a fine-looking man but more than that, he's been a rock through all that my sisters and I have been through."

Wanting to get off the subject of Gage, Melanie said, "Since you were an only child when we were kids, I'd like to meet your sisters and hear that story."

A couple came up behind them, the man's shopping basket heavy with jars of jam and honey.

"It's a good story," Delaney said. "We'll catch up when we get together. Let me get your buckets."

***

Monday morning was a lot easier when you worked from home. Gage still had to work, but he could sit around in sweats if he wanted. Not that he did, but the option was there.

This morning, he spent a chunk of time on the phone with Phil, potential client and CEO of a logistics company located in Reno. Gage's job was to convince Phil that if he hired Landry Investigation and Security, LIS could handle not only the recent physical breach at the company's headquarters, but also set up cyber protections.

Since the company's physical security consisted of deadbolts and a few cameras, anything would be an upgrade.

Gage had been developing LIS over the past year and, with approval from the Bureau, already had clients and employees. With his separation from the FBI finalized, he was ready to expand. Most of his services were of the cyber variety, but LIS also did physical threat assessments. He had two guys working with him, both former FBI agents, and once he added a few more clients, he'd hire another. He and Phil finally came to terms and Gage scheduled Dinh to fly to Reno.

Dinh did good work. If Phil was impressed, he might recommend LIS to his network of clients. That kind of word-of-mouth could be the difference between barely scraping by and building something solid.

He grabbed his coffee mug and headed for the kitchen. Sprawled in her bed, Pancake went from comatose to alert in less than a second and scrambled to follow him. Deciding to switch to tea, he filled the kettle. Waiting for the water to heat, he looked out the window. As was becoming habit, instead of taking in the view, his eyes drifted to Melanie's place.

He liked catching glimpses of her taking out her trash or raking leaves. There was something about the way she moved—competent, confident, a little guarded—that made it impossible not to watch. Add dark hair, big eyes, and curves he couldn't help but notice, and yeah. He was hooked.

She'd surprised him with that kiss. He wouldn't mind a repeat—with a bit more heat.

That morning Pancake had waited on the patio until Addy came out, dressed for school. The kid wore a puffy pink coat and a backpack that looked too big for her tiny frame, her dark hair in braids and a purple beanie on her head. Melanie had followed her out of the house still pulling on her coat.

Pancake had minded her manners. Mostly. There'd been a slipup when she'd swiped her tongue over Addy's chin. It did something in Gage's chest when he saw the girl wrapping her arms around the dog and Melanie giving Pancake a good head rub. Then all three rounded the corner of the house and disappeared down the driveway on the way to the bus stop.

Now two hours later, there was no Melanie outside. Her car was parked in front of the garage, though, so he guessed she was in the house. He poured hot water over the teabag and let it steep. Mug half-raised, he slammed it to the counter, tea sloshing onto the tile. Two men had come up the driveway to the back of Melanie's house. One wore dark clothing with a black watch cap, and the other a navy sweatshirt with a big Nike swoosh. Nike guy disappeared around the far corner and Black Hat cupped his hands around his eyes to peer through a window.

His gut clenched and a jolt of fear ripped through him. Fear for Melanie.

He punched 9-1-1 into his phone and hit speaker. Drawing on his training, he locked his emotions down tight. Movements calm and practiced, he went to the downstairs safe and retrieved his Glock 19, strapping on his shoulder holster and securing the weapon. When the call connected, he relayed what he'd seen, identified himself as former FBI, and that he was armed and going in. The dispatcher confirmed units would be sent.

He'd been on plenty of high-stakes operations before, but none had ever felt this personal. This wasn't about duty, it was about protecting Melanie.

He jammed his feet into his boots and bolted out the door, leaving a whimpering Pancake locked inside. Phone to his ear as he ran, he called Melanie. She picked up as he hit the bridge over the creek.

"Hello?"

"Melanie, listen carefully. Go into your bathroom and lock the door. There are two men behind your house who look like trouble. I called 9-1-1 and am on my way."

"Are they armed?"

He felt a flicker of appreciation. No panic, but sharp thinking.

"Not that I saw, but that doesn't mean they're not carrying."

"I'm going to look out the window and—"

"Melanie. Don't." He slowed his pace as the trees thinned. "Do what I said. Now. I don't have time to argue, and I can't afford to worry about you while I'm dealing with these dirtbags."

A beat of silence. Then a sigh.

"Dammit." She released a heavy sigh. "Okay. I want to take care of myself, but I'm not FBI trained and I'm not stupid."

He got that. Wanting to handle your own shit was hardwired into him too. Thank god she was smart enough to know when to stand down.

Over the phone, he heard a door shut.

"I'm in the bathroom," she whispered. "The door's locked. I grabbed a hardback book. It's the only heavy thing I could find. You'd better call out if it's you coming through this door, because I'm swinging for the fences."

"That's my girl."

"I think I hear someone," she breathed. "Be careful, Gage."

"I will."

The call disconnected. He estimated it had been less than eight minutes since he'd first seen the two men—but now neither was visible.

Staying low, he moved cautiously across the open stretch between their houses, eyes scanning from the barn to the back of the house.

The sliding door stood wide open.

CHAPTER EIGHT

Fuck.

Gage could wait for the cavalry, but help was still ten minutes out, maybe more. That was too long with Melanie in danger. Weapon in hand, he crept to the door and slipped silently inside.

The kitchen was empty. A few dishes in a drainer. Kid art was stuck on the fridge with heart-shaped magnets.

Heavy footsteps sounded from the front of the house.

Gage ducked behind a dividing wall as one of the intruders appeared. Black Hat, the one he'd seen peering through the windows. The man passed within arm's reach, heading down the short hallway.

Gage stepped in behind him, voice low and commanding.

"Stop. Don't move. Put your hands behind your head and get on your knees. I've got a Glock aimed dead center on your back."

The man froze mid-stride.

Gage's voice sharpened. "You so much as twitch wrong, I shoot. You follow my directions, you live. Hands behind your head. Now."

"Shit." The word was full of reluctant defeat. Dude dropped to his knees.

"Now on your stomach, hands behind your back."

Gage held his aim, tense and focused, as the man complied.

Only then did he take a breath.

Gage wished he had handcuffs or zip ties.

His gaze swept the room. A basket of yarn sat next to the couch, knitting needles poking out the top. Did people still knit?

He grabbed a ball of yarn and began unwinding it. Doubling the strands for strength, he secured the guy's wrists behind his back. Not ideal, but it'd hold.

Eyes scanning for signs of the second intruder, Gage did a quick pat down. He came up with a tactical folding knife, car keys, and a phone. No wallet. No ID.

White male, early forties. Prison tattoos covered most of his exposed skin.

"Thanks for the knife," Gage muttered as he used it to cut excess yarn. "You want to tell me why an ex-con is breaking into my neighbor's house?"

"Fuck you."

"Wrong answer. Somebody send you here?"

"I want a lawyer."

"You're gonna need one," Gage muttered, tying the man's ankles with the yarn. He pocketed the knife and stood.

The phone buzzed in his hand.

"How about that? No password. Helpful."

"You got a warrant?" the man sneered.

"Not a cop, pal. Don't need one." Gage scrolled the message. "Huh. It's your buddy in the barn. Wants to 'light it up.' Says that'll 'make the point.' Also wants to know if you're done scaring the chick. Guess he means my neighbor. Never liked the term 'chick,'" Gage mused.

He tapped out a reply. 'I'll text him back to say fuck no and you're coming out in five."

Phone still in hand, he looked at the guy on the floor. "So. Want to tell me what point you're trying to make?"

The man curled his lip. "Fuck off."

Gage hadn't expected Black Hat to spill his secrets, but Nike's text proved this wasn't some random burglary.

"Better hope your buddy doesn't torch that barn," Gage said coolly. "You two are already in deep enough shit without adding arson. And it's a damn good thing you didn't touch the woman. I'd have fucked you up for that."

He left the man hog-tied on the floor and resumed his sweep, weapon drawn, every sense alert. He trusted Melanie to stay put in the bathroom, but he wasn't about to assume the danger was over. Two suspects spotted didn't mean there weren't more.

He cleared Addy's room. Checked her closet, under the bed. All good.

Next was Melanie's. A couple boxes were stacked near the wall. She'd prioritized her daughter's space before her own.

The bedrooms and closets were clear and the door to the master bath shut. He paused, tempted to check on her, but held back. She was smart. She'd wait.

He edged toward a window, staying to the side, and scanned the narrow side yard. Nothing moved.

A small room next to kitchen looked like a home office. He swept it quickly.

Phone in hand, he hit redial. Melanie answered on the first ring.

"Gage."

"You good?" Gage moved to the French door that opened to the patio, his gaze searching the area behind the house. Bushes bordering the yard, garden area, barn, but no sign of Nike.

"I'm fine. Where are you?"

"Your office. One subject came in through the slider. He's down and tied up in the entryway. The rest of the house is clear. The other subject's outside so that's where I'm going. Stay where you are."

"Dammit. Okay."

"Good girl."

"Shut up."

He barked out a laugh. "Fair enough."

There was a pause and he thought she'd hung up.

"Gage? I know you're trained, but don't be reckless. I don't want you hurt. Let him go if it comes to that. I mean it."

"I'll be careful."

He pocketed his phone and eased open the door to step outside. The wail of sirens echoed off the mountain. Backup was close.

Nike must have come to the same conclusion. He broke from the trees between their properties and fled down the driveway. Taking off in pursuit, Gage reached the road just as Nike reached his car.

Gage didn't break stride. He launched forward, slamming into the suspect and driving him to the ground with a bone-jarring tackle.

By the time the sheriff's vehicles got there, Gage had his suspect with his face in the dirt and his arms behind his back.

Sawyer exited an SUV and tossed Gage a pair of handcuffs. "What's the situation?"

After securing the cuffs, Gage and a deputy pulled the suspect to his feet. The deputy did the pat down and netted another knife and a pack of Lucky Strikes. No ID.

Gage narrowed his eyes as recognition clicked. "This is the guy driving the Tundra. He was up on the ridge watching Mel's house."

"Don't know what you're talking about. Never been on any ridge." The guy's voice rasped like he smoked a couple packs of those Lucky Strikes a day.

"It's him," Gage said flatly. "He was taking pictures of her."

"I want a lawyer."

Sawyer snapped a quick photo of the guy and directed the deputy to take him to the station.

"Come on," Gage said, motioning Sawyer and another deputy up the drive. "Melanie locked herself in the bathroom. The other intruder's detained inside. House is clear."

They approached the open slider. A thump and a sharp voice echoed from inside.

"I told you not to move, jackass. That's on you."

Gage sprinted through the house.

The little table in the entryway was overturned. Black Hat had managed to flip himself to his side, legs awkwardly bound in yarn. It wasn't clear where he thought he was going, but Melanie stood over him with a thick hardback in her hand like she meant business.

Relief hit Gage hard, sharp and unexpected. Long legs, ruffled hair, and brown eyes that sparked with enough heat to start a blaze hit him as crazy sexy.

He crossed the room and caught her arm, drawing her away from the intruder. "You hit him with that book, sweetheart?"

"I saw from the bathroom window you had the other guy. You said this one was restrained." She lifted her chin. "When I walked past, he kicked at me. Tried to knock me down. So yeah, I hit him."

"I told you to stay put."

"I did. As long as I could."

He bit back the urge to argue. She was here. She was safe. That's all that mattered.

Sawyer spoke into his shoulder mic. "Scene is secure." He tipped his head to Melanie. "Good to see you, Mel. Been a while."

"Hey, Sawyer." Melanie gave him a wan smile.

Sawyer gestured to the deputy. "Get him cuffed and read him his rights. Cut that yarn and haul him out of here."

He smirked at Gage. "Yarn work something they teach you feds at Quantico?"

"They teach us resourcefulness, smart-ass." He righted the table.

An image caught his eye. He took the book from Melanie.

"*Behind the Shadow Throne*. I know this book." He blinked, stunned, like the world had shifted under his feet. His gaze locked on Melanie's. "Holy shit, you're M. Brennan."

Sawyer peered over his shoulder. "You write books, Mel?"

"Um…yeah." She looked caught. "Romantasy."

Sawyer frowned. "What the hell's romantasy?"

"Romance and fantasy," Gage said quietly. "This story is incredible."

"You actually read my book?" Her absolute shock couldn't be faked.

He shrugged. "My mom just married a guy with a goth granddaughter. Fifteen, wears all black, more piercings than I can count. She told me if I didn't want to be an ignorant idiot, I had to read it. So I did. Got hooked and blew through books two and three."

He raised a brow. "When's the fourth coming out?"

"Soon, I hope. As soon as I finish writing it." She looked dazed. "I can't believe you read it. You're not exactly my target reader."

"I'll read anything but crime thrillers. They hit too close to home."

Sawyer squinted at the cover. "Dude on the front kinda looks like you."

Gage studied it. "I don't see it."

"I do," Sawyer said. "Dead ringer."

Blushing, Melanie snatched the book back and set it on the table.

More officers entered the house. Sawyer led the team processing the scene, snapping photographs and inputting notes into a tablet. Melanie confirmed the glass back door had been unlocked and nothing appeared to have been stolen.

"You recognize the guy Gage tied up with yarn?" Sawyer asked.

She shook her head. Gage and Melanie had moved into the kitchen, and were leaning against the counter. Sawyer showed her a photo of Nike. "What about him?"

Her eyes widened. "Oh my god. That's the guy who was in the truck taking pictures of me." She swallowed, her voice tight. "Did he say why they broke in?"

She'd wrapped her arms around herself, brows drawn, aftershocks starting to show.

"They're not talking," Sawyer said.

"This dude?" He tilted his head toward Black Hat, who now stood cuffed. "His job was to scare the shit out of you. I intercepted a text from the other guy. He was thinking about lighting up the barn. Said it would 'make their point.'"

Melanie's voice was steady, but her eyes told a different story. "What point?"

"These two are small-time. My guess? Somebody hired them to make sure you knew you and Addy aren't welcome here."

Her face might have gone pale, but there was a fire in her eyes.

Sawyer stood with his hands on his hips. "Both have prison tats. We'll run them and see if we can get them to talk."

"They've already lawyered up," Gage muttered. "They're not giving us a goddamn thing."

"Figures." Sawyer tipped his head toward the door. "We're wrapping up here. Keep your doors locked, Mel. Think about getting a security system."

"I will. Thanks, Sawyer."

He nodded and stepped out, leaving Gage alone with Melanie in the suddenly quiet kitchen.

He studied her. "You good?"

"No. What if you hadn't seen them? What if Addy'd been here?"

He'd been asking himself the same damn thing. "Sawyer's right, you need security. Residential's not my specialty, but I know a guy who's an expert. He's a friend of Owen's. He'll put in a good system and give you peace of mind. I'll call him."

She hesitated. "I don't want to live in a cage."

"You won't. Luke will set you up with a system that works with your lifestyle."

Her sigh was heavy. "I hate this. Addy's only six, Gage. I don't want her to be afraid that there are people who would hurt her."

"She doesn't have to be afraid. You're doing everything right. But I get what you're saying. She's got a sweetness she should never lose."

Melanie nodded. "I'm not telling her what happened today."

"Agreed. And about the security system? Let me reach out to Luke, work through the options."

"I can call him. I hadn't budgeted for security. It'll mean reprioritizing my home improvement list."

He jammed his hands in his pockets. "Mel, let me talk with him. This is what I do. I'll work with him to figure out the best system."

"Okay," she sighed. "But I'm in on every step. This is my home, my kid."

He nodded. Then his tone shifted. "If I'm right and those two were hired to rattle you, it means you coming back to Sisters made someone nervous."

He wished he could ease the troubled look on her face.

"You think it's connected to the assault on me?"

"It's possible. Which lends credence to the theory the guy's still around and worried you'll remember something."

Her expression reflected uncertainty. "What if moving here was a mistake? What if I've put Addy in danger?"

He stepped closer and cupped her shoulders. "You didn't make a mistake. We'll figure this out and I'll make damn sure you and Addy are safe."

"If you hadn't seen them…" Her breath caught. "Gage, I don't even want to think about what could've happened. Thank you."

"You don't owe me anything," he said quietly. "But you're welcome."

He should have stepped back. Should've left it at that. Because once he acted, there'd be no going back. He wasn't sure either of them was ready for what came next.

But he ignored the voice of caution and pulled her to his chest, pressing a kiss to the top of her head, his heart beating fiercely.

CHAPTER NINE

Melanie needed to tell her mom about the break-in, though she dreaded making the call. It would only heighten Donna's anxiety about her daughter and granddaughter's safety.

Before reaching out, she heard from Luke Ballard and scheduled an appointment for his initial assessment. She texted the time to Gage. It felt good knowing he had her back.

At least now she had something concrete to show Donna, that she was taking action and handling things.

Her mom picked up on the first ring. "Hello, my girl."

"Hi, Mom. How's it going?"

"We're good. Let me sit down and put you on speaker." She sounded out of breath.

"What'd I interrupt?"

"Dean and I broke down the pop-up tent we use for the vaccination clinic. We had over thirty people bring in their pets to get shots, and one couple fell in love with a little kitten and adopted it." Donna volunteered at the local animal shelter. "All around, it was a good day."

"Good for you."

"What's going on? I can hear something in your voice." Donna had a highly tuned antenna where her daughter was concerned.

Melanie told her about the break-in. Donna's reaction was strong as expected.

"Good lord in heaven, Mellie. Those men could've hurt you. Thank god Gage was there. What if Addy had been home? The thought of something happening to that little girl scares me like nothing else."

"I know, Mom, but I've got a plan."

"I do too. You and Addy can move in with me and Paul until the police learn why those men targeted you. We have plenty of space and you'd be welcome here."

Melanie knew good and well if she and Addy moved in, her mom would hold on fast and tight, and it would be doubly hard to leave again. Melanie couldn't sacrifice her hard-earned independence.

"No, Mom. Addy and I are staying here."

"Hear me out. This house has two guest rooms so you and our girl could each have your own room. We're closer to the elementary school so the bus wouldn't be an option, but Paul and I can help with drop-off and pickup. You know we'd do anything for you and Addy."

Melanie had heard variations of Donna's proposal since she'd made the decision to return to Sisters.

"I know you would, Mom. You're a big part of why we moved back. But we're staying in our house. I contacted a home security specialist who's coming out to give me a quote." She didn't like using Gage as a guarantor of her safety, but these were desperate times. "Plus, Gage is right next door. He's former FBI and has his own security company. He recommended the security guy I have an appointment with."

"Thank goodness for Gage. Next time I see him, I'm giving that man a big hug. In fact, maybe I'll bake him thank-you cookies."

"Mom, you don't need to do that."

Melanie could almost hear the wheels in Donna's head turning. "You're right. *You're* going to bake him cookies. Or invite him to dinner. Because that's what you do when a handsome, single man saves your life."

"I told him thank you." Melanie cringed at the petulance she heard in her own voice.

"I raised you to have better manners than that."

"Right." Dammit. "I'll do something, Mom. Promise."

With Addy's bus due any moment, they rang off. Donna was in full agreement that Addy didn't need to know about the events of the morning.

That afternoon, as Addy lay on the living room floor with her colored pencils and a unicorn coloring book, Melanie found herself having trouble focusing.

She sat on the loveseat with her laptop balanced on her knees. But instead of working on her manuscript, she'd spent the past ten minutes searching chocolate chip cookie recipes. Oatmeal chocolate chip cookies would be good, especially if she added chopped nuts.

After dinner, Melanie and Addy trekked across the footbridge over the creek. Mel carried a flashlight and Addy carried the container of oatmeal chocolate chip cookies—they'd each sampled one and deemed them gift-worthy. The sun had disappeared beyond the mountains in the west, and the brightest stars were beginning to emerge. Security lights came on as they climbed the slope to Gage's house. A muted woof sounded from inside.

"I hear Pancake," Addy exclaimed.

A moment later Pancake nosed her way through the dog flap in the side door to bound across the driveway. Addy clutched the cookie container to her chest when Pancake sniffed it.

"It's not for you, Pancake. Chocolate chips are bad for dogs."

The door opened and Gage leaned against the frame like he had all the time in the world. Hair finger-combed back from his forehead, broad shoulders filling the space, long legs casually crossed. His eyes, dark and direct, zeroed in on her beneath a furrowed brow.

Her heart fluttered in her chest and Melanie couldn't help but think *no, no, no*. Her attraction was over the top and it scared her. She and Addy were fine on their own. She didn't need a man in her life. And yet, every time she saw him, she fell a little deeper.

He'd risked himself this morning. He could have called 9-1-1 and let law enforcement handle it. But no. He'd run headlong into danger to keep her safe. Brave, capable, protective. Of course, he was the kind of guy who took on two intruders single-handedly.

"Hi, Gage, we brought thank-you cookies 'cause Mom says you helped her this morning."

Addy beamed, holding up the plastic container like a prize.

Gage's gaze rested on Melanie, and she gave a quick shake of her head. She hadn't told Addy about the break-in.

He didn't miss a beat. He took the cookies, holding them up to the light. "Cookies. I like the sound of that. What kind we got here, sunshine?"

"Oatmeal chocolate chip," Addy said. "I helped Mom bake them. We tested them to make sure they taste good."

Gage grinned. *That grin.* Melanie barely resisted a groan. It'd been a long time since she'd been attracted to a man.

"Quality control is important," he said solemnly. "And the verdict?"

"Yummy," Addy announced, her gap-toothed smile lighting her face.

"Come on in. I want to try these."

"Oh, we don't want to intrude," Melanie said quickly, trying to rein in what she could control.

"But I want to see Pancake's house." Addy bounced on her toes.

Gage shot Melanie a smug look and opened the door wider so Addy could enter.

He met Melanie's gaze over the container. "You coming?" She had the uncomfortable feeling he knew exactly why she hesitated.

Outmaneuvered, Melanie stepped past Gage into a small room off the kitchen. A washer and dryer sat beneath a long counter, with a basket of clean clothes perched on top. Across from it was a bench with cubbies for shoes and hooks for jackets. A red leash hung beside a familiar black coat. In the corner, Pancake's food and water dishes sat on a gray mat.

"You have an actual mudroom," she said, pausing to take it in. "Why doesn't every house have one? I have mudroom envy."

"Didn't even know they were a thing until I stayed at Shane's," Gage said. "And I agree, it's a useful space." He pointed to the hooks. "You can hang your jacket there."

She added her bright red puffer next to his. The contrast made her feel weirdly domestic.

He led them into the kitchen, U-shaped, with clean lines and cool gray quartz counters. While it wasn't fancy, it was neat and efficient. The window over the sink looked toward her house.

At the far end, a cozy nook held a wooden table framed by large windows that brought in the outdoors.

He set the cookies on the counter.

She stooped to pick up Addy's pink coat where she'd dropped it and took it to the mudroom.

In the nook, Addy was on her knees next to a basket overflowing with dog toys. She held up a bright blue ball. Pancake locked in on it, tail thumping the wall.

"Addy, not in the house," she warned.

"Can I take it outside?"

"It's dark."

"The outdoor lights are on," Gage said. Maybe he'd caught Melanie's clutch of panic because his voice softened. "They'll be safe."

She gave a small nod.

Gage turned to Addy. "Stick to the upper driveway. If you bounce it high, Pancake'll try to catch it."

Melanie helped Addy on with her coat and Gage opened the door to let dog and child out. Melanie watched from the window as Addy did what Gage suggested. Pancake leaped into the air to snag the ball and Addy let out a peal of laughter.

"Coffee? Tea?" he asked.

"I didn't mean to barge in on you after taking up your whole day."

He raised a brow. "You and little miss sunshine showing up with cookies? I'm not complaining."

"That's gracious of you. Um, tea then. Thanks."

He filled a kettle and set it on the range, then gestured toward an open cabinet filled with various tea boxes. "Pick what you want."

She raised her brows. "I pegged you as strictly a coffee guy."

"If I want to sleep I switch to tea by midafternoon." He shrugged. "Also Emery, Shane's wife, drinks tea. I keep a couple boxes of what she likes on hand."

She picked a bag and dropped it into a ceramic mug while Gage did the same. Outside Addy and Pancake played in the spill of light from the back porch.

Gage popped the lid on the cookies and shoved a whole one in his mouth. He chewed slowly and swallowed. "Damn good cookies. C'mon. I'll give you a tour."

He pointed to stairs near the front door. "Basement's down there."

"You have a basement? In California?"

"Unusual, right? The space needs work. It's currently a home gym."

She nodded as she glanced at the window yet again. "They're fine," she said aloud, mostly to convince herself.

"We can bring them in if you're worried."

"No. I'm fighting the instinct to keep her glued to my side. I know that's not good for either of us."

"You're doing great."

"Show me the rest."

The house was L-shaped with the kitchen forming the short leg and the living room and bedrooms the long. They moved into the spacious, minimally decorated living room. The showpiece was a picture window framing the western sky still holding a hint of lavender from the sunset.

The couch faced a fireplace and a big-screen TV. Gage opened a sliding door to a deck beyond. "I need to get furniture for the house, but I like sitting outside so I started here."

Melanie stepped out onto the wide deck with cushioned seating and a metal fire pit. "This is nice, Gage. You've got an incredible view of the mountains by day, and the amazing night sky after dark."

"Yeah. Being close to the outdoors sold me on this place." He took her hand, leading her back inside, and slid the door shut. "And being up against the national forest means no neighbors behind me. Owen and Keeley have a similar setup not far from here."

She liked the way his big hand wrapped around hers made her feel grounded at the same time her heart sped up from the contact.

"Bathroom, my bedroom with a master bath, guest rooms, my office." He gestured as they went. "Nothing fancy, but it works for me."

She peeked into the rooms as they passed. Sparse but clean. "You've got a good house, Gage. I like the open layout." Personal touches were minimal. A few photos or prints would add warmth, but the bones were solid. "How long have you lived here?"

"A little over a year. I didn't bring much from my apartment. Emery, Delaney, and Cam staged an intervention. I was told I couldn't keep living out of boxes and needed a bed that wasn't inflatable. I let them pick out furniture and outfit the kitchen. Best decision I ever made because I don't have a clue there."

"They care about you."

"They do. Nosy as hell, but they're good people."

Back in the kitchen, the kettle was whistling. Gage poured steaming water into her mug. She walked to the mudroom and opened the door. "Addy, time to come in."

"Aw, Mom. Me and Pancake are having fun."

"C'mon, kid," Gage spoke from over her shoulder. "Someone's got to help me eat these cookies."

Addy's cheeks were ruddy from the cold as she trailed Pancake inside.

"Hang up your coat, Addy," Melanie reminded her.

Gage pointed to a plastic container on a shelf. "Grab a biscuit for Pancake. It'll keep her from having cookie envy."

After Addy washed her hands, Gage set her up with cookies and a glass of milk at the kitchen table. Overhead lights cast a golden glow. Melanie felt another hard tug on her heart. Sharing the quiet of the evening with Gage felt exactly right.

Melanie sipped her tea and let herself breathe, relaxing for the first time since Gage's call that morning. Addy giggled at something Gage said, and the corners of his eyes crinkled when he smiled. Her gaze drifted to the rough scars circling his wrists. Something had happened to him, something violent that had left physical evidence as a reminder.

When they'd finished their cookies, she said, "Time to head home, baby. Let's take our dishes to the sink and get our coats."

"Okay." Addy's voice drooped with reluctance.

"Pancake and I'll walk you back," Gage said, his tone casual, but the look in his eyes as they met Melanie's made it clear: he wasn't about to let her go home alone.

He'd picked up on her nervousness about returning to an empty house.

They walked back together with the wind whispering through the pine trees and the glow of the moon rising from behind the mountain. Addy kept up a running monologue as she walked ahead with Pancake, one hand buried in the dog's fur.

Gage reached for Melanie's hand, their fingers lacing together like it was the most natural thing in the world.

"Nice," he murmured.

Too nice. The kind of nice that slipped past defenses and made Melanie forget all the reasons she should be careful.

Her heart edged closer to something dangerous.

Something she wasn't sure she could stop.

CHAPTER TEN

Gage pushed through the back door of Easy Money. Tuesday afternoon, small crowd, classic rock humming in the background. Owen's place had the right mix of atmosphere and great food.

Gage had put out a call through the group chat. Everyone but Shane was coming.

Owen stood at the bar filling shot glasses and gave Gage a chin lift.

Jen leaned over the bar with a wink and a grin as she wiped down the polished wood. "Hey, handsome. Been a while. How's it going?"

"Good. Busy." He loosened his collar with a tug. He wasn't sure why the hell he suddenly felt hot.

"Even busy boys need a break. Why don't you pick me up after my shift? I haven't seen you and Pancake in ages."

He ignored Owen's speculative look. Jen was nice and their easy, uncomplicated relationship meant easy, uncomplicated sex. No promises. No pressure.

So why did it feel like stepping off a ledge to say, "Can't. I, uh… I'm seeing someone. Sort of." Could he be any more of an idiot? Whatever was building between him and Melanie had him off balance.

Jen's smile didn't falter. "Aw, that's sweet. Another good one off the market."

Funny. He'd never thought of himself as *on* the market. Melanie had upended that without even trying. The way she looked at him. The way she fought to protect her kid. The way she'd stood over a restrained intruder with a damn book. Yeah. Something had shifted. He was willing to sacrifice easy and uncomplicated without a backward look.

Jen moved down the bar to greet a trio of middle-aged guys in matching beer league shirts. Gage took a quiet breath and scanned for Keeley. No sign. Thank god. If she got wind of why he'd called the men together, she'd bust their asses, then she'd tell Delaney and Cam and they'd bust their asses too.

Owen finished lining up a shot tray and handed it off to a server. He turned to Gage. "What'll you have?"

"The Cider Mill Hard you've got on tap. And since I called the meeting, I'll take a platter of hot wings with another of onion rings."

"You got it, brother." Owen passed the food order to the kitchen and pulled Gage a glass of amber cider. He said something to Jen and, after filling a glass with soda water, came around the bar. "Jen'll bring out the order. Let's grab a seat on the restaurant side where it's quiet."

Easy Money had become a gathering point for the men Delaney called her dudes. It still surprised him to find himself part of that group. Delaney, Cam, Emery—they'd banded together to strong arm him—always with a smile—into becoming a member of what was essentially extended family.

They slid into a booth. Owen leaned back, resting his head on the cushion, eyes closed.

"Late nights behind the bar wearing you out, old man?"

Owen cracked one eye open and smirked. "Old man, my ass. It's not the bar that's occupying my nights."

"You work late, then spend the rest of the night doing the deed with your little ray of sunshine?"

Owen grinned. "What can I say? She's insatiable."

"Asshole." The expletive lacked heat.

"You're jealous."

Sawyer dropped into the booth next to Gage. "Why is Owen an asshole this time?"

"I'm not an asshole. Our boy's jealous I'm getting laid regular. He needs a woman."

"I thought we're here because of his woman." Owen moved over so Walker could sit.

Gage was grateful Jen arrived with the hot wings when she did. It spared him the guaranteed round of shit the guys would've thrown his way. She passed out plates, set down a stack of napkins, and turned her grin on Walker and Sawyer.

"What are the McGrath brothers drinking today?"

"Cider Mill Hard," Walker said. No surprise there since he'd developed the label and produced it at the farm. Sawyer echoed the order.

Jen shot Gage a wink before heading back to the bar.

Sawyer dunked an onion ring in creamy dip and ate it whole. After swallowing, he pointed at Owen. "Enjoy the alone time while you can. Once that baby is born, you'll have to get creative about getting time with your woman."

"See," Gage muttered. "I'm not the only one not getting laid."

"Didn't say I wasn't getting laid," Sawyer said, lips twitching. "We just have to get...strategic. Our kid has crazy internal radar. Wakes up wailing at the wrong moment. Every single time. He must not want any siblings. I swear he's doing it on purpose."

His phone buzzed and he glanced down, then grinned as he showed them a photo. "I wouldn't change a damn thing. Cam and JT? They're everything."

Gage stared at the picture longer than he meant to. Cam, glowing. The baby all chubby cheeks and bright eyes. The ache that hit him was quiet, but real. A year ago, that kind of life would've been the last thing he wanted. Now... He wasn't so sure.

"Speaking of kids," Walker said, licking sauce off his thumb, "I've got an hour max before I need to be back. Clara's with Harper while she naps, but I need to be there when she wakes up." He nodded to Gage. "What's going on?"

Gage scanned the faces around the table. These men weren't just backup—they were steady. They showed up. Every damn time. Exactly what he needed.

"Melanie Brennan," he said. "My new neighbor. She and her daughter moved in about a week or so ago."

"I told Walker what happened with her yesterday," Sawyer added. "You need to bring Owen up to speed."

Gage did that, walking through the break-in, the texts, the suspects. He paused as Jen returned, sliding glasses of cider in front of Walker and Sawyer. They waited in silence until she left again. "Now Sawyer can fill us in on what they've dug up on those two assholes."

"We confirmed their IDs," Sawyer said. "The guy Gage tied up inside is Darrel Franklin. The other one, the Tundra driver, is Keith Boner."

Owen snorted into his glass. "Bet middle school was a bitch."

Sawyer shrugged. "Would explain the attitude. Anyway, they've got records, petty stuff going back to their teens. DUI, shoplifting, simple assault. They shared a jail cell in Sacramento County and have paired up since then."

"Motivation?" Walker sipped his drink.

"They're claiming they were looking to score easy-to-fence goods," Sawyer said.

"I'm not buying it," Gage's voice was low, rough. "Boner surveilled Melanie's house. If they were after loot, they'd wait until she was gone. But they came when she was home.

And that text I intercepted? Their job was to scare her."

"I'm with you," Sawyer agreed. "We don't have a warrant for their phones yet but they're burners. If they're working for someone, my bet is the phones won't contain anything that could link them to whoever payrolled them."

"Or," Walker added, "this could be a stalker situation. One of them's obsessed and pulls in the other to help."

"Maybe. Mel could've been followed from Stockton," Gage said.

"But you don't think so."

Gage shook his head. "It's possible, but unlikely. She spotted Boner watching her from his truck. If she'd had issues in Stockton, she would've said something. I checked with Stockton PD. She's never filed a stalking complaint. Her only contact with them was nearly four years ago when she was in a fender bender with an uninsured motorist. No restraining orders, no complaints, no red flags."

"So no history to suggest she was followed from Stockton," Walker said.

"Which leaves us with the more likely theory," Owen said, leaning in. "She comes back to town and someone wants her gone."

Gage met Owen's gaze and nodded. "That's what I'm thinking. Her being here makes someone nervous."

Walker straightened. "You think the guy watching her is connected to her assailant." It wasn't a question.

Gage nodded. "Yeah. Melanie wants the case reopened. She's on a mission, and I don't blame her. She made a spreadsheet listing every person she remembers from that party you yokels call a bootlegger. She's planning to talk to each one of them, hoping to shake something loose."

"Solid start," Sawyer muttered, "but fuck."

"Fuck is right," Owen agreed, voice grim. "It's no secret she moved back. If the guy who attacked her has been keeping tabs, he knows she's asking questions. I respect her for going after the truth, but she's painting a target on her back. You're the law school grad." He pointed at Gage. "What's the law say? If she IDs him, can the fucker still be charged?"

"She was seventeen," Gage replied. "The law on the books at that time gives minor victims until age forty. She's got time. She could also file a civil suit."

"So if he's still around and she's asking questions, he's got incentive to make her stop," Owen said.

Gage nodded once. That's the part that killed him. He admired her strength. He respected her refusal to back down. But now there were break-ins, threats of arson. And Addy was in the crosshairs too. Justice mattered, but not at the expense of their safety.

He raked a hand through his hair, then looked around the table. "She shouldn't do this alone. That's why I need your help."

"You've got it," Sawyer said without hesitation. "What's she learned so far?"

"She's just getting started, so not a lot yet. Melanie remembers seeing Rhonda Lockwood from the bank hanging out with Chase Bradford and a guy named Greg Delano. Says Rhonda and Greg were all over each other that night. But when she asked Rhonda, she denied being with them."

Walker frowned. "I was there but don't remember anything about Rhonda. Delaney might."

"The question is why lie? The reason could have nothing to do with the attack on Melanie, so who knows." Gage moved his plate to the side. "The same day at the bank, Bradford cornered her and asked her out. She agreed to meet, said it felt like a chance to dig into what he knew about that night. He thought it was a date. She didn't."

"Our boy didn't like that," Owen said with a grin, wiping his fingers on a napkin. "Gage had his eye on her all evening, then stepped up when Bradford stormed out without walking her to her car."

"Damn right I did," Gage said. "And Bradford left because Melanie asked about the night she was assaulted. That rattled him. Another thing, he's got a record of violence. Shane and I stepped in once when he hit his wife. I doubt it was the first time."

Sawyer nodded grimly. "Sheriff's department was called to their place a few times. She wouldn't press charges. Then he hit her in public and you two intervened. That was apparently the last straw. Still no charges, but she divorced him and has full custody of the kids. Tells you something."

Gage drained the last of his cider. "His record with women, plus how upset he got when she asked about the party. That's why he's top of my list." Chase being named in the confidential FBI target letter was another strike against him.

"You all know he pulled papers to run for county supervisor?" Sawyer asked.

"He'll never get elected," Owen scoffed. "Too much of a self-important dick."

Walker snorted. "You're forgetting how many self-important dicks get elected."

Gage turned to Walker and Sawyer. "You knew him back then. Do you think Bradford could've been the one who assaulted Melanie?"

Sawyer nodded slowly. "Yeah, I do."

Walker leaned forward, elbows on the table. "I knew him a little, and yeah, I wouldn't put it past him. But if it was Bradford, why the hell would Neil Grafton destroy his own career to protect him? What kind of leverage or loyalty explains that?" He drummed his fingers on the table. "Grafton had a grudge against me, but I think fucking with me was a side benefit. Protecting the rapist's identity was more important."

"That's what I want to find out," Gage said. "I'm starting with Bradford. We're looking for evidence of what he was up to the night of the assault, and any connection between him and Grafton."

"Another element to consider, the Bradfords are plugged in socially and politically in this area," Sawyer said. "George Bradford, Chase's old man, was on the city council, even did a stint as mayor. In fact, he was mayor when all this went down. And when he stepped down as president of Sierra Valley Bank, he handed the reins to Chase."

Gage cocked his head, considering. "Sheriff is an elected position. Let's say George Bradford used his money and influence to support Grafton's campaign. Grafton gets elected and owes him. Then the rape kit comes back and implicates George's son. Grafton swaps out the name, pins it on Walker, and has the added bonus of putting a punk kid he sees as a troublemaker behind bars."

Gage continued. "That tracks up to a point. But once Grafton's career tanked, he still chose to protect the rapist's identity. Even when it meant prison. You don't take that kind of fall to repay a political favor. His career was already in the toilet, but he still chose to keep the name secret. There's got to be a stronger motivation."

Owen stacked the now empty platters and leaned back. "So where do Boner and Franklin fit in?"

"Not sure yet," Gage admitted. "Bradford is our primary suspect, but we can't rule out other possibilities. One of them could've been the assailant. Got wind she's back in town and wanted to shake her up a bit, scare her into leaving again."

Sawyer shook his head. "After you called me with that theory, I ran their records. At the time Melanie was assaulted, Franklin was in lockup in a cell in Oakland awaiting arraignment for auto theft. Boner was in Marine Corps boot camp in San Diego. He got kicked out a few months later for dealing weed."

"Then they were hired," Owen said.

"Exactly," Gage replied. "Boner scopes her out, snaps a few pics to confirm it's her, then they stage a break-in. Franklin's job was to scare the hell out of her. Maybe they torch the barn if she didn't get the message."

"That fits," Sawyer said. "Which means the person who assaulted her is still watching her."

Gage's jaw clenched. "That's why we protect her."

"Agreed," Sawyer said.

"Luke Ballard's coming out for a consult on installing a security system for her. He said he'll work her in, but he's a busy guy."

Somewhere in the last twenty-four hours, Gage had crossed an invisible line. Not that he'd ever stood by when someone was in danger—but this wasn't anyone. Melanie and Addy were more to him than just neighbors. They were his to protect.

The realization had crept in slow and steady, but now that it was here, it settled deep. And became unshakable.

Sawyer finished off his cider and set the empty glass back on the table. "The department will do what it can with extra patrols, but with you out on the edge of town, resources are limited."

"Understood."

"You got a plan?" Owen asked, leveling a steady gaze at Gage. "And how can we help?"

"We run our own investigation. Melanie sent me the spreadsheet. I've already done background checks on everyone listed. Besides Bradford, a few have records. One guy was picked up for domestic violence. I'm digging deeper into him."

He paused, then added, "Next step is interviewing them. I'll handle that. Any of the dudes could be her attacker and I don't want Melanie talking to them alone."

Sawyer lifted an eyebrow. A knowing look passed among the men.

"What?" Gage asked, annoyed.

"Some things you gotta learn the hard way," Owen said, grinning.

Gage didn't have time to deal with Owen giving him shit. "This is how it'll work. Her spreadsheet's the starting point. Once we ID the fucker who hurt her, we'll deliver him to the sheriff tied up with a bow."

"Make sure it's by the book. Last thing we want is for the case to get tossed on a technicality," Sawyer advised.

"You said you've already looked through department records?" Gage asked.

"I have. But I'll go back through them, see if anything rings a bell that didn't before." Sawyer's tone was cautious. "Still, we've reviewed that case a dozen times. When it came out that Grafton falsified the rape kit ID, everything was reopened. We never found anyone in the department willing to admit they knew what he was doing."

"Maybe that's changed," Gage said. "Time has a way of loosening tongues. Someone might talk now."

Walker nodded toward his brother. "Our grandfather and Delaney's grandma got the case reopened. I was exonerated. But even then, no one came forward. Grafton kept his circle tight— maybe it was only him."

"Then we go back to the list of men who gave DNA samples. One of them was a match. That's where we start." Talking it through had Gage feeling more confident he was heading in the right direction. "Melanie wants to talk to Grafton. She's reaching out to see if he'll agree to a prison visit."

"Worth a shot," Walker said. He checked his phone and stood. "I gotta head out. I'll call Grafton's old secretary. She's been helpful in the past. If she remembers anything new, I'll let you know. Thanks for the grub."

He raised a hand in farewell and headed for the door.

Owen leaned back, arms crossed. "You gonna loop Melanie in?"

Gage shook his head. "I told her I'd help and I'll share what I've got from the background checks. But she's got an independent streak a mile wide. For now, I'm holding off on mentioning the rest of you."

Owen and Sawyer exchanged a look.

Gage frowned. "What now?"

"You're going all-in on this and keeping the person at the center of it in the dark?" Sawyer pointed out. "Why not bring her in? Hell, bring all of them in. Keeley and Delaney were at that bootlegger. They'll have different insights. Might even add names she missed."

"And if you don't tell her," Owen added with a smirk, "you'll get your ass handed to you when she finds out. Deservedly."

Before Gage could respond, Keeley appeared and slid into the seat beside Owen. Gage didn't miss how they immediately linked hands. "Why are we handing Gage his ass?"

"Because he's got a lot to learn about women," Sawyer said, pushing back from the table. "And speaking of women, mine is at home and I want to see her."

After Sawyer left, Keeley turned her full attention to Gage. "What are you up to?"

"I'm not—" Gage sighed. He hated sounding defensive. "I'm trying to protect someone."

"Don't bullshit me, Gage."

Owen kissed her hand. "Give him hell, princess."

"What happened to you being all sweet and sunshiney?" Gage grumbled.

"Curiosity wins over sunshine. Does this have anything to do with Melanie and Chase Bradford?"

"Jesus, does anything stay quiet in this town?"

"Nope," Keeley said cheerfully. "Also, you were practically shooting laser beams at Chase on Friday night."

"Laser beams?"

"Yeah. If looks could kill, you'd have incinerated him with your laser beam eyes."

He rubbed a hand over his jaw. "Melanie wants to find the fucking bastard who assaulted her. I'm *concerned,*" that was a better word than "afraid," "that poking around could put her in danger."

Keeley's gaze softened. "Aww, you like her and want to protect her."

"I'd protect anyone in her situation."

Keeley's stare was unwavering. She'd have made an excellent FBI interrogator.

"Fine, I like her. But don't go blabbing everywhere, okay? I'm only getting my head around it myself and have no idea if she's interested." Except that she'd kissed him. That gave him some idea.

Keeley's face lit up so brightly it was like she had emoji hearts in her eyes. "I'm so glad, Gage. You need someone and Melanie is a good person. Since we're not in junior high, I won't tell my besties, but you should definitely work with her on the investigation." She glanced around. "Seeing Walker and Sawyer on their way out, I'm deducing you're including all our dudes. The women shouldn't be shut out, not only because you're not a sexist jerk and shouldn't act like one," she said sweetly, "but because Delaney and I were at the bootlegger and we know just about everyone in town. We'll help with anything that brings Melanie justice."

Which only confirmed Sawyer's advice. He pinched the bridge of his nose, then speared her with a look. "I'll talk to Melanie. But

Keels? If things get dicey and there's a threat to any of you, the women are out." He pointed a finger at her when she opened her mouth. "That's not me being sexist. That's me being trained and realistic. You're pregnant. The others are mothers. None of you have law enforcement training."

"He's damn right about that." Owen's tone was dead serious.

Keeley nodded slowly. "Fair. But Gage, make sure you don't protect her so much that you take away her power. That man took something from her. Don't take her agency too."

Gage left them at the table, Owen and Keeley murmuring to each other like they were on a date. At the bar, Jen rang up his tab. He paid, left a generous tip, and stepped out into the crisp autumn air.

He had a lot to think about, including a conversation with Melanie.

CHAPTER ELEVEN

Gage unlatched Pancake's harness from the seatbelt in the backseat of his SUV. The dog scrambled out and over to the dirt where she squatted. She had a bladder the size of a peanut. He grabbed his laptop case and duffel from the back and stepped out of the garage and into a brisk wind. Clouds gathered to the west. His weather app had shown rain heading toward Sisters. He punched the button on the control panel and his garage door rumbled closed.

Being pulled into an unexpected trip to the Bay area had put the conversation with Melanie on hold. He could've called, but he wanted to talk with her face-to-face.

Dinh had called Tuesday evening.

Working for Gage allowed Dinh to supplement his retirement income while enjoying the perk of taking time off when he needed it. Time he used searching for his birth mother. He'd been brought to the U.S. in the 1970s, one of thousands of orphan children born to American GI fathers and Vietnamese mothers during a senseless war.

The phone call? Dinh had located a woman who might be his aunt. Someone who could possibly help him find his mother. As a result, Dinh needed to move up a planned trip to Ho Chi Minh City, which meant Gage had to cover a scheduled training for a new client plus an on-site assessment for another. Both were in San Francisco.

That had given Gage the opportunity to stay with his mom and Stuart in Oakland. He'd crashed in their guest room last night, Pancake snoring beside him on the ridiculously cozy bed Judy had made: layered blankets stacked like a throne littered with about a half dozen toys.

Lying in bed, Gage texted Melanie to let her know he and Pancake were out of town. Nothing more than a simple courtesy. He was *not* checking in like they were in a relationship.

She'd replied with a thumbs-up.

That should've been the end of it, until she sent a picture of Addy and Olivia holding wooden pails stamped with the Cider Mill Farm logo. The buckets were full of apples, and also twigs, leaves, and acorns. He'd responded with a picture of Pancake eating pancakes because, again, his mom.

He'd spoken with Luke so he knew he'd been out to Melanie's house to assess her security needs. Gage texted asking her about the meeting, and was relieved to learn she was leaning toward the system he thought would work best for her.

Melanie'd followed that up with pics of her and Addy assembling the desk. He grinned at the one of Mel using Gage's screw gun, which she'd captioned "girl power."

Then he got pissed because the kid who'd been harassing Addy had, as Melanie put it, "accidentally on purpose" spilled milk all over Addy's clothes. The texts kept flying drifting from topic to topic, until Melanie finally signed off with a sleeping emoji.

He'd been shocked to realize he'd spent nearly an hour texting with her.

Now he was back home and wanted to check in with them. Make sure they were okay. See the desk in person. Pretend he wasn't falling for them both.

With the dog at his heels, he lugged his gear to his backdoor. Kid voices carried from the creek. Pancake froze, ears up, then went charging down the slope and through the trees. That was followed by excited shouts and Pancake barking her head off.

A glance toward the house had Gage stopping in his tracks. Yeah, Melanie was there, leggy and gorgeous as usual. It was the A-frame ladder she was carrying down the driveway that put him on alert. He disarmed the alarm and stashed his bags inside the door, then moved down his own driveway to see what she was doing.

She set the ladder under the eaves at the front of her house. It was made of wood and had to be decades old. She moved it around to stabilize it. Even with the distance he could see the ladder was wobbly, but she put her foot on the first rung and climbed right up.

"Oh, fuck no." He headed for the trail across the creek. Kids and dog were at the bridge.

"Hi, Gage. Pancake is causing mayhem." Addy gave him her dimpled grin, Olivia at her elbow. "Olivia and me are making fairy boats, but Pancake sank Jordy's."

Pancake sat on the sandy bank of the shallow creek, paws muddy and showing no remorse. The girls both wore rainboots while Jordy's sneakers were coated in mud.

Jordy looked up from where he knelt next to the grinning dog. "Pancake didn't mean to sink my boat. She got excited."

Olivia held up a mess of twigs and leaves. A plastic doll with a tiara sat on top. "This is the fairy princess. Her name is Keyara and this is her boat that will carry her to fairyland. We're almost ready to sail it."

Gage tried to keep the skepticism out of his voice. "Good luck with that."

"Mine was a pirate ship, *not* a fairy boat. I'm making another one." Jordy had a row of sticks about the same length and a long piece of twine he was using to lash them together. Expression serious, he said, "Girls are crazy about fairies. I don't get it."

"Well, *you're* crazy about pirates," Addy retorted.

"She got you there, pal." Gage left the kids and climbed the embankment. He crossed to Melanie's driveway and followed it to the front of her house.

Screwdriver in hand, Melanie stood near the top of the ancient ladder, leaning over way too far to do whatever she was doing to a sunshade attached to the facia board. She would likely have been fine if the ladder had been made in the current century. The high eaves made it even more of a stretch to reach the sunshade.

"What the hell are you doing?"

He realized his mistake instantly. She jerked in surprise and the rickety ladder wobbled, giving a loud creak. The screwdriver clattered to the ground and Melanie grabbed for the roof edge. The rung she was standing on gave way with a splintering of wood, and Melanie let out a shriek as the ladder toppled over, leaving her hanging.

He leapt over the ladder to wrap his arms around her legs from the front. She'd caught herself with one hand on the roof edge and the other entwined with the shade that looked brittle from sun exposure. "I got you."

"I'm gonna fall. I'm gonna fall. Oh damn, I don't want to break a leg."

"You won't fall. I got you. Let go, Melanie."

She didn't let go. "Dammit, Gage. Why'd you scare me like that? I'll break a leg." Her voice sounded strained. "Mom will have to move in to take care of me and that'll only prove I made a mistake buying this house."

"Jesus Christ, woman. We can talk it to death when you're safe on the ground." He angled his head back. Both her hands now gripped the edge of the roof. "I got you. Let go."

"I'm heavy. You'll drop me."

"I won't drop you."

"Are you sure?"

"Positive. Let go, sweetheart."

He could feel her take a deep breath, then release her hold. He took her weight and eased her down. His hands on her ass and her breasts in his face would have made his day in any other circumstance, but he was too relieved and too pissed to enjoy the moment.

Her arms circled his shoulders in a death grip. "Holy crap. Thank you, Gage. I didn't want to die."

He lowered her until her feet touched the ground.

"What were you doing up there?" he growled. "If you hadn't climbed up there on a shit ladder, you wouldn't have been in danger of breaking your leg."

Her arms remained clamped around his shoulders. Her chest rose and fell as she gave a shuddering breath he felt against his skin as she'd burrowed her face into his neck.

"You can yell at me later, but give me a minute, will you?" Her words sounded muffled. God, she felt good. And safe. She couldn't get hurt if she was in his arms.

That one snuck right under what was left of the shields guarding his heart. The anger drained away and he held her tighter, lowering his head next to hers and breathing her in. "I didn't mean to startle you. I'm sorry," he murmured. "You scared the shit out of me."

"I scared the shit out of me too." She gave a shuddering breath. "I'm okay now."

"Yeah, you are."

She tipped her head back and their gazes locked, her close call heavy between them. Something shifted and with it came a feeling like he was staring at his destiny.

Sanity seemed to have escaped him because he made no effort to stop himself from dipping his head and taking her mouth. Her lips parted, his tongue sought hers, and the kiss skipped slow and casual and rocketed straight into intense and hot.

Her taste, dark and seductive, contrasted with her scent, which reminded him of the freshness of first rain. Add in the feel of her body clamped against his, and the parts of him that had been closed down for too long roared to life.

The kiss felt inevitable and the assault on his senses made him ravenous for more. Her mouth moved with his like she was savoring the kiss as much as he was. A hard frozen knot deep inside his chest felt like it was warming for the first time in more years than he could count.

The thought flashed that he was well and truly fucked, and there was no going back. She went still and her breath hitched. He had a *hell no* moment because he didn't want it to end, but then her tongue slid over his and she let out a purring groan that had his blood draining straight south.

Her hands fisted in his shirt and she pulled him closer. Cupping her face, he buried his fingers in the silky thickness of her hair. He tried to ignore the message his brain was sending: a giant neon light blinking *mine* surrounded by caution tape.

They broke apart and realization seemed to strike each of them at the same moment. She stared at him with a deer-in-the-headlights look. He lifted his hands carefully as if she was unstable dynamite. They each took a step back.

He needed to think, to put this moment in perspective, but the wind ruffling her hair distracted him. He never thought short hair would do it for him, but god help him, he found it sexy as hell. Tousled on top and falling over her forehead in choppy bangs, it somehow made her eyes look big enough to drown in. And the bare slope of her neck? Next opportunity he had he was putting his mouth right there. Now that they'd had a taste of what they'd be like together he didn't think either of them would be able to resist going for more. Lots more.

"Looking like you want to eat me alive isn't making this any easier." Her throat moved as she swallowed. "That was a heat-of-the-moment kiss, right?"

"If that's what you want to tell yourself."

"Yes, I do. It's way safer than the alternative."

"No doubt. But me? I like direct." He took a breath and went for it. "There's something about you that's grabbed me and it's not letting go."

"Oh shit."

If that kiss had hit her like the freight train that had flattened him, he figured she understood. "Yeah, oh shit."

She opened her mouth, but Pancake barked and there was the thunder of racing feet and then they were swarmed by dog and kids and the moment was gone.

"Mom, Mom, Mom. Guess what? Me and Olivia's fairy boat sank but Jordy's pirate ship didn't sink. Can we follow it down the creek and see how far it goes?"

Canine and kids all had muddy feet and happy faces. That kind of carefree happiness should never be taken for granted.

Melanie cleared her throat. "No, it's a school night and almost dinner time." She glanced at Gage, then the kids. Jordy was examining the ladder resting on its side.

"Jordy, help me break that ladder apart and we'll get it in the trash."

Melanie bent to retrieve her screwdriver. "I'll do it. It's mine to deal with."

Addy piped up, "Us too. Me and Olivia want to help."

Gage couldn't help smirking when he caught her gaze. "Ball's in your court."

She rolled her eyes and he stifled the desire to laugh. He couldn't shake the feeling of being in tune with her, like he understood her on some fundamental level. He didn't know her well enough for that, but that didn't diminish the feeling.

"Girls, the ladder is a two-person job so we'll let the boys take care of it. You can help me clean Pancake's feet and we'll rinse off your boots."

He watched them retreat up the driveway. Two little girls, the dog, the woman who'd seeped into his skin, and need pulsed through him. His own childhood had been traumatic, and he'd made the choice early on never to risk the heartache certain to come if he had his own family.

But deep inside he craved the warmth and sunlight he was missing.

***

Melanie tasted the soup, added more salt, and stirred. The task didn't occupy her mind nearly enough to keep her from replaying that kiss. She'd never experienced a kiss that so completely *consumed* her. Made her feel like every cell in her body was on fire. Made her want to explore a man's body with her lips, her tongue, her fingertips. Not any man's, only Gage's. And that erotic image had no place in her head when she was standing in her kitchen making dinner.

She dumped a bowl of chopped spinach into the steaming pot. It would cook down enough Addy would deem it edible.

She'd managed to keep her few boyfriends at a safe emotional distance, but with one kiss Gage had obliterated every barrier she possessed. It scared her at the same time it thrilled her.

Setting down the spoon, she peered through the slider to the patio. She hadn't heard a peep from her girl since Jordy and Olivia had left for home. The rumble of thunder echoed off the mountain.

She slid a tray with a bake-at-home loaf into the oven before going in search of her daughter. The deep timbre of Gage's voice carried from the front of the house, followed by Addy's lighter tones. A glance through the living room window had Melanie making a beeline for the front door.

Addy and Pancake sat on the front stoop while Gage stood on a ladder—this one sturdy and made of aluminum—with pliers in his hand.

"What the hell are you doing?"

He glanced at her, the corner of his mouth lifting before returning his attention to pulling out the staples holding up the sunshade. "Back to that, are we?"

"Yes. Why are you doing that?"

"Gage is helping us, Mom."

He pulled out another staple, dropped it in a small tub, then addressed Addy. "Shade's coming down, sunshine. You and Pancake stay put." Addy tightened her arm around the dog.

Gage pulled out the last staple and let the screen fall to the ground.

"Mom said 'hell.'"

"I heard that. She allowed to swear?"

"No, but she says 'shit' sometimes too."

"No kidding?" Gage's grin had Melanie's stomach doing a slow roll.

"Way to rat me out, kid," she muttered. Telling herself to stay focused, she said, "Addy, it's time to come in. Dinner's ready."

It was getting dark and thunder rumbled again. Like a switch flipped, rain began pelting the ground from the heavy gray clouds overhead. Pancake whimpered.

"Poor baby, she's scared." Addy moved farther under the overhang, keeping a hand on Pancake's collar.

"Addy, take Pancake inside until Gage is ready to take her home. She'll feel safer. Remember to wash your hands and set the table. I put the dishes on the counter." Melanie opened the door and Pancake bolted inside, followed eagerly by Addy.

Mel turned back to Gage. He collapsed the ladder and leaned it against the wall under the eaves. "I didn't ask for your help getting the screen down."

"No, you didn't. I'll put it in my trash can."

"I can deal with it. I was going to borrow a ladder from Paul to finish the job."

"Now you don't have to." He climbed the steps to stand on the small, covered stoop, dark gaze assessing. The rain came down in a curtain behind him, filling the air with the smell of wet earth. "I have a ladder. I've got pliers. Your trash can is full since Jordy and I filled it with the pieces of the other ladder and I have space in mine. I don't see the problem."

She heaved out a frustrated breath and closed her eyes. "I'm the problem. Dammit." She opened them again to find he'd taken a step closer. She tilted back her head to meet his gaze. "I'm grateful for your help, Gage. But this is my house, and I need to do things myself. I knew going into it there'd be maintenance I'd have to take care of." She pointed up. "The eaves and facia board need to be painted, which is why, besides being hideous, the screen had to come down. I don't want to rely on friends or family to take care of things like that."

"So you watch how-to videos."

"It's not like I don't know how to do anything, but yeah, pretty much."

"I've got nothing against learning from videos. Do you plan to do the painting yourself? There's a lot of prep work, and painting takes skill. That's besides being backbreaking work and risky if you're working from a ladder, even a good one."

"Hold on, I never said I was doing the entire project. Addy's school friend Lucy's two moms own a house painting business. They call it

Roller Girls. Jessica is coming tomorrow to give me an estimate. She said she'll give me the friends and family discount. That's why I wanted the screen down."

"Next time ask me."

"Next time I'll make sure I have a sturdy ladder and do it myself."

"Uh-uh. I don't want you getting hurt."

"You can't tell me what to do, Gage."

"All that means is I need to keep a closer eye on you." He shook his head as the words left his mouth. "I don't mean that as bad as it sounds. I want you safe." He jammed his fingers through his hair and looked like he wanted to say something else but stopped himself. "I'll get Pancake and head home. The ladder and screen can wait until it's not raining."

A woof followed by Addy's giggle sounded through the door that had been left ajar.

Melanie rubbed her arms against the chill and looked out into the pounding rain that had dropped the temperature. Bringing her gaze back to his, she said, "This doesn't mean anything in the context of, um, what happened earlier, but if vegetable bean soup sounds good, you're invited to stay for dinner."

"You mean in the context of the blow-my-socks-off kiss we shared?"

"Yeah, that. You and Pancake will get soaked if you try going home now."

"Okay."

"Okay?"

"Yeah. I'd like to stay for dinner."

That's how Gage ended up sitting at her small kitchen table across from Melanie and Addy while they ate soup and crusty bread. Rain drummed against the roof, the aroma of fresh-baked bread scented the air, and the soup was warm and savory. She wondered if Gage was affected by the coziness of a scene that felt very much like a family sharing a meal at the end of the day.

Addy chattered nonstop, thrilled to have guests for dinner. She'd wanted to feed Pancake soup until Gage warned her onions weren't good for dogs. Now Pancake sat looking forlorn.

"We need to get treats for Pancake for when she visits, Mom."

"We can do that."

Gage spread butter over his bread. "Give her a carrot and she'll be fine until I feed her."

Addy looked skeptical. "A carrot? Dogs don't eat carrots."

"Wanna bet? Pancake loves them."

"Then you should have called her Carrot."

"She likes pancakes more."

Giggling, Addy got a carrot from the fridge.

She held it out and Pancake took it carefully and began crunching.

"She likes it." Addy beamed at Gage as she returned to her seat. "What other vegetables do dogs like?"

That question was followed by a discussion of foods dogs could and could not eat.

Since the blow-the-socks-off kiss had left Melanie feeling off-kilter, she was happy to let Addy keep the conversational ball rolling.

They finished dinner, Gage and Addy both having seconds, and then it was time for the evening routine to get her little girl settled in bed after which Melanie would have a couple hours to work on her manuscript.

They rose from the table and Gage took the empty bowls to the sink.

"It's getting toward bedtime, sweet child of mine," Melanie said. "Say goodbye to Gage and Pancake. Tonight's bath night so take your pj's to the bathroom. And don't forget to lay out your school clothes for tomorrow."

"Can't I stay up since Gage and Pancake are here?"

Gage tugged her braid "We're going, sunshine. It's getting toward Pancake's bedtime too."

Addy's shoulders slumped. "Okay." How could she make a simple word sound so sad? "Bye, Gage. I like it when you and Pancake have dinner with us."

Gage met Melanie's gaze over Addy's head. "It was nice. Thanks for having me." Melanie didn't miss his surprise when Addy wrapped her arms around his waist in a hug. He hesitated, then dropped a hand to rub her back. Addy released him to fling her arms around Pancake, who swiped her chin with her tongue.

When the hug looked to stretch indefinitely, Mel urged her along. "Go on, Addy. I'll be in to run your bath in a minute."

Dragging her feet, Addy headed for her room.

Melanie retrieved her car keys from a dish on the counter and held them up to Gage. "It's pouring. Take my car."

Gage raised his brows. "You sure?"

"Positive. You and Pancake will get soaked and muddy if you walk. If it's still raining in the morning, though, I'll need you to bring the car back before eight so I can drive Addy to the bus stop."

"I can do that." He took the keys. "Thanks."

He made no move toward the door. "Look, I want to talk with you when you have time." He glanced toward the hallway. "But not when Addy needs your attention."

"Okay. I could call you after she's in bed."

He shook his head. "How about tomorrow? I'd rather we talk in person."

"Is this about my, um, project?" she asked, in lieu of a better word.

"Yeah. I've done preliminary research on the people listed on the spreadsheet."

"Okay. Come over whenever. I'm home all day." She cocked her head. "Another thing. Delaney texted earlier and invited me to the farm on Monday. It's tentative because her baby has a cold plus she's teething and everyone is feeling it. You're invited too, if you still want to come. You don't have to, you know. But if you do…"

His gaze dark and watchful, he said, "I'll be there. And Mel? Dinner was good. Real good. Thanks."

It was there again, the heat of attraction that made the protective barriers she'd built around her heart wobble.

His hand was on the doorknob when he paused. Turning back, he cupped her jaw and kissed her. A swift press of his lips to hers that felt like a promise.

Then, with Pancake trotting at his side, he disappeared into the rainy night, leaving her to wonder how a man she hadn't known existed only weeks ago could suddenly feel so essential to her world.

CHAPTER TWELVE

Melanie sat on the floor, her phone in her lap and a box from the stack in the corner of the living room open in front of her. Gage had dropped off her car early and said he had meetings most of the morning. They'd agreed he'd come over in the afternoon.

Putting in earbuds, she tapped on the phone number from her favorites list. Esme answered with a cheery tone. "Hey, best friend. You caught me on my break. I'm walking around the block to try to get my steps in. How's life in the outback?"

"Quite civilized. We even have indoor plumbing."

"Ha ha."

"I'm tackling the stack of boxes in my living room so you can tell me about your date while I sort through them. It's been a while since we talked."

"Okay, let's see. We had to postpone the first time because Isla had a fever and the second time because my sitter cancelled, but we *finally* went out Tuesday evening. Oh my gosh, Mel. It was so worth the wait and Andres is so nice. But not too nice, you know what I mean? He's sincerely interested. He asked how I got into marketing, and he told me about his work as an analyst, and we talked about our girls. The conversation flowed so easily, and we had such a good time. There are definite sparks."

"Oh, I'm so happy for you. Do you have plans to get together again?"

"We do. Get this, he said he'd call me the next day and that's exactly what he did."

"Calling when he says he will cannot be overrated."

"Tell me about it. The plans are to take the girls to the children's museum. We're coming to see you at Halloween so it'll be after that."

"That sounds like a fun time." Isla's father had been volatile and controlling, and Melanie had been relieved when her friend had finally left him and filed for divorce. It'd been a tough few years for her and Isla. Esme dating a decent guy felt like a win.

Melanie stared at the contents of the box. Dead batteries, charge cables that didn't fit anything, old keys. She'd been rushed to get out of the apartment and ended up dumping the entire contents of her junk drawer into the box.

"I heard that sigh. Why are you sighing?"

"Because I'm looking at a box and have no idea why I bothered moving it to this house. It's everything from the kitchen junk drawer and absolutely none of it is worth keeping. Why did I box up expired coupons and dried-out markers?"

"Dump it all in the trash and be done with it. Isla has been talking nonstop about Halloween. Does Addy have a costume?"

Deciding Esme was right, Melanie took the box to the kitchen table, where she pulled out the loose batteries for proper disposal. "Addy wants to be a fairy princess, which is pretty easy since she has enough in her dress-up drawer to outfit an entire kingdom of fairy princesses. I'll get her some face glitter and we can make a wand."

"Our girls are like carbon copies because Isla also wants to be a princess, albeit a mermaid princess, which complicates matters a bit. Face glitter is a good idea."

"Addy's school has a carnival Saturday afternoon so you and Isla can come with us."

"The girls will be out of their minds with excitement all day."

"That is a good prediction."

"Now tell me about the hot neighbor with the cute dog. Anything happening with our handsome Alaric look-alike?"

"He's read my books."

"I'm not surprised. M. Brennan is an amazing author."

"*I'm* surprised. Stunned is more accurate. He said a teen relative challenged him to read the first book, and he's since read all of them.

I haven't had a chance to talk with him about them, but he used the word *incredible*."

"That's the best kind of validation, Mel."

Melanie leaned against the kitchen counter, rubbing her eyes. "It adds layers to the attraction. I don't think either of us is looking for a relationship, but there's something there."

"Define this something. I need details."

"He kissed me."

"What?!?" Melanie pulled out an earbud when Esme screeched the word. "If I didn't need to get my steps in, I'd have to sit down. Tell me about the kiss."

"Actually, I kissed him first. Just a peck. Then last night, he kissed me, and boy, did I kiss him back. It was sexy and hot, and now I think I've lost my mind because I can't think of anything else."

"Oh my *god*, Mel."

"I know. And up until recently, he was an FBI agent." Another squeal from Esme. "Put those together and I'm not sure what to make of him."

"FBI is way cool, but what does that have to do with you two locking lips?"

She deemed it safe to return the earbud. "I think his background makes him protective. I have to tell you what happened on Monday."

"Your tone says it's something serious. What happened?"

Melanie told her friend about Gage's call to lock herself in her bathroom, and how he'd subdued both intruders single handedly. "So you see what I mean about him being protective? I think it's encoded in his DNA and is probably why he joined the FBI. He now owns his own security consulting firm. I told him about the assault and how I want to find who did it."

"Okay, so he's protective, which is uber hot. But again, what does that have to do with kissing you?"

"I don't like the idea that being attracted to me is somehow mixed up with thinking I need his protection." Melanie sighed. "And now that I've said it out loud it doesn't make as much sense as it did in my head."

"Maybe one doesn't have anything to do with the other. It sounds like being protective is part of his nature and he can't help extending that to you. I bet he's attracted despite that."

"Maybe," she said.

"You shared your history with him, which means you trust him. That's a good start for any relationship." Esme called out a hello to someone. "Now I want the good stuff. How did you end up locking lips with Special Agent Gage? What's his last name?"

"Landry."

"Okay, with Special Agent Gage Landry. Was the kiss amazing?"

"Oh yeah." Melanie described the ladder mishap. "I was using a screwdriver to pry out staples holding the screen up and I would have been *fine,* but then Gage comes up behind me and demands to know what the hell I'm doing. He'd been on an overnight business trip and we'd spent at least an hour the night before texting. I'd been thinking about him and then all of a sudden he's there and startles me. I'm near the top of the stupid ladder, which I should've realized wasn't strong enough. Then the step breaks under my feet and the ladder falls."

This time Esme's squeal wasn't quite as loud. "Oh my god. You must've been terrified."

"Tell me about it. I'm hanging on to the roof and I think I'm about to die, but he grabs me. Good thing he's tall and has excellent muscles because he's got his arms around me and I basically slide down his body. All of which leads to this moment when I'm looking in his eyes and he's looking in my eyes and the next thing I know, we're seriously kissing and it's amazing."

"Holy shit, Mel. First off, be more careful. Second, how amazing is amazing?"

"Off the charts amazing. I've never felt like that with a kiss. There was the sexy part of it, because good lord that man is sexy down to his bones. But there's the other part too. I'm scared to put it into words, but it's like something inside me recognized him as mine, like he belongs to me, and I belong to him. Which sounds dumb when I say it out loud."

Esme's sigh carried over the connection. "Oh, that's so romantic. You found him, Mel. You found your man. I have dibs on maid of honor."

Melanie snorted. "Slow down, friend. As in way down. I feel something. He flat out said he does too. But that's chemistry. No one's thinking marriage. All it means is we'd have really good sex. After the super-amazing kiss, it was raining and I didn't want him and Pancake getting soaked if they walked back home, so I invited him to stay for dinner. I'm grateful Addy isn't shy because that kiss muddled my brain and she kept the conversation going."

"You had him to your house for dinner? That's a date."

"No, no. I wouldn't call it a date. It was more an impromptu sharing of soup. I don't know that I'd want to date him. I don't want to subject Addy to men coming in and out of our lives. She's so sweet and I can already see her falling for him. It's not fair to her." Melanie huffed out a breath. "Beyond that, I get the feeling he's careful about relationships. You can see why I'm conflicted."

"I do. We've talked about protecting our girls. I have strict rules about introducing the men I'm dating to Isla. It's different with Andres, though, because we were with our girls when we met. If this thing between us gets serious, I'll have to think about how to let him be a part of my life. But Mel, you don't want to be single forever, and it sounds like there's a good chance Gage is *the one*."

"There is no *the one*. That's a myth."

"It's not. You've been hurt badly and don't trust guys. I get that, so I'm saying this as a friend who loves you. You keep dudes at arm's length to protect yourself." She spoke fast as if trying to make her point before being interrupted. "You haven't found someone who's strong enough to break down those protective barriers and prove he'll stand with you. Until Gage. I think he could be that guy."

"I don't know, Es. Addy and I are fine the way we are."

"You are, but that doesn't mean you couldn't be better."

She'd have to think about that. They chatted a few minutes more before disconnecting. Melanie took the junk drawer box out through the slider. The pumpkin from the garden sat on the little patio table to be carved after school. Melanie toted the box to her trash cans at the side of the garage. She dumped the contents in one and then flattened the box and put it in the blue recycling bin.

The sound of a vehicle had her looking up. A large SUV with a light bar across the top pulled to a stop in her driveway. Sawyer McGrath stepped out. Tall, broad-shouldered, and handsome as sin.

He strode up the driveway in his sheriff's deputy uniform. "Hey, Mel."

"Hi, Sawyer. I should've said the other day how sorry I was when I heard your grandfather passed. He was a good and kind man."

"He was. Thanks." He cocked his head as he studied her. "You settling in?"

"I still have boxes from the move. It's slow going making my way through them, but it'll happen." She gave him an inquiring look. "Do you have any more news about the two guys arrested on Monday?"

"Gage didn't talk to you?"

She shook her head. "He was away on business and when he came back, we, um, didn't have a chance to talk." She could feel warmth spreading up her neck.

"We've identified them as Darrel Franklin and Keith Boner. Boner was the guy in the Tundra taking pictures. They're both lawyered up and aren't talking."

"Okay." Something about his expression had her asking, "Is this an official visit or were you in the neighborhood?"

"You got a minute?"

Her stomach dropped. His non-answer meant it was official. "Um, yeah. Would you like to come inside?"

"Sure."

She led him to the back door and into the kitchen.

Sawyer motioned to the table. "Mind if we sit?"

If this had been a social call, she'd offer him something to drink. But he was making her nervous, so she sat across from him, her hands clenched under the table. He glanced around and she chewed her bottom lip. He'd been there the other day so she wasn't sure what he was looking for. There was a fruit bowl on the table with shiny red apples from the farm. Addy's colorful drawings were displayed on the refrigerator. A notepad and pen were on the counter for the grocery list she'd started. Normal stuff.

"You want to call Gage and see if he can come over?"

Call Gage? Fear slammed through her and she felt the blood drain from her face. She gripped the edge of the table. "Did something happen to Addy at school? Is she hurt?" Her lips felt numb as she formed the words even as her heart slammed in her chest.

"No. Shit. I'm sorry. I didn't mean to scare you. Addy's fine."

A sharp rapping had her gaze flying to the glass door. Relief flooded through her when she saw the tall man on the other side. She jumped to her feet, then had to grab a hold of the chair as a wave of dizziness washed over her. Sawyer surged to his feet but Gage pushed open the door and reached her first, immediately putting an arm around her shoulders.

"What the fucking hell, Sawyer?" He bit out the words, but when he spoke to her, his voice was infinitely more gentle. "Sit, sweetheart, before you fall down."

She sat, Gage's hand resting on the back of her neck, his thumb stroking into her hair. "I'm fine. I got up too fast."

He turned on Sawyer. "What'd you say to her?"

"Gage, he didn't say anything. He was so serious I thought something had happened to Addy. I jumped to conclusions and it's not his fault."

Sawyer closed the slider and returned to his seat. "Again, I'm sorry. Can I get you tea or water or something?"

"No, thanks. I'd rather you tell me why you're here."

Gage pulled a chair to sit next to her. He took her hand in his. Maybe he thought she'd collapse onto the floor without his support. She hated looking weak.

Sawyer sighed. "Look, I'll level with you, Mel. There's been an anonymous complaint against you."

Melanie shook her head, not sure she'd heard right. "A complaint? About what? I moved in two weeks ago. I can't imagine what anyone would have to complain about."

His gaze remained steady. "Child neglect."

She sucked in a breath and tried to speak, but what felt like an iron fist had gripped her lungs so she couldn't get her breath.

"Addy's not being neglected," Gage growled. "What's going on, Sawyer?"

"We have to investigate if a complaint's been filed. Children's Services got the complaint. They called the sheriff's office to ask someone to do a check. I know Melanie so I volunteered."

Finally able to breathe, Mel spoke. "What was in the complaint?"

"That you're mentally unstable and the child is neglected and living in unsafe conditions."

Shock was still there, but now there was anger. The words came out rapid-fire when she spoke, though her voice shook. "Addy is healthy and loved and cared for. I don't know how anyone could think otherwise. And I am *not* mentally unstable. Talk to her teacher, talk to my mom and stepdad. Talk to Addy's father if you want. I'll give you the number of my therapist in Stockton. No one will tell you any different. I'm a good mother and my daughter is thriving."

"The complaint is bullshit, Sawyer." Gage glared at the other man. "Melanie is as steady as they come, and that kid is happy. You were here the other day. Use your goddammed eyes." He waved his hand toward the kitchen. "This place is clean and feels like a home. I looked in Addy's bedroom when I searched the house. The kid's got a bed and clothing and toys and every damn thing she needs. Open the fucking refrigerator and you'll find the leftover soup her mom made last night."

Sawyer held up his hands in a placating gesture. "I believe you." He sighed. "Like I said, if someone makes a complaint, it has to be investigated. Addy's at school."

It didn't sound like a question. "She is." Melanie struggled to gain her composure. "The bus will bring her home in about an hour. Poke around my house if you need to, Sawyer, but I'd like you to be gone by the time my daughter gets home."

"Fair enough, but full disclosure, another officer has gone to the school. They'll pull Adelyn from class to talk with her."

Melanie made a supreme effort to contain the rage that was building before it could erupt in a scream of defiance. Some nameless, faceless person had made a false accusation and now the cops were questioning her daughter and searching their home. Gage had moved his hand to her back. She focused on the movement of his thumb as he stroked her neck.

"I don't want my child scared." Her voice firmed. "I don't want some person in a uniform pulling her from class and scaring her."

"We don't want her scared either. Deputy Beth Guerrero went in plain clothes, and she'll make sure Adelyn is comfortable." Sawyer rose to his feet. "I need to take a look around so I can fill out the report."

She nodded numbly.

"While I do that, give some thought to why someone would call in a bogus complaint of child neglect."

Gage shadowed Sawyer as he moved through the house. Their voices carried from the back rooms. Melanie stayed at the table, arms crossed in front of her, the hard knot in her belly making her queasy. Returning to the kitchen, Sawyer opened cupboards and the refrigerator. Gage returned to sit next to her, his arm resting across the back of her chair.

Sawyer sat again. "Sorry about all this, Mel. Gage confirms Adelyn is a normal, happy kid and everything I'm seeing here supports that. Once we get Beth's report, we should be able to close the case." He frowned, his expression thoughtful. "You're trying to find the person who assaulted you."

"I am. You think this complaint has something to do with that?"

"I don't know, but it's a possibility. Whoever attacked you all those years ago could still be in Sisters. Finding out you've moved back could have him spooked. Add on that you're asking questions, and he's got an incentive to try to drive you from town."

"By having me questioned about child neglect? No one who takes one look at Addy would think I'm neglecting her."

"It's harassment," Gage growled. "Fucker is trying to rattle you."

"He succeeded."

Sawyer shook his head. "Shook you for a minute, but you're steady now. Tell me what Chase Bradford said when you talked with him Friday night."

"How do you know about that?"

Sawyer nailed Gage with a look. "You didn't tell her we'd talked?"

"No time." He turned to Melanie. "I don't like you going after the person who attacked you on your own. I met with the guys because you need backup."

Her tone cooled. "Oh really."

"Yeah, really. I planned to tell you about it but haven't had the opportunity."

She raised a brow. "There's this thing called a phone, which you were using to text me the night before last. You couldn't have included that tidbit of information sometime in that roughly one-hour period when we were texting? Or called when you were driving home? Or told me before you left here last night?"

"I wanted to talk with you in person and last night wasn't the right time."

"You screwed up, man," Sawyer muttered.

Ire fueled Melanie's clipped tone. There was nothing she disliked more than someone deciding they knew what was best for her.

"Sawyer was at this important meeting. Care to share who else was there?"

Gage gave her a look. "Owen and Walker."

"But not Keeley, or Delaney, or her sisters. Or myself, for that matter. None of the *women* were invited to discuss my business, which you decided to freely share."

Gage scrubbed a hand over his chin. He hadn't shaved and his stubble made a raspy sound "I admit I called the men together, and I know that sounds bad. I want a deeper investigation than what you can do on your own. Keeley figured out what we were doing and busted my chops."

"You should've talked with me first, Gage."

"Look, the guys have expertise the women in our group don't have. Sawyer, Owen, myself, we all have years of law enforcement experience, and even if Walker doesn't, he could take on the rest of us together and still come out on top."

"It sounds like a tidy boys' club."

He sighed. "I know it looks that way, but I wanted their skillset, not their Y chromosomes. I fully intended to talk with you today, but Sawyer beat me to it."

"Glad to help you out," Sawyer grumbled. "Mel, tell me about Bradford. Gage says you asked him about the night of the bootlegger."

She held on to her temper. Being upset over Gage's methods didn't mean she'd dismiss the help that might come of them. "I didn't tell Chase about my plan to find who assaulted me and expose them. I simply asked what he remembered about the night I was attacked. My goal is to talk with every person I remember being at the bootlegger that night. I only started with Chase because I ran into him at the bank and he asked me out. It made it easy."

"His response?" Sawyer asked.

She shrugged. "He acted upset and didn't want to talk about it."

"What exactly did he say?"

She tipped her head to the side, remembering. "He'd been relaxed up to that point but then tensed up. He said it was a long time ago and I should move past it and not let it bother me."

Gage muttered an oath under his breath.

As she spoke, she rubbed at a blue streak on the table from a crayon. "Chase sat up straight, and his jaw was clenched so tightly I could see a muscle ticking. He said innocent people could get hurt if I stirred things up." Her voice sounded tight to her own ears. "He used Walker as an example. He all but said that me reporting the assault is what got Walker wrongfully convicted." She lifted her gaze. "That was hard because I already carry guilt over that."

"Asshole," Gage growled.

"Agreed," she said. "Anyway, he said he had nothing to tell me about that night. Then he threw some money on the table and stalked out."

"You don't have any guilt where Walker's concerned," Sawyer said. She didn't say anything. Her feelings were her own. "Gage has already done a preliminary background search on the people you listed on your spreadsheet. Why don't you hold off talking to folks until we can do more digging? I'm with the department's Special Investigations Bureau and have access to the files surrounding your case. Let me do that and then we can all meet and discuss our findings."

She considered his comment but shook her head. "Honestly, Sawyer? While I trust you, I don't have confidence in the sheriff's department. When Sheriff Grafton was found guilty of framing Walker, they reopened my case. Nothing came of it then and I'm not expecting anything different now. We need to find new evidence. You can go through the files again, but I'm doing my own investigating."

Gage and Sawyer shared a look that had her scowling. "I saw that." She pointed between them. "It means you'll talk later and decide what to do between you. You don't get to do that. I'm not a little lady to be placated and pushed to the side. I won't sit back and let bad things happen to me and my daughter. I don't know who called in the child neglect claim, but they're trying to mess with me. You can help me, but you're not standing in my way."

"You're right, Mel," Gage said. "But let us help out. We're in this together."

"Okay. But no holding back information. I want to know what you know."

Sawyer rose. "Agreed." He handed Melanie his phone. "Put in your number, then I'll text you mine."

Numbers exchanged, Melanie and Gage walked out with Sawyer. After he drove off, Gage stood with Melanie in the driveway, his hair tossed by fitful gusts of wind. He laced their fingers together and moved to stand facing her. The corners of his eyes crinkled when he spoke. "You're badass, you know that?"

She shook her head. "I don't feel badass. I want to find the man who hurt me, and I want him in prison. Then I'll be happy to live a quiet life with my daughter, writing my books."

"That's what makes you badass. You stand up when someone is trying to intimidate you. Same thing Addy's doing with that punk kid at school." He brought her closer until their lips were a breath apart. "You're also beautiful and I can't get you out of my head." Then he closed the gap and his mouth was on hers, his tongue seeking, hers savoring. His hands slid under her sweater to move in firm strokes over her back.

Her skin tingled wherever he touched. Warm, sure, and when she pressed her body to his and felt the growing ridge of his erection, a growl rumbled low in his throat. They broke apart, and she thought she probably looked as dazed as he did.

A shaky breath blew through her lips. "We can't make out in the driveway. I don't want to give the neighbors a show."

He sighed and stepped back.

There was a rumble followed by the sound of air brakes. "That's the bus. I need to get Addy. I hope being questioned by Deputy Guerrero didn't traumatize her."

"Addy's tough like her mom. She'll be fine."

They started to walk down the driveway when a howl carried from his house.

"I need to let Pancake out before she loses her mind."

"Let her come to the house with us. Addy and I are carving her pumpkin this afternoon and Pancake can keep us company."

"Okay. And Mel? There's something between us. We'll have to decide what to do about it."

CHAPTER THIRTEEN

Monday evening, Melanie sipped tea from her mug, her laptop balanced on her knee. The planned gathering at Cider Mill Farm had been postponed until the next day because Harper was still recovering from a bug.

With Addy in bed, Mel was curled up on her small couch, staring at her spreadsheet. Focus was difficult. She was so damn furious.

That afternoon she'd stood at the end of her driveway watching Addy get off the bus. She'd trudged up Bluebell Lane, shoulders slumped, and when she'd reached Melanie, had immediately burst into tears. Once inside and calm enough to talk, the story came out of how Liam had called her an ugly name and told other kids to do the same. The teacher on yard duty had made Liam sit on a bench for the remainder of recess.

Gage had nailed it by calling Addy "sunshine" because her girl radiated sweetness and warmth, and some bully kid had no right to steal that light from her. Getting benched at recess wasn't nearly good enough. Melanie could feel herself getting angry all over again. It wasn't lost on her that both she and her daughter were dealing with harassment. Maybe they'd both come out stronger from the experience, but right now it sucked.

After setting Addy up with hot chocolate, cookies, and a video, Melanie'd taken a minute to calm herself before texting her teacher. Mrs. Delgado called back immediately and promised to monitor Liam any time he and Addy were in the same vicinity. She also promised to talk with Liam's teacher. Melanie thanked her but let her know she planned on calling the principal. While she trusted Mrs. Delgado, teachers were busy and simply monitoring Liam didn't address the underlying issue of the kid's bullying. So next she called the school secretary requesting a conference with the principal and Liam's parents.

She'd done what she could but was still steamed. The meeting was scheduled for the next afternoon, and Donna had offered to come with her. Mel would have liked the backup but didn't want to pull her mom away from the animal shelter and leave it short-staffed.

All this was after Addy'd been questioned by Deputy Guerrero at school on Friday. Melanie had been ready for her to be upset, but according to Addy, it'd been no big deal. Not wanting to make it a big deal, she hadn't pressed for details.

All of which meant she was keeping a close eye on her daughter. Gage's suggestion that the child neglect complaint was an attempt at harassment made sense, which only made her more watchful.

One good thing was Sawyer had texted to tell her Child Services had closed the case against her.

Her phone chimed with an incoming text. She glanced at the lock screen. Chase Bradford. Crap.

She'd have to decide how to move forward with him. Maybe he'd cooled down and they could have an adult conversation. But first she'd make it clear she wasn't romantically interested in him. She closed her eyes and leaned back against the cushion. She'd read the text in the morning.

While no longer feeling like punching someone, the pent-up anger over Liam's behavior had given her a low-level headache. Maybe she'd do yoga before bed. But until then, she needed to focus on her project.

She checked her email, not really expecting a reply to the message she'd sent Neil Grafton and cc'd to Gage. She'd probably written more than she should have, but she wanted him to know how his actions had affected her, and how she wanted to hold the person who'd assaulted her to account. Then she'd requested permission to visit him in prison so they could talk.

There was no reply. She had no idea how often prisoners had access to the internet, so she was prepared for it to take weeks to hear back. If she ever did.

She clicked to open the spreadsheet. For the hundredth time, she went over the list of people who'd been at the bootlegger, trying to picture who'd been there in case she'd missed anyone. There were columns for arrival and departure times, and one for relationships – who'd been with who, what the friend groups were, who'd been dating. Delaney might be able to provide phone numbers or email addresses.

A knock at her front door had her sitting up. Setting her laptop on the coffee table, she rose to her feet. She hesitated at the door. She didn't have a peephole and no way was she opening the door without knowing who was on the other side. Luke from Ballard Security was squeezing her in as a favor to Gage, but it would still be the end of the week before the system could be installed.

"Mel, it's Gage."

Her breath left her with a whoosh. The worry she was being targeted was wearing on her. She worked to smooth out her features before turning the deadbolt and opening the door. Gage wore a heavy sweater open over a gray knit shirt, his long legs encased in faded blue jeans, and leather boots. Pancake standing at his side with a doggy smile only made the man more attractive. He finger-combed damp windblown hair back from his forehead as he studied her, eyes dark and searching.

Maybe it was because she felt wound up emotionally. Maybe it was because something about him called to her on an elemental level. Or maybe it was because Gage was so damn appealing. Whatever the cause, the result was desire curling through her as seductive as a whisper.

He crossed the threshold, his hands settling on her shoulders. He bent his knees to look her in the eye.

"What is it?"

No way was she telling him she had a bad case of lust, so she shrugged.

"Addy okay?"

"Um, yeah. She's asleep."

"You're upset. What happened?"

Which only proved she had zero poker face. Resigned, she stepped back. "Come in first."

Gage grabbed Pancake by the collar and Melanie closed the door.

"You got a towel? It's still wet out." A storm late in the afternoon had sent thunder echoing off the mountains and brought an intense downpour followed by a persistent drizzle.

"Yeah, give me a sec."

In the service porch she took a moment to calm herself before grabbing a towel from a stack she used for cleaning. Gage was like the thunderstorm, wild and electrifying. It made her wary of getting burned.

Returning to the front entry, she handed him the towel. Once Pancake's paws were dry and she was free to roam, she nosed around the living room before heading for the kitchen.

"She's looking for Addy." Gage pulled off his boots and set them beside the door.

"Yeah, she is," Melanie agreed. "Do you want tea? I don't have beer or wine."

"No, thanks. I'm good." He caught her hand. "You hurt pissed or mad pissed?"

There it was again – that support and quiet insight that steadied her at the same time it made her heart yearn. She fought back the urge to move in for a hug, to wrap her arms around his solid strength and hold on, knowing doing that was a slippery slope she might not be able to climb back from.

"Is there an FBI class on reading people?" she muttered. "You're annoyingly good at it."

He brushed the back of her hand with his thumb. "It's a special skill. And I'm dogged, not annoying."

She rolled her eyes.

"But you're deflecting. What's going on?"

Melanie stepped back and he released her. She led the way into the living room, where he sat next to her on the loveseat, knees brushing. Yep, she needed more seating because being this close was way too cozy. She curled her legs under her and leaned back against the cushion.

Tea mug cupped in her hands, she said, "Remember when I told you about that kid Liam?"

"You mean the little fucker who pushed Addy? Yeah, I remember."

"You can't call a child a little fucker, Gage."

"A kid pushes Addy, he's a little fucker. He still harassing her?"

She told him what happened and felt herself getting steamed all over again. "So now I have a meeting with the principal tomorrow afternoon."

"Will the kid and his parent be there?"

She shook her head. "I asked for that, but maybe they think I'll go off on the boy because the secretary said that's not happening. I don't even know if they'll talk to his parents. They should because he needs therapy."

Pancake returned, looking unhappy at not finding her bff. She commando crawled into the space between the loveseat and the coffee table before settling herself with a sigh. Melanie reached down to give the dog a good rub and Pancake stretched under her touch. "Hey there, Pancake, make yourself comfortable."

"She likes it here." He drummed his fingers on his knee. "You know the kid's last name? I'll find the parents and have a chat with them."

"Really? You'd do that? Is that legal?"

"Yeah, really, and yes, it's legal."

"Wow, okay, but no, thank you. I'll get Liam's last name tomorrow, but I want to give the school a chance to deal with him." Addy was lucky to have Gage solidly in her camp.

"Let me know if you change your mind."

The quiet stretched between them, not uncomfortable, but...waiting.

She wondered what had brought him over and if he was thinking about kissing her because she really liked kissing him, and in that moment, it was all she could think about. His gaze snagged hers and her cheeks warmed.

Her phone chimed, breaking the moment. A glance at the screen had her groaning. "It's Chase again. It's the second time he's texted this evening."

"He bothering you? He's one of the reasons I came over. What does he want?"

She set her mug on the coffee table. "He's not bothering me. Tonight's the first I've heard from him since that night at Easy Money and it's been over a week." She tapped the screen and gave an incredulous laugh when she read the messages. "Get this, in the first text he says he had a nice time when we got together. In the second he's inviting me to his house so he can cook for me."

"Oh hell no."

Melanie tapped her lip with her forefinger. "I can't see why he thought our evening was so great, but I want to talk with him again. That'll be easier if we're somewhere he feels comfortable."

"Bad idea, Mel. He acted defensive when you brought up the night you were assaulted. That's a signal he could be hiding something."

"Which is all the more reason for me to try again. Maybe he has a suspicion about who attacked me."

"Or maybe he's the attacker. Not happening, sweetheart."

She narrowed her eyes. "Don't 'sweetheart' me, Gage Landry. I'm not reckless or careless. I agree going to Chase's house isn't smart. I don't want to be alone with him. Plus, cooking for me smacks too much of romance and I'm not interested in him that way."

"Damn straight you're not," he growled.

"I'll suggest we meet for coffee at the bakery," she decided, ignoring his comment. "It's a comfortable space and it'll give me another chance to learn what he knows." Her gaze locked on his. "Why do you two dislike each other so much?"

"Besides him being a pretentious dick, Shane and I intervened when he hit his wife. They'd been out to dinner at Easy Money. Asshole was drunk."

"He hit her? In public?"

"Yeah, and that's why I consider him the most likely suspect from your list." His eyes glittered with intensity. "You're right not to trust him."

"Is this what you came to tell me? You could have texted me."

He gave a humorless laugh. "There's not much I'll put in a text. Bradford reacted strongly when you brought up the assault. He mostly held it in, but he was angry. I want you safe and that means being careful in your dealings with him."

"Okay." She couldn't argue with his logic. Her thumbs flew across her phone screen as she typed out a response. She held it up and leaned toward Gage, angling the phone so he could see the screen. "See? I suggested we meet at Three Sisters Bakery at one on Friday so we can talk. It shouldn't be crowded then. Hopefully, he can take a late lunch." He nodded and she hit send.

"Someone from our group should be there. Not with you, but at a table where they can keep an eye on things," Gage said. "Bradford and I irritate the hell out of each other so it's better if it's not me."

"What did he mean about you playing ranch hand?"

He shrugged. "I worked on Shane's ranch when I first got here. Bradford assumed that was my primary occupation. I didn't set him straight. Beyond being honest work, it's none of his fucking business what I do. Plus, it was hard to resist giving him the opportunity to show the world he's an asshole." He drummed his fingers on his thigh. "Keeley and Delaney would be better backup."

"I don't know. I've only recently reconnected with those two. I don't want to impose. If you think it's important, I can ask Mom or Paul."

"You could, but I'm positive Keeley and Delaney would like to be there for you. Like I said, Keeley already laid into me about excluding the women from our investigation."

"I'll have to thank her for that. We're seeing Delaney at the farm tomorrow. I'll see how that goes before asking her." She shifted so she was facing him. "I don't think you're wrong to suspect Chase. It's awful to think he's capable of doing what was done to me. If it's true and he's exposed, it'll shake up this town. The Bradfords have been a big deal in Sisters for a long time."

She narrowed her eyes at his change in expression. "What's that look about?"

"Nothing I can talk about."

Realization dawned. "That night at Easy Money, Chase claimed the FBI was harassing him, and you said they tried to limit their harassment to criminals. Is the FBI investigating Chase?"

"Good memory, but I still can't talk about it."

She nodded slowly. "Wow. That makes things more complicated." She picked up her phone when it signaled. "Chase says Friday at one at the bakery is fine."

"He accepted damn quick," Gage muttered.

His arm rested along the back of the couch. She shifted under his watchful gaze, worrying he could see more than she wanted to reveal. She set her phone on the coffee table. "Anything else bring you here tonight?"

"Besides you? I want to go over what I'd found in my initial search of the people on your spreadsheet."

Besides you? Why did a throwaway comment like that make her feel all sparkly inside? She gave herself an internal *get it together* admonishment. "Right. Why don't you add what you found to the spreadsheet? I made it so you could edit it too."

He shook his head. "Nope. Not putting anything in a document someone with the hacking skills of a third grader could get into."

"Do third graders have hacking skills?"

"You'd be surprised. I investigated a case where a twelve-year-old hacked his school's computer system. He changed his bully's name to 'Imma Asshole' and his grades to straight Fs."

"Maybe I could hire him to transfer Liam to one of the other elementary schools."

"He probably could do that for you."

"Yikes."

Gage pulled his phone from his pocket and moved closer until they were shoulder to shoulder. He angled the screen so she could see and opened an app. "This app allows you to store and manipulate data and provides encryption. I transferred the information from your spreadsheet and added notes on what I found. You'd listed twenty-one people. There are a few with red flags."

"What were you looking for?"

"Criminal records, court and civil records, police reports, complaints. Anything that suggests a pattern of violence against women."

"This seems intrusive, like an invasion of privacy."

He gave her a *you've got to be kidding* look. "Cops would do this and more if they were to reopen the case. That's what you're aiming for, right?"

"I guess so. I don't have the full plan worked out yet, but I figured I'd start by talking with Delaney, see if she knows who still lives in Sisters and reach out to them. She might be able to help me identify others I missed and, hopefully, give me contact info for them. Once I have that, I'll start making calls."

His green eyes were sharp as he studied her. "The information I found indicates most recent known addresses and should inform who we look at first and what we ask them."

"We?"

"Yeah, we. We're doing this together." She must be softening because she didn't even bother protesting. Somehow she'd acquired a hunky ex-FBI agent security consultant whose expertise could mean the difference between success and failure in her quest.

He went on, "Download this app. I'll authorize you on my account and we can share information that way."

"Right." She reached over a snoozing Pancake to retrieve her phone. She downloaded the app. "You move fast, you know that?"

"This is important."

Melanie filled in the required fields, then handed over her phone so Gage could link the app to his account.

With that done, he pointed to the screen. "Tap here and you'll find my notes on each person. One subject died in a car accident about six years ago and one from an overdose a year and a half ago. Of the couples you identified, three married, and a fourth married and divorced. One female subject was arrested for DUI and a male subject served time for domestic violence. Only fourteen from the list still live in Sisters."

"Oh man. Pete Orona is the one who died in a car accident. He was a nice guy. At least I think he was." When she spoke again, her voice was subdued. "The person who attacked me grabbed me from behind and put a hood over my head. I never saw him. One of the awful consequences is I suspected everyone. Any one of those guys I knew could act like a normal guy, but it could be a mask over an evil soul. It makes it hard to trust anyone."

"You say that, but you trusted Walker enough to testify in his defense."

"True. But I knew Walker from being friends with Delaney. He's always had this unshakable integrity. During my sophomore year I had a flat tire on my way home from choir practice at the high school. It was dark, the road was deserted. He came by on his motorcycle and stopped. He changed the tire and loaned me his cell so I could call Mom. And all the while he was changing the tire he talked about Delaney."

She shrugged. "During our senior year, he would pick up Delaney after school on his motorcycle. He had this hot bad boy vibe. You'd think he was in a boy band because the girls *loved* him. One day there was a group of senior boys, Chase Bradford, Greg Delano, and some others, making crude comments to girls as they walked by. Walker was pissed. He confronted them and whatever he said shut them up."

He gave her a considering look. "It took a lot of faith in Walker to stand up in court and defend him."

"I did have faith in him. I can't see a rapist acting like he did. But that's not all. Walker's a big guy. He's tall and has big hands. The man I fought against that night didn't seem as big. But because I couldn't see anything, the prosecutor was dismissive of my claims."

"Which made you feel powerless all over again."

She nodded, surprised at his insight.

"Tell me more about Chase in high school."

She sorted through her memories. "He was popular, especially our senior year. The football team made it to the state championships, and he was quarterback. They'd only had one loss all season, which was attributed to a bad call on his part. In fact, the bootlegger was the day after that game."

"Any questionable behavior you know about?"

She told Gage about Chase defending Thad Stimson only to later slam the boy into the lockers.

"Sounds like a fucking narcissist."

"You're probably right." Melanie leaned her head back against the cushion. "Oh, I almost forgot. He asked me to prom junior year. I turned him down. He seemed okay about it but that afternoon he was in an awful fight with another boy. Broke the kid's nose. The football coach got Chase out of any punishment. I don't know if that's connected."

He gave her a you've-got-to-be-kidding look. "Hell yeah, it's connected. It shows you had his attention and his use of violence when he's thwarted."

"I thought he was a jerk but didn't see it as a pattern."

"Crushing on you is motive, so we'll be looking hard at him. You were the girl he couldn't get any other way. That said, I don't want tunnel vision and miss clues that might lead us to someone else, so we'll keep our scope broad."

"It makes me sick to my stomach to think he could have done that to me."

Gage caught her hand and brought it to his lips, where he pressed a kiss to her palm.

"I'm sorry, baby," he murmured. Their gazes caught and held. "I should get going." He didn't move, and neither did she. "And you need something for that headache."

Her hand tightened around his. "I'll take something before I go to bed. I'm glad you came over."

The tension, energy, whatever it was that heated the air between them flared and all she could think was how much she wanted to lead him to her bedroom and dive into something deeper. Despite the temptation, she couldn't violate her hard and fast no-sex-when-Addy-is-home rule. Until now, a rule she'd never been tempted to break.

Gage cleared his throat and nudged his dog with his toe. "C'mon, Pancake. We need to go home."

Pancake opened an eye, yawned, then closed it again.

Melanie laughed. Letting go of Gage, she swung her feet off the couch and gave the dog her own nudge with a stockinged foot. "Pancake, where do I put my feet? You're taking up all the space."

Pancake didn't even twitch.

"She's fake sleeping. She thinks if she's asleep I can't make her leave. You and Addy are the cool kids and she likes it here."

"Addy asked if she could invite Olivia and Pancake for a sleepover. She has it all planned, including pancakes for breakfast."

"That kid kills me. She knows Pancake's a dog, right?"

Melanie smiled. "She does, but the line between dog and human isn't so clearly defined for her. She measures a good day by how many dogs she gets to pet. Pancake has upped her good day count exponentially."

Gage stared at her. "Do you ever feel like you created a perfect human? How do you live with yourself knowing that?"

Take a guy who was already appealing on so many levels and add that he thought her child was perfect? Melanie was falling for him and it terrified her. She desperately needed a parachute to slow her descent.

"Addy's done nothing but make the world a better place since she was born. I'm lucky to be her mom."

"That kid Liam needs to leave her the hell alone. We're going to the farm tomorrow, but we'll wrap up our discussion in time for you to make the meeting with the principal."

He pushed back the coffee table to make room and got to his feet. Melanie took his extended hand, his grip firm as he helped her step over the fake-snoozing dog.

Instead of letting go, he pulled her closer, the air between them thickening.

She knew when a man wanted to kiss her. She put a hand on his chest, only barely restraining herself from rubbing the solid muscle under his shirt. "Gage, I'm not looking for a relationship. Or a hookup." She ignored the voice in her head telling her that was a big fat lie. "I'm good with it being just me and Addy."

"Yeah, me either. Wasn't looking for a relationship. Got plenty on my plate without having to consider another person, and you're not one person, you're two."

Her brow winged up at that even as he cupped a warm hand behind her neck, his fingers sliding into her hair.

"I'm two people?"

"A relationship with you means a relationship with Addy. It makes me cautious."

"I see."

"Cautious because I won't be reckless around that little girl. She matters. But that doesn't quell this craving I have for you." He dipped his head, gaze heated, his lips a breath from hers. "You feel it, Melanie? This thing between us? Scares the shit out of me."

She did and it scared her too. She tried to remember her reasons for not wanting to get involved when he made everything inside her come alive.

"You guys are kissing."

Swelling anticipation burst like a popped balloon. She rested her forehead against Gage's chest for the briefest moment before taking a deep breath and straightening, his hand still warm on her neck.

Pancake scrabbled to her feet. Addy stood in her unicorn pajamas clutching her stuffed mermaid. "And Pancake's here. You invited Pancake when I was in bed?" Addy's expression reflected utter betrayal. She dropped to the floor and wrapped her arms around the dog.

Gage pressed his lips to Melanie's temple before releasing her.

He crouched down next to Addy. "Hey, sunshine. Pancake and I dropped by uninvited. Not your mom's fault." He rubbed Pancake's neck. "Do you have a problem if I sometimes kiss your mom?"

"Gage."

He shot Melanie a frank look. "I like direct, remember? Addy saw what she saw. I want to be up front with her."

"You can only kiss her if she wants to be kissed. That's what Mom always says."

"She's right about that. I promise to only kiss her if she wants me to." He rose to his feet. "Pancake and I need to get back home and I think you're supposed to be in bed."

Addy angled her face up to Gage. "Will you tuck me in?"

Melanie nodded slowly when he sent her a questioning look.

He turned back to Addy. "Sure. Lead the way, sunshine."

She took his hand to lead him to her room. Melanie followed, watching from the doorway. Gage tucked the blankets around her little girl and dropped a kiss on her forehead. After Addy blew Pancake kisses, he shooed the dog and walked out, Melanie quietly closing the door.

In the entryway, he scrubbed a hand over the back of his neck. "I'm fucked."

Melanie crossed her arms over her chest. "Dammit, Gage. This is why I don't do relationships. I won't have Addy getting attached to men who won't be around long term. It's bad enough her father is in and out of her life. I don't want her thinking that's how relationships are."

He bent to pull on his boots. "I know. I don't want to hurt her either." He straightened and said flatly, "It would help if you two weren't so damn appealing. See you in the morning."

Gage and his dog stepped through the door. Melanie found herself once again watching them retreat until they were swallowed by the dark.

CHAPTER FOURTEEN

"You don't need to drive. We can take my car," Melanie said, shifting from foot to foot beside Gage's SUV. "Since I'm dragging you along, it's the least I can do."

She never fidgeted. Seeing Mel nervous surprised Gage.

Temps overnight had dropped to near freezing and it was damn cold. Melanie wore a black leather jacket over a red sweater and black stretchy pants. Her head was bare and the breeze ruffled her dark hair.

"You're not dragging me anywhere," he said. "And we're taking my car. Pancake's gear is already loaded."

He watched her hesitation. "You worried about not having an escape plan?"

A furrow formed between her brows. "No, not exactly. But what if it goes badly? What if they blame me and it's awkward and I want to leave?"

"You've already talked to Delaney and Sawyer. Did it feel like they blamed you?"

She hesitated. "No."

"Then don't borrow trouble. Grafton's the one responsible for what happened to Walker, not you. But if you want to leave, say the word and we'll go."

To end the debate, Gage opened the back door. Pancake leapt in and settled in the center of the backseat, already alert and staring through the windshield. She'd go nuts once she realized their destination was the farm. Cider Mill Farm was doggy Disneyland. The place wasn't open to the public until Friday, so she'd be able to run through the orchards and fields and splash in the creek with the other dogs. He attached her harness to the seatbelt and Pancake gave them a *c'mon* look before turning to stare ahead again.

Melanie let out a breathy laugh. "Okay, you win. But I have to be back in time to grab my car and meet with the principal at three. I need to catch Addy before she gets on the bus."

"We'll be back in time."

"Right," she said, and slid into the passenger seat. Her tone was light, but he knew this wasn't about transportation. It was about facing ghosts. And she was doing it anyway.

Soon they were on the road, the SUV speeding past towering pines lining the highway like sentinels, their dark silhouettes etched against a sky of endless blue.

Gage glanced at Melanie, then back at the road. Having her with him felt...right. In fact, he felt better than he had in ages.

It took him a couple minutes to recognize the feeling. Peace.

Maybe it was the mountains. They'd always grounded him. But this was something more. After his father's death in a car accident, Janie's cancer fight, Rafe's murder—for as long as he could remember he'd thrown himself into whatever came next to try to keep the people he loved safe. The FBI had honed that purpose. But somehow, Melanie stilled the chaos he'd carried for years.

He'd felt it the first time they'd shared a meal at her kitchen table, seen it in Addy's dimpled grin, and felt it settle deeper every time he held Melanie close.

She tipped her head, eyes on the scenery rushing past. "It's so beautiful here. I want to take Addy hiking. There's a trail that starts at the farm. It leads up a canyon to a waterfall. Delaney and I used to hike it when we were teenagers." She smiled softly. "Addy would love it."

"I know it. It's a good hike." He had to fight against inviting himself along, not wanting to push Melanie into thinking their relationship was too much, too fast. Though that ship had probably sailed.

Pancake poked her head between the seats, tongue out, tail thumping. Melanie chuckled but rubbed her belly where her hand rested.

"You good?"

She nodded, then hesitated. "I'm nervous about seeing Walker. I'll admit it. I feel like butterflies are swirling madly in my stomach."

"It's okay to be nervous," he said, glancing at her. "But you're not walking into this alone. Not sure who'll be there, but they're all good people."

"Oh my god. You think it'll be more than Delaney and Walker?"

"Delaney texted you to come to the big house, right?"

"Yeah. So? That's where she lives."

"No, she and Walker live in the cabin at the north end of the farm, the one Walker's grandfather lived in. Cam and Sawyer live in the big house. Unless they're working, I expect they'll be there. You remember Clara?"

"Sure. Delaney's grandmother who raised her."

"Yeah, but not only Delaney's grandmother. Cam and Emery's too. She still lives in the big house."

Melanie slumped back in her seat. "Maybe this isn't such a good idea."

He reached over and gave her hand a reassuring squeeze. "You'll be fine."

Instead of keeping her hand in his like he wanted to, he let her go. She was already on edge and he didn't want to make it worse. She was more uncertain than he was, and with good reason. If anyone could understand how the past could linger and wound, it was him.

Gage turned onto Mill Creek Road, and Pancake gave a happy bark.

"She's excited."

"Yeah. She recognizes where we're going."

"Do you know Sawyer and Walker through Shane? Do you hang out with them?"

"Yeah. You know Shane?"

"Some. He was friends with Sawyer, so I'd see him occasionally when Delaney invited me over. They graduated several years before me so we weren't in the same social circle."

He nodded. "I stayed at Shane's ranch for a year. That wasn't long after Delaney and Walker married. Then Shane and Sawyer fell like dominos for Emery and Cam."

"That must've been fun to watch."

"Shane literally falling flat on his face for Emery? It was classic. Then with Keeley being tight with Delaney, she and Owen are also part of the group."

"Found family."

He took his eyes off the road to glance at her. "What's that?"

"It's the family you make rather than the one you're born with."

He grunted. "Yeah, I guess that's what we have. Though there's blood ties in there too."

"How'd you end up staying with Shane?"

"I was on extended leave." He tapped his fingers on the steering wheel. He didn't like talking about himself but found he wanted her to know. "I had a case go bad. Real bad. Shane showed up at my hospital room when I was being discharged. Said he was taking me to the ranch to recover. I wasn't in any condition to argue. I was shitty company, but they made me part of that found family anyway."

He could feel her gaze on him. "Is that where the scars on your wrists are from, the case that went bad?"

Trust her to notice. "Yeah. Fuckers in the cartel killed my partner." He clamped his mouth shut. He hadn't meant to tell her that. That peaceful feeling he'd worked hard to give her, especially on this day, got lost in his past. Being around her was messing with his head.

He turned onto the farm road and took the fork that wound around a hill. He pulled up beside two trucks already parked near the big house. Pancake looked eagerly out the window, whining as the muffled sound of barking carried from the house.

Melanie reached for his hand, pulling up his jacket sleeve. She ran the tip of her finger over scars that were finally starting to fade. "Let me see your other arm."

He showed her his left arm with its matching marks, and they received the same light touch. She turned his hand to trace the puckered skin around the back of his wrist. *Fuck me.* Her touch felt like a healing balm that soothed more than the scars.

"You were restrained, weren't you? You tried to save your partner. They shackled you but you tried to break free to save your partner." The gold in her eyes glinted with compassion. "Am I right?"

"Something like that. Didn't do any good. Rafe still died."

"A man like you, a protector? That hurt would cut deep."

Pancake thrust her face between them, and Melanie let go of him. He was grateful for the diversion. She'd brought a sheen of acceptance over memories that'd brought guilt and rage, and he wasn't sure how to handle it. "Let's go."

He opened the back door and wrestled with a wiggling Pancake to unclip her. Once free, she leapt out of the car. Shiloh, Sawyer's big-ass German shepherd, bulleted around the corner of the house and they chased each other around the wide yard.

Gage caught Melanie's attention. "Are we doing this?"

"Yeah," she said, nodding. "I'm glad you're with me."

He put out his hand. After a brief hesitation, she clasped it, holding tight as they approached the house.

***

The front door opened and two dogs ran down the porch steps, one so tiny Mel worried it might get trampled. The other, medium size with mottled fur and bright eyes, leapt off the porch to catch up with Pancake and her friend.

Delaney followed the dogs onto the porch, a blonde-haired woman with a baby on her hip coming out with her. Melanie climbed the stairs, Gage a solid presence at her side.

"Hey, you two." Delaney waved them forward. "Mel, this is my sister Cam and her boy JT, boycotter of naps. You missed seeing her at the farm the other day."

"Oh, boycotting naps is not good. Nice to meet you, Cam." The little boy studied Mel solemnly. "JT looks big enough he should be carrying you."

"No kidding. He's not even a year old and already wears a two-year-old size."

The little boy switched his attention to Gage.

"Come on, bud. Let's give your mom a break." JT put out his arms and Gage released Mel's hand to hoist him up.

Melanie didn't know why it surprised her that Gage was so easy with a child. "JT looks like Sawyer's mini-me," she observed.

"He does, except for his eyes," Delaney agreed. "That aqua color is all Cam. You're a natural with him, Gage."

"What can I say? Little dude likes me. Harper, on the other hand, acts like I'd eat her for breakfast."

"It's not only you. The people allowed to hold that girl are me, Walker, and Gran. If she's feeling generous, her aunties. She's taken the stranger-danger concept to heart. And," she added, "we're fortunate she's napping because she's been cranky with a tooth coming in on top of getting over a cold."

Some of Mel's anxiety lessened with the easy welcome. "I don't miss teething. They're just so miserable." Mel crouched down when the tiny dog with a sparkly lime-green collar sniffed her shoes. "This is the most adorable dog I've ever seen. Is she a Morkie?"

"Yep," Cam said. "That's Willa. Would you mind bringing her inside? We don't let her run around with the big dogs. I'm afraid a hawk will think she's a snack-size treat."

Mel scooped up Willa, who licked her hand. "You, little thing, can't weigh more than a newborn baby. My daughter would go nuts over Willa," she told Cam.

Cam smiled as she led the way into the house. "You're welcome to bring her over so they can meet. Willa loves kids. Come on in. The guys are out back." She waved behind the door. "You can leave outerwear on the hooks."

Melanie set Willa down and she trotted to a small bed next to the hearth. Gage took Mel's jacket and hung it beside his. Cam led the way to a bright kitchen that had been remodeled since Melanie had been there last. She'd been inside the big house many times as a child. The home now had a brighter, more open feel than it had back then.

Freshly baked turnovers cooling on wire racks smelled heavenly.

A woman with silver hair rose from a chair at the table and came forward using a cane. Regal and reserved, Clara Bryant had raised her granddaughter while Delaney's mostly absent father had crisscrossed the globe working as a photojournalist.

"Hello, Mrs. Bryant."

"It's good to see you, Melanie. I'm pleased you're home in Sisters."

Clara Bryant, who had every reason to judge her harshly, grasped Melanie's hand briefly before releasing her. Melanie swallowed against the sudden rush of emotion tightening her throat.

"This is where you and your little girl belong," Clara murmured. "I spoke with your mother the other day. She and Paul are so glad you're here."

"Thank you. It's good to be back. It feels like home."

"That's because it is. Now, I know you young people want to talk. I'll leave you to it." With that she made her careful way from the kitchen.

Cam secured JT in a high chair with a teething ring. "Gran, I'll bring a turnover and tea to your sitting room."

"Thank you, dear."

The back door opened and Walker came in, followed by Sawyer. The McGrath brothers together made an impact. Both were well over six foot and shared the same dark hair and strikingly handsome features. Seeing Walker for the first time in over a decade had Mel's insides roiling with anxiety.

He and Sawyer had lived with their grandfather in the cabin on the farm. She remembered him as a boy, then as a teenager. There'd been a wildness to him that only Delaney had been able to calm.

Walker's gaze took in Gage, who'd moved to stand at her side, then locked on hers. This man had spent over two years in prison for a crime against her, a crime he hadn't committed. Two years in a cage, being treated like a wild animal.

She'd last seen him at the trial, a young man with his whole life ahead of him, until that future had been ripped away. The memory of the jury foreman reading the guilty verdict was etched forever in her brain. Walker's face had turned to stone. He'd stared straight forward, refusing to meet anyone's gaze, until being led from the courtroom in handcuffs.

Now in his mid-thirties with a wife and child, he wore a layer of maturity that looked good on him. She took a deep breath, hoping it would ease the nerves bubbling under her skin, but it didn't. "Hello, Walker."

"Melanie. It's been a while."

"Yes." She sucked in a shaky breath. "I'm sorry. I'm so sorry. I should've been able to convince the jury it wasn't you." She blurted out the words in a rush of emotion. "I knew it wasn't you, but I couldn't get anyone to believe me."

Walker looked startled, his forehead furrowing as he raised his brows. She should've eased into what she wanted to say, not ambushing him the moment she laid eyes on him. The guilt she'd been living with for so long couldn't be contained.

Except for JT fussing in his high chair, every person in the room had stopped what they were doing, their eyes on her and Walker.

"What the hell?" Walker studied her with a frown. Delaney came to stand beside her husband. Melanie didn't miss how their hands brushed and held before releasing.

"Have you been carrying that around all this time, the idea that somehow you're responsible for sending me to prison?"

She nodded slowly.

"You were never the reason, and I never blamed you." He scrubbed a hand over his face. "Good god, Melanie, you were a traumatized kid. The DA wanted a conviction, not justice. You and I were sacrificial pawns."

"You had to blame me. I couldn't convince them of the truth."

He shook his head. "I didn't. I was so damn grateful you had the guts to testify on my behalf. Not many did." He huffed out a breath and opened his arms. "Come here."

Melanie hesitated, then walked into his embrace. When his arms closed around her, some of the pain she'd held inside loosened, then began to melt away. He relaxed his hold. When she stepped back, he muttered, "We good?"

She brushed a tear from her cheek. "Yeah, we're good."

"Let's sit at the table." Delaney's tone lightened the mood. "Cam made turnovers. We have coffee and there's hot water in the kettle for anyone who prefers tea."

As people moved around them, Gage dropped a hand on her shoulder and guided Melanie into the living room. She wiped at her cheeks again. Crying was for wimps. "I'm fine," she muttered.

"Want to take a walk, see what the dogs are up to?" His thumb stroking the back of her neck helped to settle her.

"No. Truly, I'm fine." She shook her head and cleared her throat. "I didn't mean to dump that on him without warning. I've been thinking about it for so long it just tumbled out."

"Understandable. But Mel, you're too hard on yourself."

"Maybe I have been. Even with therapy I hadn't been able to let that go. I guess I needed to hear it from Walker." She felt steadier. "I'm better now. Thanks for standing by me, Gage."

"Always."

She had a feeling he meant that.

They returned to the kitchen, where JT's fussing had turned to howling, his face scrunched up as he banged his teething ring on the tray in front of him. When Cam moved toward him, Sawyer stopped her. "I got this guy."

He lifted the little boy from the high chair, and the fussing immediately stopped. "Time to try that nap again, kid." Sawyer patted his back, and JT laid his head on his dad's shoulder, his eyes already drooping. Moving to the doorway, he murmured something to Cam, then walked out of the room with his son.

Gage ran his hand down Melanie's arm. "You want tea?"

"Yeah, thanks."

"I'll get it," Delaney said. "You two have a seat."

"Sit, Laney," Walker growled. "You were up last night with Harper. I can bring stuff to the table."

"Well, okay then." She took the chair across from Melanie.

Once everyone had their beverage, they sat around the table. Melanie cut off the corner of her apple-berry turnover and bit into the flakey goodness. "This is delicious, Cam. Where'd you learn to bake?"

Cam leaned back in her seat, a mug of coffee cradled in her hand. "I worked at a bakery in college, then learned more following bakers online and experimenting with recipes."

She looked up as Sawyer returned, a baby monitor hooked to his belt. He dropped a hand to her shoulder and brushed his lips to the top of her head before moving to the counter to pour coffee into a mug. Melanie saw so much communicated in that moment: you're my person, I love you, our child is settled. We're in this together.

The pang of longing startled her. She never once regretted not staying with Addy's father, but there were times she yearned for someone to share that connection, who would be for her what Sawyer so clearly was for Cam.

Taking a fortifying sip of tea, she turned to Delaney. "I'm curious how you, Cam, and Emery found each other."

While everyone enjoyed their pastries, Delaney told the story. "That was all Gran. After Dad died, I read his journals and learned he had two other daughters. He was a love 'em and leave 'em kind of guy. When Gran found out, she made it a mission to find my sisters. She hired a private investigator who tracked down Emery and Cam." She went on to relate how Emery's work for a developer had brought her into direct conflict with Shane Keller of Lone Pine Ranch, which shared a boundary with Cider Mill Farm.

Delaney continued, "But before Emery came on the scene, Cam started working for us under an assumed name. I had no idea she was my sister."

Cam took up the narrative. "I was in a bad situation in Oklahoma and ended up having to run for my life. I'd gotten a letter from Gran inviting me to Cider Mill Farm. That gave me a destination. I didn't feel safe revealing my identity, but Delaney still hired me without official ID or a Social Security number." She eyed her husband. "But Lieutenant McGrath was suspicious and kept poking around."

Sawyer caught her hand and gave her a satisfied grin. "I got you, didn't I?" His gaze shifted to Melanie. "She thought she could fool law enforcement, but I was on to her."

"Wow, it's amazing how it turned out," Melanie said. "Clara must be thrilled to have her granddaughters all living in the area and marrying local boys."

"That's a definite yes," Delaney agreed. "I didn't know I needed sisters, but now I can't imagine my life without them. Gran brought us together and we're here for her whenever she needs us."

"I'd like to meet Emery." She glanced at Gage. "I recognized Shane Keller at Easy Money the other night, so I'm assuming that was Emery with him."

"That was Emery. She's been good for Shane."

"He looked happy."

"I'm looking forward to us being friends again, Mel." Delaney looked at Walker, then spoke when he nodded. "Walker says you're working to identify the man who assaulted you. We'd like to help with that. It has to be hard knowing he never faced justice and is out there free to live his life."

Mel nodded. "It is. One reason I returned to Sisters was to reframe the narrative and find the man who did this to me. Mom and I moved away because I was ashamed and embarrassed about what happened. I feel coming back is reclaiming my right to be here."

"That's important," Cam said. "You shouldn't feel ashamed. Shame belongs on the person who assaulted you."

"Exactly. I think bringing him to justice will help me find closure." Her gaze met Walker's. "I think for you too."

Walker sipped his coffee. "What he did affected me, Delaney, my family. It's time we got some answers."

"Which brings me to contacting the people who'd been at the bootlegger," Melanie said. "My car ran out of gas after I left the party that night, even though I had half a tank when I left home." She gripped her mug with both hands, appreciating its warmth. "I was only a block from my house when it stalled. I decided to cut through the park, which sounds so stupid now. But I'd been to that park so many times and our house was just on the other side, and it was a long walk around. The attacker put something over my head so I couldn't see and only spoke in whispers. That makes me think he knew I'd recognize him."

"Sawyer told us you have a spreadsheet listing the names of the people who were there that night," Delaney said.

Melanie felt relief talking about it, putting into words the thoughts that had been swirling in her head for so long.

Sawyer tilted his head. "You think gas was siphoned from your car and then you were followed?"

"I do. I didn't notice anyone following me, but I don't know that I would have."

Sawyer nodded. "It's been a long time. People's memories will be hazy, especially if they were under the influence. But asking if they recall someone near the cars is a place to start." He drummed his fingers on the table. "I've been combing through department records. So far, nothing new."

"Thanks, Sawyer."

Melanie still felt shaky as she pushed back on the emotions threatening to swamp her.

When she'd first decided to dig into the past, she'd assumed she'd be on her own. But looking around the table, seeing the determined faces of the people beside her, she felt anything but alone. They formed a solid unit of unexpected support. It made her feel stronger, and she didn't take it for granted.

Gage slid his plate aside, bringing his coffee mug in front of him. "When we figure out who the assailant is and how he was tied to Grafton, we'll have our motive. From what you've all told me, the sheriff wanted an arrest and a conviction, but he also had someone to protect. Framing Walker let him accomplish all three."

"How was Walker finally exonerated?" Melanie asked.

"Gran, Sawyer, and James, Walker's grandfather, hired a lawyer who was able to prove Neil Grafton put Walker's name on the DNA match. Once his conviction was overturned, Walker took off." Delaney gave her husband a pointed look. "He spent several years roaming the country, working. Avoiding me."

"Didn't think Delaney tangling up with an ex-con was good for her," he told Melanie. He raised a hand when Delaney opened her mouth. "I know, I'm not an ex-con if I was exonerated, but I was so fucking pissed. If I'd come back, I'd have burned down the town. I had to get that rage out of my system, and I didn't want to hurt Delaney or my family."

He glanced at his wife. "When I finally did come back, I still wanted retribution, but I wasn't reckless."

"I can understand that," Melanie said. "I was angry too, and ashamed. Mom made sure I got therapy, and that helped. It took a while before I had perspective on what happened to me and Walker. Like Cam said, I shouldn't feel ashamed because I was assaulted. The person who attacked me should be ashamed. *He* should be in prison."

"We all have a vested interest in finding him. I want to work together on this," Walker said.

Melanie nodded. "My original plan was to find any information the detectives might have missed. Once I identify a suspect, I mean to bring that evidence to the sheriff's department and ask them to reopen the case." Melanie looked around the table. "But I hear there was a little meeting among the guys," she said pointedly, "and now the plan's evolved."

"I heard about that." Delaney gave her husband a narrow-eyed look.

Walker held up his hands. "Hey, don't blame me. I was lured there with promises of alcohol and hot wings."

When Cam raised a brow at her husband, Gage let out a sigh. "That one's on me. Keeley already let me have it. In my defense, every woman in our group is a mom or soon to be, and I don't want any of you in harm's way."

"Good for Keeley," Delaney shot back. "But discussing the case doesn't equal danger, and we're more than capable of deciding what risks we're willing to take."

"Moving on," Gage said, looking like he'd rather be anywhere than in the crosshairs of Delaney McGrath. "Bottom line, we follow the evidence. And after talking with Mel, and considering his record of domestic abuse, Chase Bradford's my top suspect."

The conversation shifted back to the bootlegger party. Melanie appreciated how Delaney and Walker helped clarify her list, adding a couple names and filling in missing connections.

Delaney confirmed seeing Rhonda with Greg Delano.

"I definitely remember Rhonda with Greg," Delaney said. "They were against a tree. She was in his lap, and he had his hand up her shirt." She frowned. "I think they disappeared for a while, but I'm not sure. I know his sister and I'll get his contact info from her."

Once they'd mapped out next steps, Melanie pushed her chair back. "We should get going."

She paused, her gaze sweeping over the people seated around the table. "When I first came back to Sisters, I wasn't sure I'd ever find the evil bastard who hurt me. But now I believe I will. And it's because of all of you. Thank you for your help, and for being here."

"We're in this together," Delaney affirmed.

A cry coming over a baby monitor had her pushing to her feet. "That's Harper." She gave Melanie a hug, then Gage. "We'll touch base in a couple days and see what we've found."

CHAPTER FIFTEEN

Gage steered the SUV back the way they'd come, Pancake sprawled across the backseat like she'd just finished a marathon. Beside him, Melanie sat quietly, gaze fixed on the road ahead. Pensive. He was beginning to recognize that was how she processed.

The day had warmed enough for them to shed their jackets, and he cracked the window to let in the scent of pine. He liked seeing her with the people who felt like family to him. She belonged. She had a history with them and was reconnecting. Which only made her feel more right for him. She and Addy would fit perfectly into his world.

The truth was settling in: he didn't just want her in his life—he wanted a life with her.

The thought scared the hell out of him, but losing her because he couldn't get his shit together was not an option.

Desire wasn't the problem. He wanted her in his bed, in his arms. Bad. And yeah, he figured she knew it. But he'd let her set the pace. That part he could wait for. But not for much longer.

What haunted him was everything that came after. What if they were together, what if they got *married,* and something happened to her? They'd have Addy, maybe more kids. What if something happened to them? Kids were tiny disasters. Terrible things could happen to them. What if they built a life together and then lost it?

His dad, his sister, his partner, they'd all died. Each ripping a gaping hole in his heart. He couldn't imagine surviving another blow like that. Not again.

But lately, another voice had started to make itself known. The quieter one. The one that asked *What if nothing bad happens?*

What if Melanie was the real thing? What if he got to raise Addy, not from the outside looking in, but as her dad? What if he and Melanie could grow old together, side by side?

That voice was getting harder to ignore, and it was beginning to sound a lot like hope.

Gage was about to suggest they grab lunch before Melanie's appointment when her phone rang.

"It's the school," she murmured, swiping to answer.

She pressed the phone to her ear. He went on high alert when her voice sharpened. "How can you not know where she is?"

Alarm shot through him. Without a word, he cut across a lane and took the turn toward Mill Creek Elementary.

She listened for a beat, then turned to him, her face pale. "Gage, the principal says Addy's disappeared."

Just like that, the air went thin. His worst fear—*not again, please not again*—roared to life in his chest.

"Put your phone on speaker," he said, hands tightening around the steering wheel.

Melanie tapped the screen. "You're on speaker so my friend can hear."

"Hello, this is Susanna Majors, principal of—"

"Have you contacted the sheriff's office?" Gage cut in, his voice clipped.

"No, we wanted to inform her mother first. We don't have any reason to believe Adelyn left campus. We're currently searching the school."

Gage gripped the wheel tighter, his mind already racing through protocols. But the only thing he could hear was that whisper from earlier: *What if you lose her too?*

"Were there any reports of unfamiliar adults on or near campus?" Gage asked.

There was a pause. "I'm sorry, who am I speaking with?"

"Gage Landry. I'm with Melanie. Former FBI agent. We're on our way to the school now."

"I see." The principal's voice lost a bit of its edge. "No, there have been no reports of unidentified adults, and no visitors signed in within the past hour."

"How long has Addy been missing?"

"She didn't come in from recess so about twenty minutes."

"Call 9-1-1," Gage ordered. "Melanie will give you a clothing description for dispatch."

Melanie sat straighter, her voice steadier. "Addy's wearing black leggings and a purple sweatshirt with a unicorn on the front. She has on shearling boots and a puffy pink coat. Please check if her backpack is still in her classroom. It's pink and green."

"I need to inform you, Miss Brennan, there was an incident on the playground involving Adelyn and another student," the principal said, clearly flustered. "I know we're scheduled to meet this afternoon about the same student. I'm putting you on hold to check if her backpack is still in the classroom."

The cheerful hold music was jarring.

Melanie's hands fisted. "Liam is still bullying her."

"Yeah, that's going to stop."

"What if she's been kidnapped?" Her voice wavered. "What if whoever made the child neglect complaint grabbed her during recess?"

"Mel, listen to me," he told her firmly. She looked pale, but her jaw was set. "The school is fenced, and visitors have to check in at the front office. There's supervision on the playground. This sounds more like Addy got fed up with the little fucker hassling her."

The principal came back on the line. "Her backpack's gone. It's not in the classroom."

"Call the sheriff's office now," Gage said, "and we'll be there in a minute."

Melanie ended the call, her lips tight. "She could've grabbed her backpack and taken off."

Gage eased off the gas as they entered the neighborhood around the school. "Keep a lookout. There's a back exit to the school somewhere around here. It should be locked this time of day but if Addy jumped ship, she could have gone out that way.

Melanie rolled down her window, her head swiveling as she searched. "She could be anywhere, Gage."

Pancake stuck her nose out the window as far as her seatbelt restraint would let her.

"I know, sweetheart. We'll find her."

Gage turned onto a street where houses shared a back fence with the playground. The next turn would take them to the front entrance of the school.

From the corner of his eye, he caught a flash of green and pink. "Jesus Christ." He whipped the SUV to the side of the road, jamming the transmission into park. "I see her."

He was out of the car and running up a gravel path. He could hear the slamming of the car door behind him and Pancake's excited bark. Addy'd climbed over the gate and he'd seen her backpack as she'd dropped down.

"Gage," Addy screamed his name, then she was racing to him, arms outstretched. He swung her up, and her arms and legs went around him, her backpack dropping to the ground. Her little body shook with tears he could feel soaking his shirt. He closed his eyes and breathed deep.

"I'm sorry. I'm sorry," she hiccoughed.

"It's okay, baby. You're safe. It's okay." He rubbed her back while she sobbed.

Melanie reached them and he brought her into the hug. They stood like that, arms around each other. "She's okay," he murmured, voice hoarse.

Holding on to a little girl he'd come to love, and her mother, who he'd fallen for, hard, solidified what he'd been feeling: Addy and Melanie were his. This little girl, this woman, they'd become the focus of his life. He wanted them to be together as a family. Addy? She seemed to be on board. It was her mother who might need some convincing.

He kissed them each on the forehead before transferring Addy to her mother's arms.

He picked up the backpack. Melanie set Addy on her feet and tipped her head up with a finger under her chin. "We need to talk, Adelyn, but first I have to call Mrs. Majors and tell her we found you."

Addy drew in a wobbly breath and wiped her eyes. "Was she looking for me?"

"Yeah. It's a big deal when a kid goes missing."

"Am I in trouble?"

Melanie sighed. "You might be. I need to know what happened first. But, Addy? What's most important is that you're safe. You scared me."

Addy ducked her head. "I was *trying* to be safe."

Melanie made the call and Pancake cried pitifully in the car.

"Pancake's here? Can I go to her? Please?"

Gage thought time with Pancake would do them all good. "In a minute, sunshine."

Melanie assured the principal they'd bring Addy to the school, then disconnected the call.

"Do we have to go back?" Addy asked.

"Yeah, we do." Melanie rested a hand on her shoulder. "But first I want to know what happened. It's not safe for you to run away from school, Adelyn."

Addy sent pleading eyes in Gage's direction. He crouched down. "What happened? Why'd you run away?"

"Liam tripped me at recess and I scraped my knee. See?" She pointed to a hole in her leggings and the torn skin beneath it. The sight of the bloody little scrape had Gage seething.

"Me and Olivia told the yard duty teacher, and she made Liam sit on the bench. But when the bell rang, he ran over and said he was going to beat me up after school."

She looked at her mom. "I didn't want to get beat up."

Melanie kept her voice even though Gage could see she was as angry as he was.

"I don't want you beat up either. But, Addy, grown-ups can help only if they know what's going on. If you told Mrs. Delgado that Liam threatened you and you were scared of getting beat up, she would have helped you."

Gage rose to his feet. "What was your plan after you got over the back gate?"

"To hide until the bus came and then sneak on without Liam seeing me."

"Didn't you remember that I was meeting you at school for our appointment with the principal?" Melanie asked.

"No." She shook her head. "I forgot."

Gage rubbed a hand over his face. This beautiful child shouldn't have to devise plans to avoid getting beat up.

He caught Melanie's gaze. "I'll drive you around to the front of the school. If you give me your keys, I'll go home and bring back your car with the car seat."

"Me and Pancake want to come with you," Addy pleaded. "Please."

"You and Pancake, huh? Sorry, sunshine. The farthest I'm willing to go without you in a car seat is around the block."

Melanie was giving him a measured look. He raised his brow in question. "Good with you?"

"If we're holding you up," Mel said, "Mom has a car seat and can come get us. She's at the animal shelter for another couple hours but Addy and I can hang out here to wait for her."

He shook his head. "It's not a problem."

"Okay," she muttered. He knew she had an independent streak a mile wide, and he had the feeling she didn't like relying on him. Or maybe men in general.

Addy took Melanie's and Gage's hands and they walked together back to the car.

The little girl looked up at him and gave him a sly smile. "Can Pancake stay with Mom and me until you come back? She can keep me company when Mom talks to Mrs. Majors. That would make me happy."

He barked out a laugh. "No doubt, but I don't think your principal is ready for Pancake-level mayhem."

***

Melanie closed the book and set it on the nightstand. Gage had brought over a stuffed penguin with a purple bandana to replace the one Pancake had mauled. Addy was tucked under her blankets with the penguin curled in her arm. Pancake lay on her back in the middle of the floor, paws hanging in the air.

Gage leaned against the door frame, his arms crossed over his chest.

It was unnerving to admit how much they felt like a family. How much Gage had become central to their lives. It felt right and that scared her senseless. No man had ever been a reliable presence in her life. Feeling like she was waiting for the other shoe to drop was making her antsy.

Addy rolled onto her side. "Can we read another chapter? I don't want to go to sleep." She may not want to go to sleep, but heavy eyelids and a big yawn gave her away.

"We'll read the next chapter tomorrow night." Melanie straightened the comforter. "It's been a tough day. But you know what? I'm proud of you. You told Mrs. Majors everything Liam has done. You stood up for yourself."

"Is he going to jail?"

She caught Gage's quick grin. "No, they don't put kids in jail." Melanie weighed how much Addy needed to know. "Mrs. Majors called a little while ago. She'll make sure Liam doesn't bother you anymore."

Melanie had found Mrs. Majors fair-minded and empathetic. She'd assured Melanie that Liam would be evaluated and receive the services he needed, including counseling and mental health support.

Liam's parent was informed that any further incidences of bullying would result in more serious consequences. Mrs. Majors had also stressed to Addy that any adult on campus would help her and she was not to run away from school ever again.

"If Liam does anything, Addy, and I mean *anything*," Melanie emphasized, "you're to tell a grown-up immediately."

Addy plucked at her blanket. "He's sneaky. But Jordy said he's gonna tell Liam to knock it off or he'll clobber him. I think clobber means beat up so maybe that's not a good idea."

"I'll talk with Jordy," Gage said.

Melanie brushed the hair off Addy's forehead. "Addy, Liam will be getting help so he can learn how to treat people with kindness. Kids aren't all bad or all good. Liam was behaving badly, but he can learn to be a better person. But no more running away from school, okay?" Melanie leaned down to kiss her girl.

"I guess so." Addy shifted her gaze to Gage and gave him a sleepy smile. "Will you kiss me good night?" Any thought that Melanie could prevent Addy from falling for Gage was officially quashed.

"Sure thing."

Gage moved to the bed and bent over to kiss Addy on the forehead. "Sweet dreams, sunshine."

"Pancake has to say good night too."

Pancake gamely rolled to her feet and Addy looped an arm around her in a hug. The dog gave her a tongue swipe.

"Sleep now, Addy," Melanie said quietly.

Addy settled on her pillow and Melanie turned out the lamp on her new desk. She followed Gage and Pancake out of the room, shutting the door softly behind her.

Gage took her hand and when they reached the living room, pulled her to him. Pancake gave a noisy yawn and collapsed on the floor. Melanie tilted her head back to look into dark eyes that held a look that set her nerve ends tingling.

Having the undivided interest of a man like Gage gave her a heady feeling. He bracketed her face with his hands, his long fingers in her hair while his thumbs caressed her cheeks. "What am I to do with you?"

"Kiss me?"

"Yeah, that's exactly right."

She thought he'd dive in, but instead he nipped her chin, then pressed his lips to the corner of her mouth. "These dimples drive me crazy, you know that?"

"You've got cute dimples of your own."

He moved back enough to look her sternly in the eye. "Not dimples, creases. Rugged, not cute."

"No, of course not. They're exceptionally manly."

"Damn straight."

He pressed open-mouth kisses along the line of her jaw and it felt like he was worshipping her with his tongue and mouth.

He nipped at her earlobe then moved to savor the sensitive skin below her ear. Then finally, *finally,* returned his attention to her mouth. She groaned when he slid his tongue past her lips, and she could taste the hint of chocolate from the ice cream they'd had for dessert.

Her hands clutched his belt, pulling him fully against her, his arousal a hard ridge beneath his jeans. He deepened the kiss, his groan vibrating through her as she gave in to temptation and rubbed against him. He slid his hands under her loose sweater, his fingers stroking up her rib cage to the swell of her breasts. She followed his lead, her own hands equally as busy as she slid them under his thermal to caress the warm skin of his back.

He brought his hands back to her face and, with a final kiss, stepped back. She drew in a deep breath, trying to calm her racing heart. Her arousal was echoed on his face.

"When this is done, when we figure out where the threat to you is coming from and neutralize it, I want more time with you and Addy. Normal time."

She smiled. "I'd like that."

CHAPTER SIXTEEN

Addy was in bed, which gave Melanie time to sit at her kitchen table, her laptop open, and the printed spreadsheet next to it. She'd called three people on the list. Two hadn't answered, but with the third she'd had a nice conversation with a woman who'd graduated from high school the year before her. Sarah Jacoby told her what she remembered of the bootlegger, which wasn't much. But they'd chatted and Melanie learned Sarah also had a daughter in first grade who attended a different elementary school in Sisters. They made tentative plans for a play date.

The next number was one Delaney had texted her earlier that day. Greg Delano. Memories of Greg were indistinct. Medium height, medium build, sandy hair. He'd been on the football team but hadn't stood out. Part of the jock crowd, she remembered him as more of a follower who'd remained in Chase Bradford's shadow.

As with the other men she'd called, there was that moment when she wondered if the person she was calling was the attacker. The man responsible for creating the jagged line dividing her life into before and after. Pushing aside the thoughts, she dialed the number.

Forty minutes later, she disconnected the call, mind spinning. When it rang in her hand she startled, fumbling the phone.

Gage's name flashed on the caller ID.

"Hey."

"Melanie." Gage's voice instantly grounded her, stopping the spinning thoughts. "Want some company?"

"This is becoming a regular occurrence."

"Is that a problem?"

"I'm having a hard time keeping an emotional distance from you." The words were easier to say over the phone than if he was standing in front of her.

"Yeah, same. Doesn't keep me from wanting to be with you, though."

"Come on over, but Addy won't be happy if she finds out you were here or, god forbid, Pancake."

"We'll be quiet." His statement was followed up by a knock at the slider. "We're here."

She couldn't stop her grin as she slid open the door. "That was mighty quick."

"We were counting on you saying yes."

Pancake nosed her way past Melanie. Gage slid the door shut behind them, shutting out the cold. His gaze on hers, he pulled her into a kiss so dreamy it made her sigh when he finally released her.

Judging by his heavy-lidded gaze, Gage was equally affected. "I missed you today."

"I texted you. You texted me. About a dozen times."

He shook his head. "Not the same." He nipped her lips again before she moved back. It was then that she noticed the bag decorated with a smiling apple in his hand.

"Is that what I think it is?"

"If you think it's apple pie cinnamon rolls from Cider Mill Farm, you'd be correct."

"We better hide the evidence or we'll be in trouble. Addy and I brought some home when we visited the farm and Addy's decided they're her favorite treat, even better than the cider donuts, which were also a hit."

"I've got the kid covered. There's one for her too."

Melanie filled the electric kettle while Gage got mugs and plates from the cupboard. Pancake planted her butt next to the table, head moving back and forth as she watched them.

Melanie ripped open a treat pouch she'd picked up at the grocery store. "Hey there, Pancake. I've got something for you." She picked out a bone-shaped dog cookie and offered it to Pancake, who settled with it on the rug in front of the slider.

"How did your meetings go today?" Gage had texted that morning to say he had back-to-back-to-back video conferences scheduled with his team and prospective clients.

"All good. One of the potentials is a solid yes, the other is considering her options. I'm confident she'll go with us."

"Why'd you choose this line of work?" She eyed the huge rolls he took out of the bag. "Half for me."

He shrugged as he got a knife. "I know myself well enough to know it's a way of doing what I couldn't as a kid."

She poured hot water over teabags, then leaned back against the counter to study him. "A way of protecting people?"

"Yeah."

"Who needed protection when you were a boy?"

He leaned against the counter beside her. "My dad died when I was a little older than Addy. Killed by a drunk driver."

"Oh no. Your family must've been devastated."

"We were. It was hardest on my mom. I was old enough to realize she was struggling, but couldn't figure out how to help her."

Moving in front of him, she laid her hands on his chest. His dark eyes held a storm of emotion.

"You can't think you could've protected your dad from a drunk driver. Or your mom from that pain."

"Our emotional baggage isn't always rational. I remember Mom wrecked with grief and nothing I could do made it better. My sister Janie was a toddler and needed to be looked after. I tried my best to protect her, but she died too "

"What happened to Janie?"

His gaze was on his fingers as he threaded them through her hair. "Fucking cancer when she was twelve. Her diagnosis was acute myelogenous leukemia."

Melanie took his hands, holding them to her chest as she moved between his legs. She understood him enough to know revealing vulnerability wasn't something he did easily.

"Oh Gage. I can't imagine how awful that was for you and your mom. How old were you when Janie died?"

"Seventeen. And yeah, it was hard. Janie always seemed frail, even when she was a baby. I remember sneaking into her room at night to sleep with her because I was worried she'd need me, and I wouldn't be there for her. Then there was a period when she was five or six and she would sleepwalk. I was afraid she'd fall down the stairs so I'd sleep on the floor in front of her door. Figured she'd have to get past me to get to the stairs."

"But she still died."

"Yeah, she did."

"And your partner died."

He nodded. Melanie let go of his hands so she could wrap her arms around him. It felt perfectly natural when his arms circled her, cradling her against him, her head tucked under his chin.

"You're hardwired to be a protector, Gage. You won't like it, but I think it's noble."

He shook his head and held her closer. She had the uneasy feeling that her feelings for him were speeding past like and admiration and catapulting straight into love. She'd always safeguarded her heart, but Gage had managed to blast through those fortifications as if they were made with balsa wood.

"You feel it, Mel? What's between us?"

How could she deny it? Face pressed to his chest, she nodded. "It's so damn scary."

"I know. It's scary for me too," he whispered. "I won't let you down."

Listening to the steady beating of his heart, she held tight. He gave really good hugs. She wanted to believe he wouldn't let her down. It was hard when a voice in her head kept reminding her to be cautious, to be careful about trusting someone, that the stakes were too high.

She didn't know how long they stayed like that until he loosened his hold and pressed a kiss to her forehead. "Tea's getting cold."

She pushed aside the spreadsheet and her laptop. They brought the steaming mugs and plated cinnamon rolls to the table.

"You were making calls this evening. Turn up anything?"

"As a matter of fact." Melanie forked up a bite of pastry and groaned as she chewed. "Let it be said, Cam is a genius. Apple pie cinnamon rolls are the best."

"Agreed."

She sipped her tea. "Still no response from Grafton."

"His access to email will be limited, and he may not have a way to respond. Generally, emails are printed and delivered to the inmate."

She sighed. "It's worth a try. But I did make contact with someone else on our list. I talked with Greg Delano. He was on the football team and a friend of Chase's."

"What'd you find out?"

"He lives in Denver and confirmed he'd hung out with Rhonda Lockwood at the bootlegger. Turns out Greg always had a thing for Rhonda and when she showed up that night without Josh, he figured it was his chance."

"They hooked up?"

"They did. In the back of his daddy's Chevy pickup where Greg had a sleeping bag."

"Romantic."

"Only the best. Rhonda had come to the bootlegger with Josie Whitlock. Those two were the heart of their own little mean-girl pack at school."

"I know Josie. She worked at Easy Money until Owen fired her."

"I bet she hit on you."

"Big time. Not my type."

"According to Greg, he and Rhonda climbed into the bed of his pickup while Josie paired up with Chase."

"They're not the first teenagers to do the deed at a party. Why do you think Rhonda refused to admit she'd been with Delano?"

"Because she'd lied to Josh Lockwood and said she was staying home that night with a headache. According to Greg, Rhonda and Josh had only recently gotten back together after breaking up a month or so before."

She waited expectantly for him to say something. "Aren't you going to ask why this is important?"

Gage chewed thoughtfully. "If I had to speculate, it's because she got pregnant."

Melanie gaped at him. "How'd you guess?"

He shrugged. "Has to be something big if she's still nervous about it after all these years. Delano didn't stand up for her?"

"He wanted to. Greg says Rhonda came to his house a couple weeks after they'd been together. She'd found out she was pregnant and was a hot mess. He had a big-time crush on her and figured a baby meant they'd be together. Since he'd committed to the navy and was set to go to boot camp after graduation, he felt he could support her and a baby. He wanted to marry her."

"I take it Rhonda didn't want that." Gage pushed his plate away.

"Nope. Greg sounds bitter. He thinks she decided Josh Lockwood's prospects were better than his. Josh was popular and was on his way to becoming valedictorian, his family was wealthy, or at least everybody thought so.

"A kid from a working-class family wasn't going to provide for Rhonda in the manner to which she wished to become accustomed." Melanie sipped her tea. "The irony is the Lockwood family was struggling. They operated a sawmill outside of town. The logging industry was in decline and they ended up shuttering the mill and declaring bankruptcy."

"So no more family business?"

She shook her head. "According to Greg, no. I'm not sure what Josh does for work, but he's not working for Lockwood Lumber."

"Assuming she kept the baby, did Delano say whether Rhonda tried passing it off as Lockwood's?"

"Rhonda was adamant she wanted to keep the baby. Greg thinks claiming the baby was Josh's is exactly what she planned, though he hasn't talked with her since and doesn't know for sure. He does know her parents kicked her out and Rhonda went to live with a relative in L.A. until she had the baby." She gave a heavy sigh. "I can't imagine parents treating their daughter like that."

Gage nodded. "Society is more forgiving now, for the most part."

Melanie continued. "Greg said his sister told him Rhonda and the baby returned to Sisters and moved in with the Lockwoods, and eventually she and Josh got married. Greg promised Rhonda he wouldn't tell anyone they'd hooked up. I think the dam broke when I called him. All this bitterness spewed out. He regrets keeping his promise as long as he did. Chase and Josie would know, though."

"Josie would probably keep her mouth shut for a friend. But what's Bradford's motivation, especially if he was friends with Delano?"

"Good question. But there's more. Greg said Chase's vehicle was parked close to his. He heard Chase and Josie arguing, and then Josie stormed off and went back to the party."

"So no hookup there. And Chase?"

"Rhonda told Greg she was going home. After they parted ways, he went back to the party. He said he wasn't really paying attention, but thinks Chase showed up again much later. Once the party started breaking up, Greg went home and doesn't have any recollection of when Chase left."

Gage leaned back in his seat, brow furrowed in thought. "At what point did you leave?"

"My curfew was eleven, but that night I was having a good time and used a friend's cell to call Mom. I begged her for an extra hour and she finally gave in. It was a twenty-minute drive back home, so I left a little after eleven thirty."

"You didn't have a cell phone?"

"No. Mom and I couldn't afford one."

"You and I were in the same boat there," he said. "What I'm hearing is Bradford was in the area where the cars were parked and there's a window where he's unaccounted for when he could have siphoned gas from your tank."

She carefully arranged her fork on her plate. "The assailant, Chase or whoever it was, could've returned to the party after assaulting me." Talking about it without shame made her feel stronger. "You still consider Chase your prime suspect?"

"I'm looking at all possibilities, but yeah." His gaze remained steady on hers. "You found useful information."

She mulled through what she'd learned talking with Greg. "I keep coming back to Rhonda. That day at the bank she'd acted like the same mean girl she'd always been, but when I mentioned the bootlegger, she seemed scared. Really scared."

"She has a secret."

"I guess that's it. But it seems like there's something more."

Gage nodded, then stood up and circled the table. He took her hand and pulled her to her feet. His gaze on hers, he dipped his head and met her lips in a kiss that left her longing for more.

"We'll have to decide where we're going with this, Mel." His voice had dropped lower and made her wonder if that was his bedroom voice.

"I know."

He called Pancake and left through the sliding door.

***

Thursday morning, Melanie strolled along the boardwalk on Main Street. Tourists snapped photos of the fall décor, probably to capture the town's mountain charm for social media. Pumpkins, plaid ribbons, and hay bales made Sisters look like a postcard come to life. She tugged her beanie lower over her ears, warding off the crisp breeze.

She'd put in a solid two hours on her manuscript. It was coming along. Addy was at school, and Mel needed a break from writing, from playing amateur detective, and from the constant loop centered on Gage Landry.

She'd even considered knocking on his door and seducing him. Just stripping away the tension and making it happen. But she hadn't. First, because he was probably working, and work-from-home was still work. But in all honesty, she was afraid. What if she made the move and he didn t want her?

She'd driven into town hoping for clarity, but maybe she was running from the fear of rejection.

That wasn't like her. Confidence usually came easy. Their kisses were like liquid fire. He was always touching her. Holding hands, nudging knees, stroking his thumb along the back of her neck.

She stopped mid-stride, eyes narrowing in thought. Oh. Oh my god.

Gage was waiting for her to make the move. Of course he was. Giving her control of when and how they became physical. Another thing that made him special it was his way of respecting what she'd lost.

The realization hit her right in the heart.

He wasn't just being patient; he was being careful, protective in a way that put her first. And knowing that, knowing he was letting her set the pace for both of them, made her certain. Gage understood what it meant for her to have that control, and he gave it freely.

She stood on the boardwalk, heart full and aching, and knew she had a choice to make.

Mulling over her revelations, she continued her stroll. She stopped in front of Retro Days, the store belonging to Antonia Reynoso. She went in, and it was like stepping onto the set of a sixties TV show. The colors, patterns, and materials evoked a nostalgia for a time before she was born.

She browsed through the vintage clothing and gave serious thought to buying a denim jacket decorated with flower power patches.

"Melanie, you came to visit me. I'm so happy to see you." Antonia stepped from a display at the back of the store. She bustled forward in her colorful muumuu and opened her arms. Melanie felt herself enveloped in a warm hug that had her squeezing her eyes shut against the rush of emotion. Then Antonia stepped back and did a top-to-toe survey. "Beautiful as ever, my girl. I love your pixie cut. Not everyone can pull that off, but with your gorgeous cheekbones, you can."

"Thank you. It's so good to see you. This is a wonderful store."

"I opened it with my Carlos, and now that he's gone, it keeps me busy."

"I'm sorry about Carlos. You must miss him terribly."

"I do, but I try not to dwell on it."

"I ran into Mateo and Juliette at Easy Money. They're such a cute couple. Have they set a date for the wedding?"

"They're looking at venues, and availability will dictate the date." Antonia's smile broadened. "I don't think I'm talking out of turn to tell you that they've been talking with Delaney and Cam about having the wedding at Cider Mill Farm."

"Oh, the farm would be beautiful for a wedding."

"Wouldn't it?" Antonia clasped her hands together. "Mateo said the only way he'd have it there is if they can hire enough staff that the McGrath clan can enjoy the event as guests."

"That's thoughtful of him."

They continued chatting, catching up with each other's lives. Antonia hugged her again as Melanie was leaving. "Next time you come in, bring your little girl. She needs to meet all her people."

"I will."

Returning to the boardwalk, Melanie knew it was a rare gift to be able to make people feel loved no matter how many years they'd been apart.

Turning into the narrow walkway between Retro Days and Three Sisters Bakery, Melanie caught the scent of roasted coffee and almost gave in, but she kept walking. She spotted Delaney and Walker beside their SUV in the rear lot.

"Hey, there," she called.

Delaney looked up from strapping a baby into a stroller. "Hey, Mel."

The little girl looked at her wide-eyed and held up a drool-covered toy key ring.

"Hello, sweet thing. You must be Harper. I'll let you keep that," Mel said with a smile. "How's that tooth coming?" she asked Delaney.

"The tooth broke through last night," she replied. "Right now, we're getting a brief break from the crankiness."

"It feels like once that first one shows up, they're teething forever." Melanie remembered those days.

Walker slung the diaper bag over his shoulder. "I was hoping it gets easier."

"The older they get the better they handle it, if that helps," Melanie said. "You guys out shopping?"

"Coffee first, then shopping," Delaney answered. She glanced at Walker. "We've got an update on our detective work."

Melanie perked up. "So do I."

Walker scanned the lot. "Why don't you join us at the bakery and we'll swap notes?"

"Absolutely."

A few minutes later, they were tucked into a corner table at the back of Three Sisters Bakery, away from listening ears. Delaney settled Harper in a high chair with a teething biscuit while Melanie wrapped her hands around a mug of hot tea.

"I forgot how cold it gets here. Addy and I are definitely in need of gloves."

"Add sturdy lined boots to your shopping list," Delaney added. "You'll thank me when the snow hits."

"Laney's right about the boots," Walker said, then nodded toward Melanie. "All right, let's hear what you found out."

"Okay. I had an interesting conversation with Greg Delano last night. He's not a happy man." Mel told them Greg's story of the night of the bootlegger and Rhonda's subsequent pregnancy. "He thinks she told Josh Lockwood the baby was his," Melanie told them. "That said, I don't know how any of this is relevant to our investigation."

"It gives us a more complete picture," Delaney said, brow furrowed. "Rhonda was a senior that year, and she didn't come back after winter break. There were rumors she was pregnant and doing adult-ed to graduate."

Melanie shook her head. "It's always women who pay the price for an accidental pregnancy."

She pointed to Walker. "Okay, your turn."

He ran a hand over his beard. "I spoke with Martha Watkins this morning. She was Grafton's secretary back when he was sheriff. Her help was key to uncovering that he falsified the DNA report." He sipped his coffee. "She told me something new. When Grafton was still a captain, there was a rumor he was having an affair."

"How long ago? Who with?" At Walker's raised brow, she held up both hands. "I'll shut up."

He flashed his lightning grin, reminding Melanie why the young Walker McGrath had made all the girls swoon.

Delaney leaned in and whispered, "This was over thirty years ago, but Martha said she saw them together."

"Ooh, now it's getting juicy," Mel said.

"No kidding. I'll let Walker finish," Delaney said as she lifted a fussy Harper onto her lap.

Walker continued, unfazed. "One night, Martha had to go back to the office because she'd left her wallet in her desk. It was dark, but she heard voices in the break room. There shouldn't have been anyone in there, so she went to investigate. The door was cracked. She saw a woman with her back to the door, blonde hair a mess, adjusting her blouse. Grafton was in uniform, his shirt untucked, and he was zipping his pants."

Melanie blinked. "Wow. Did she recognize the woman?"

"No. The angle wasn't right, and she didn't want to risk getting caught. But she did hear the woman mention a baby. Said it was hers and she'd do what was best for it, and she wasn't going to ask for a divorce. Grafton responded, but Martha couldn't make it out. The woman got louder, saying how much she liked Neil but couldn't live on a captain's salary."

"Ouch," Melanie muttered. "This is more salacious than a soap opera."

"*I know,*" Delaney breathed. "But there's more."

Mel's gaze was glued on Walker as he resumed the tale.

"The woman said it'd be easy to convince her husband the baby was his. It'd be proof their fertility problems were fixed. That's when Martha slipped out."

Melanie stared at them, mind racing. "That...that's twisted. And it sounds an awful lot like what Rhonda pulled."

"Exactly," Delaney said.

Walker took Harper and let her stand on his lap. "It may not help with what we're doing, but it paints a bigger picture."

"If that woman carried to term, her child would be about our age," Delaney pointed out.

CHAPTER SEVENTEEN

Mel stood outside Gage's mudroom, worrying her bottom lip. It was a little past noon. Lunch time, right? She raised a hand to knock, then hesitated. What if he was busy? What if she'd misread everything?

Her plan had seemed less fraught when she'd decided on it while driving back from Sisters.

Maybe she should text him first, see if this was a good time. Or she—

The door swung open and her thoughts derailed. Gage filled the open doorway, expression inscrutable and every inch the gorgeous distraction she couldn't stop thinking about. Dark jeans. Gunmetal gray shirt. Sleeves rolled to the elbows.

Would there ever be a time when the sight of him wouldn't feel like a hit to the solar plexus?

Pancake poked her head around him, tongue lolling in greeting.

"You must be psychic," she muttered. "I was just talking myself out of bothering you."

"Saw you on my security monitor," he said, then looked her over. "Nice sweater. Nervous energy. You were definitely going to knock."

"I was. Maybe." She tried to smile. "I like your shirt. You probably have Zoom calls or something. I should go."

"You could." His lips twitched. He caught her hand and tugged her inside. "Or you could tell me why you're so nervous you're nearly vibrating with it."

"I'm not vibrating."

"You so are."

The door closed behind her with a click. "Addy okay?"

"At school."

"Any emergencies?"

"No."

"Interesting."

He backed her up against the door and her heart slammed in her chest. The heat from his gaze traveling over her body held such intensity it burned.

"Why is that interesting?" She had trouble forming simple words.

He bent his head, his mouth a hair's breadth from hers. "Because it opens up possibilities."

"I like possibilities."

The air pulsed between them while he seemed to be waiting. Clearly, this was her decision.

She reached for him, fisting the front of his shirt. Their mouths collided, hunger surging to the surface.

The kiss hit like a shot of tequila—it burned, made her dizzy, and left her craving more.

His hands rested on her waist then skimmed beneath her sweater, exploring the skin at her ribs before cupping her breasts. His thumb slipped under the shell of her bra and gently traced over her nipple, making her shudder.

They broke apart, panting. Pancake slumped to the floor with a groan.

Freeing his hands, Gage brought them to her face, his voice gravelly. "Do you want this, Mel? Do you want me?"

"Absolutely. Yes," she croaked, emotion tightening her throat.

He lifted her into his arms with easy strength. "Thank god."

"You're so romantic."

"You bring it out in me."

She burrowed into his chest as he carried her through the house, her fingers fumbling with his buttons. She wanted to touch him everywhere. Nose buried in his neck, she inhaled his fresh scent.

In his bedroom, he peeled back the quilt and laid her on the bed, then joined her. The sheets felt soft against her skin.

"Flannel. Comfy," she murmured.

"I like comfy." His lips brushed her throat. "But you're overdressed."

"You should fix that."

"I intend to." He did by removing her sweater, her bra, reverence evident in every motion. He buried his face between her breasts, inhaling deeply. "You're beautiful, Mel. Everything about you is beautiful." His words were muffled against her skin. "I want to savor every inch of you." He lifted one breast and ran his tongue over its pink tip. Her breath hitched when he took it into his mouth to suck deeply.

The pulse of desire evident whenever they were together swelled to a deep ache throbbing with need.

She tugged his shirt from his shoulders. "I want more skin, more *you*."

"I'm yours, Melanie. Take what you want."

She worshipped his body, kissing, tasting, teasing, drowning in sensuality, until he quaked with need. Breath ragged, he gripped her hands.

"My turn." He eased down her leggings and underwear, baring her with tenderness and hunger. Lips, tongue, fingers—he used them all to optimum effect to pleasure her, and when she was panting on the verge of orgasm, he kissed her thighs, then straightened to reach into his nightstand.

Rising over her, condom in place, he paused, watching her, waiting.

"I want this," she murmured, "with you."

He entered her slowly, both groaning with the pleasure. She clung to him, overwhelmed, aching for more.

Gage drove deeper, pushing her higher, then higher still. Her heart swelled as she reached the crest. "That's it, baby. Come for me." He drove her harder, pummeling into her until finally, *finally,* she came apart with a keening cry.

Gage slowed, letting her ride out her orgasm. When she thought she might slide off the bed in a languid puddle, he gripped her hips, stoking her pleasure once more. "Again, Mel. Give it to me again."

"I don't think I can."

Steady, strong, determined, he worked her, mouth on her breasts, fingers moving between their bodies, forceful thrusts filling and stretching, building her desire, and once again she was on the edge of oblivion.

"It's too much—"

Gage's jaw clenched. "You can, baby. Give it to me." He thrust powerfully, holding her body tight against his, and when she shattered, he followed, burying his face in her neck, his hot breath on her skin.

They lay tangled together in the quiet. He moved a strand of hair from her eyes.

She ducked her head to rest on his chest, suddenly feeling exposed.

He brushed back her bangs. "You don't have to hide from me, Mel."

"This is scary."

Being like this with Gage could be a big mistake and leave her vulnerable to heartache on a level she'd never experienced.

"What's scary?"

"You. Us. My feelings."

Infinitely gentle, he said, "If it helps, I'm scared too. I'm falling for you, Melanie. Hard. My reasons for not getting into relationships don't seem to apply to you and Addy, because I want both of you. I want to give this a try."

Fear clutched around her heart. She propped herself on his chest so she could look in his eyes. "I'm a bad bet, Gage. I'm not ready to commit to a relationship." But even as she said the words, she realized she'd changed and what used to be true, no longer was.

"Melanie." He smiled. "Hasn't it occurred to you we're already in a relationship?"

"Maybe. I think Pancake planned this."

"Smart dog."

The temptation to say yes to all of it, to let her heart be free of the restraints of the past, nearly overwhelmed her sense of self-preservation. "Seriously, what would a relationship even look like? Becoming involved with you includes Addy. My girl has a huge heart, and I don't want to see it broken if this ends badly."

"I'd take a bullet before hurting Addy, you've got to know that. And I believe she's more resilient than you give her credit for." His gaze remained steadfast, not allowing her to look away. "Give us a chance, Mel. Give me a chance."

She sobered. "I'm still learning how to trust, Gage."

"Then let's take the leap together. Be honest. No games. Just us. And we'll see where it goes."

He brought her hand to his mouth and pressed a kiss to her palm.

Her heart ached with fear, yes, but also something beautiful. She'd fallen in love with him, loved him in a way she never thought she could.

And it terrified her.

Maybe trust wasn't the absence of fear. Maybe it was deciding to love in spite of it.

"Okay." Her breath shuddered out. "We'll see where this goes."

His arms tightened around her and he sealed their commitment with a kiss that consumed her.

***

Melanie called Esme as she walked back from the bus stop after waving Addy off. Her best friend picked up on the second ring.

"Hey, girl."

The sound of Esme's voice was like pulling on a blanket straight from the dryer – warm and comforting.

"Gage and I are together." The words tumbled out of her mouth.

Esme's predictable shriek had Melanie grinning. "How? What happened? I need details. All of them."

Melanie rattled off the events of the last couple days. When she stopped, there was a beat of silence.

"Esme? Did I lose you? Dammit." She entered her house and moved into her office, which sometimes had better reception.

"I'm still here," came the reply, softer this time. "I'm in awe, Mel. You're incredible. You wanted him and went for it. I'm so happy for you." She paused a beat. "Maybe I should try being more direct with Andres."

"How's that going?"

"Slow, but good slow. We're both recovering from not-so-great relationships. I don't want a fling, I want something that sticks." Her voice echoed with determination. "He's hot and sweet and makes me dizzy, but I want more than a hookup, so I'm holding out."

"You're being smart. Sounds like he's worth the wait."

"I hope so." Esme's voice brightened. "But back to you. Gage sounds like Captain America. Protective and impossibly sexy."

Melanie sighed. "He's got me all twisted up. I can't stop thinking about yesterday. I'm trying to figure out boundaries. I was thinking about inviting him to the school carnival tomorrow. I want him to meet you and Isla. But I don't want to be clingy, you know, that girlfriend who can't get her nails done without dragging her boyfriend along."

"Ask him. If a hundred sugar-fueled kids isn't his scene, he'll say so."

"You're right. I don't want him to think it's some kind of test he fails if he'd rather spend the afternoon watching a football game on TV. I need to stop overthinking before I ruin it for myself."

She paused. "Are you and Isla ready for the weekend? Addy's already planning to set her alarm to wake up early tomorrow morning. You know, in case you decide to arrive at six."

"We'll be there," Esme laughed. "But I can guarantee it won't be at six. Isla is so excited she probably won't sleep worth a damn tonight."

"Addy wants to introduce Pancake to Isla. Oh, real quick. If the call drops, it's because I lost service. Cell service has been inconsistent the past few days."

"A-ha. I was right. You do live in the wilderness. Got anything fun planned for today?"

"I'm writing a scene, which is work but fun work. I'm at a pivotal point between my hero and heroine. I need to decide how sexy to make it."

"I say go for all the heat. Your readers will thank you."

"Maybe. I'll see how it plays out. What's your day like?"

"Oh, you know. Work, work, and more work. I'm hoping to get off a little early so I can pack."

"Don't worry about toiletries. Use ours. We've got it all: shampoo, toothpaste, whatever you need."

"Okay. I'm pulling into work right now. Talk to you later, best friend."

"Bye, Es."

***

Two hours later, Melanie's phone chimed, making her jump and yanking her out of the scene she was writing. She glanced at the number. Her mom. It hadn't rung, instead going straight to voicemail. She'd call her back later.

Melanie refocused, her fingers flying over the keyboard. Alaric and Vaelora had squared off in a fencing duel that was more seduction than swordplay. After simmering through three books, their sexual tension had reached a fever pitch.

Was this the right moment for a kiss? Melanie could visualize them leaning forward, swords crossed between them, lips inches apart. Or maybe—

Her phone chimed again. Concentration broken, she sighed, then tapped to play the voicemail.

When it finished, she stared blankly at the screen. What. The. Heck. Donna had fielded a report of a stray mama dog with a litter of half-grown pups abandoned at the old Lockwood sawmill.

I'm at the mill now and...and I got myself into trouble. I need your help. Can you come? I found this one spot where there's cell service but it's iffy. Please hurry. I'll hold on until you can get here.

Melanie couldn't put her finger on the problem but something about the message struck her as off. Immediately, she called Donna's number, frowning when it went straight to message. Rubbing her thumb between her eyebrows, she thought through her options.

The urgency in Donna's voice couldn't be doubted, but why hadn't she explained what the trouble was? Was she having difficulty rounding up the dogs? Melanie shook her head. It had to be more than that. Her stomach twisted at the thought maybe Donna was hurt.

Mel opened her map app and entered "Lockwood Mill." She studied the screen as the results loaded. The old mill was in a neighboring valley, reachable by Route 22, a winding mountain road. It was isolated with no homes or businesses in the area. Estimated drive time was thirty-three minutes.

Dammit. She was supposed to meet Chase at Three Sisters Bakery for a late lunch and that was already giving her anxiety. Delaney and Emery had promised to hang out there while she and Chase talked.

Why hadn't Donna taken one of the other volunteers to pick up the dogs? Or called animal services? Paul was in Sacramento for the day, so not close enough to help.

Before she could close her laptop, an email notification popped up with the domain used by prison inmates. Her breath hitched in her throat. Neil Grafton had responded to her query. She opened the email and scanned the contents.

Sitting back, she stared out the window trying to process what she'd read. The ramifications had her mind spinning. But she couldn't deal with this now. She needed to help her mom, then she'd figure out what it all meant.

Melanie dialed Gage's number, whispering *please, please, please* as it rang. She'd feel a lot more confident driving into the mountains to take care of whatever was going on with Donna if he was with her. Strong, competent, capable—he made her feel safe. A hiss of frustration escaped her lips when his recorded voice gruffly told her to leave a message. Hanging up, she settled for texting her destination so at least he'd know where she was going.

Calling Donna again netted no better results.

Niggling worry had her moving quickly through the house. Grabbing a small backpack, she threw in her wallet, protein bars, a water bottle, and a raincoat. Weather in the mountains could change in the blink of an eye. At the last minute, she added the bag of treats she'd picked up for Pancake. Those might be useful.

Backing out of her driveway, she debated knocking on Gage's door. Since he parked in the garage, she couldn't tell if he was home, and no lights shined from his windows. Glancing at the clock on the dash, she shook her head. She needed to hurry if she was going to help her mom and make it back for her meeting with Chase where she hoped to get some answers.

Tapping the screen on her dash, she followed the map directions out of town.

Even on an unplanned and unwelcome errand, the scenery gave her a boost. Thick stands of aspens dotted the narrow, winding road, their golden leaves swirling around her car. Tumbling creeks formed an occasional waterfall and spectacular clouds billowed into the sky. A lot of spectacular clouds. She might need that raincoat.

The map was still getting data, though she was confident she could find the mill without it. Her stepdad had stuffed paper maps of the area into her glove box for exactly that reason.

Clouds thickened as she drove deeper into the mountains. There wasn't much this far out, only a few lakes and an occasional cabin. Dark pine forests climbed steep slopes to the timberline, the jagged peaks of the Sierras jutting skyward like defiant fists.

She tried calling Donna again. And Gage. No luck.

A message flashed on the display: GPS signal lost. Damn.

The temperature dropped as she climbed in elevation and the first drops of rain hit. She cranked up the heater. The mama dog and her pups didn't deserve to be out in this weather.

The last instructions had put the turnoff for the mill less than two miles ahead. Even watching for it, she nearly missed the faded wooden sign.

The road to the mill was rough, winding and potholed, narrowed in areas by rockslides and erosion that had chewed away the shoulder. Who'd even been out here to spot the dogs? Hikers possibly, or hunters.

She crawled along at barely fifteen miles an hour. A mile and a half later, she rounded a bend and exhaled in relief at the sight of her mom's van. The mill buildings looked derelict with faded paint, broken windows, and rusted corrugated roofs that looked ready to cave in.

Rain spit against her windshield as she pulled up beside the van. She slipped on her raincoat, zipping her phone inside a pocket.

Delaney was right, she needed winter boots. Her old canvas sneakers wouldn't hold up to mountain weather.

Leaving the car, Melanie checked out Donna's van. Finding nothing concerning, she scanned her surroundings. "Mom?" Her voice was snatched by the wind. She called again, the only reply the groan of trees and the creak of swaying limbs.

The last thing she wanted was to go poking around in a crumbling mill, but if she were a mama dog with pups, she'd head straight for shelter. Rounding her car, she opened the passenger door, grabbed a flashlight from her glovebox, and tugged on a knit beanie she found.

She circled the perimeter of the mill, looking for gaps where an animal might slip through. Rusted scrap metal and forgotten debris littered the ground, forcing her to watch her step.

"Mom?" she called again, her voice muffled by the rising wind.

She pulled the hood of her raincoat over her beanie for extra protection. Icy rain stung her face.

Another call. Then—

She froze. A sound. Faint. Indistinct. The wind whistling through the old building?

"Mom?"

This time, a reply. A cry, thin and distant.

Melanie scrambled over a heap of crumbled brick and twisted metal to the main structure, its wide bay open to the elements. She entered cautiously, gaze barely penetrating the gloom. She pulled back her hood. The overcast sky did little to light the interior. Inside was a cavernous space, skeletal beams arching overhead.

"Mom?" Her voice echoed.

There was no return call, no barking dog, no whimpering puppies.

She switched on the flashlight. The beam cut through the gloom, glinting off enormous saw blades, jagged teeth still poised to rip through logs. Hulking machines loomed eerily. Why leave this equipment behind?

Narrow staircases on each side led to an open walkway that circled the perimeter, connecting to metal catwalks above. To the left, doors stood open to what might once have been offices or break rooms.

She turned to head back outside—

Thunk. Something solid hit the floor.

"Mom?"

"Go, Melanie. Run!"

Instinct kicked in. She dropped low, heart slamming in her chest, creeping behind a towering machine. There was a rustling sound as she scanned desperately for the threat. Crouching, she darted toward an open doorway.

Donna's call had come from one of those rooms.
A shadow shifted, separating from a dark doorway.
"You should've run. Too late now."

CHAPTER EIGHTEEN

Gage slowed the treadmill and wiped sweat from his face. He needed to burn energy after sitting through a two-hour meeting. There was also the hope he could get his brain to focus. No such luck. Even when he was working, his thoughts kept circling back to Melanie.

Melanie. His girlfriend. His first in years, and if he had any say, his last.

They'd planned to work separately through the morning, then touch base before she met up with Chase Bradford in town. Which sounded reasonable except he'd woken up missing her.

They'd shared his bed for all of two hours yesterday, and already it felt empty without her. He wanted more. He wanted her. He wanted Addy. In his house, in his life. For good.

He'd come to terms with that truth. Now he had to hope Melanie wanted the same. This thing between them was so new and they still had to figure things out. What commitment would mean, how to build a life together. But he was all in.

Done with the treadmill, he capped his water bottle, chuckling when Pancake jumped. She scared herself with her own farts.

They climbed the stairs from the basement. He flicked on lights as he went. A glance through the kitchen window showed Melanie's car gone from her driveway and storm clouds piling up over the mountains. Maybe she'd gone grocery shopping ahead of Esme's visit tomorrow. Not that she had to check in every time she ran into town.

Thunder echoed off the mountain, and Pancake whimpered. A feeling of unease slithered up his spine.

He pulled out his phone, and it vibrated in his hand, the screen lighting up with a call from an unknown number.

"Landry."

"It's Paul Bukowski, Mel's stepdad. You seen her or her mom?"

Gage stood straighter. The uneasy feeling ratcheted up several notches.

"No, what's going on?"

"Neither of them are answering their phones. Donna drives a blue van. You see it in Mel's driveway?"

He didn't need to check. "No van. Melanie's car is gone too."

"Damn. I'm on my way back from Sacramento. I'll be home in twenty minutes."

"Why the alarm, Paul?"

"Got a call from the animal shelter where Donna volunteers," Paul said. "She didn't show up for her shift this morning and she's not answering her phone. I thought Mel might've heard from her, but calls to both of them go straight to message."

The unease ratcheted up, tugging at Gage's gut, and experience told him to listen.

He put the phone on speaker so he could swipe through screens. Fuck. He'd missed a call from Melanie when he'd been working out. She'd left a text.

He read it quickly and swore under his breath. "Melanie texted she's on her way to the Lockwood Mill to help Donna," Gage told Paul.

"Lockwood Mill? Why is Donna there? And help her with what?"

"She doesn't say. I don't like this. They've got no business going out to that mill, especially when there's a storm brewing. I'm calling Sawyer. I might be jumping the gun, but I don't care. You're worried about Donna. And with the threats Melanie's been getting, I'm not taking any chances."

"I'm heading home to see if Donna left a note," Paul said, strain evident in his voice.

"Good. I'll stay in touch," Gage told him.

He tried Melanie's number again. It went straight to voicemail.

Phone on speaker as it rang Sawyer's cell, Gage moved swiftly through the house. He grabbed his Glock from the safe, clipping it to his waistband, and snagged a pair of handcuffs.

"Something's going on with Melanie and her mom," Gage said the minute Sawyer picked up. He laid out the situation as he knew it. He didn't have to convince Sawyer of the urgency.

"I'll call a team together to go up to the mill. That place is derelict—those women shouldn't be anywhere near it," Sawyer said, his words clipped. "But there's something else. Chase Bradford was picked up last night. DUI. We held him in a cell overnight to sober up. Guy was a fucking mess. Wouldn't stop mouthing off."

"What about?"

"Beth Guerrero was the arresting officer. She reports he railed against a whole list of people who'd ruined his life. You topped the list. Called you the 'FBI fuck-hole.'"

Gage rubbed a hand over his jaw. "Did he mention Melanie?"

"Beth said he ranted about 'bitches' screwing him over. Could've meant Mel, his ex, or even Beth."

Gage tossed Pancake a biscuit and grabbed his keys. "He get out?"

"Yeah, this morning. Released on his own recognizance. His old man took him home."

"We need to know where he is," Gage ground out. He didn't know how Bradford could be involved with whatever Melanie was up to, but he didn't trust the bastard.

"I'll call the bank, see if he's at work," Sawyer said. "If he's not, I'll send a unit out to check his house. I'll breathe easier once we've got eyes on him."

"You think he's gone off the deep end and done something stupid?" Gage questioned.

"Don't know. He's a loose cannon, and I don't like that now we've got two women who've gone off-grid. I have Mel's number and I'll authorize a cell tower ping. I want to know where she's at, and I'm not wasting time on a warrant."

"I'll have Paul send you Donna's number. Ping hers too."

"Will do. I'll call back as soon as I get something."

Gage ended the call. He was anxious to get on the road. His head jerked up when Shane's pickup pulled into his driveway. He headed outside, locking the door behind him.

Gage punched the code into his garage door, motioning to Shane when he stepped out of his truck. "You're coming with me."

"I dropped by to get that router you're lending me. What's going on?"

Gage told him as they pulled out onto the street.

"Shit," Shane muttered. "The Lockwood Mill's been abandoned for over a decade. What would make those women go up there?"

Gage shook his head as he used the screen on the dash to call Ashley, Jordy and Olivia's mom.

"Hey, Ash. Can Addy stay with you if Melanie's not there when the bus drops her off?"

"Of course," Ashley said without hesitation. "Is everything okay?"

"I hope so. I'll explain later. Thanks." He hung up, grateful for the help.

He picked up first ring when Sawyer called. "You find anything?"

"Yeah," Sawyer said. 'Cell phone pings show both women heading northeast on Route 22. Donna first, around nine. Melanie followed the same road about forty minutes later."

"That's a road that'll take them to the mill?"

"Yeah," Sawyer replied. "Last pings for both phones are off a tower west of the Lockwood Mill turnoff. Less than three miles out. Signal dropped after that. If their phones are still on, we might get another hit if they come back in range." He paused. "There's been interest in the mill lately."

"Tell me." Gage figured the more information he had, the better he could fit the puzzle pieces together.

"The Lockwood family tried to hang on in the early nineties. Took out loans to modernize but couldn't make their payments.

Ended up losing everything. Interesting note," Sawyer added, "the family still owns the land, including a lake at the end of the valley. Josh Lockwood recently put together financing through Sierra Valley Bank to tear down the mill and build a hunting lodge and cabins."

"Not sure how that fits in, but I'm on my way there. Shane's with me."

"Good. I'll follow soon as I get my team together. In the meantime, I'm sending cruisers to check both Bradfords' homes. I want to know where they are." Sawyer's voice dropped a notch. "Be safe, brother. Storm's blowing in."

***

The flashlight beam caught the dull glint of a gun barrel pointed at Melanie. She froze. Her pulse thundered in her ears at the voice. Not identifiable, but not a man's. A woman's.

"Where's my mother?" she demanded.

"Safe. For now," came the reply, cold and steady.

Melanie's heart stuttered. The figure stepped forward into the flashlight's shaky beam. Her hair was a tangled mess, her blazer torn at the sleeve, dirt smudging one cheek. Rhonda Lockwood.

Melanie reeled. "You?"

Rhonda's eyes glittered. "All your questions. All your poking around. You couldn't leave well enough alone."

Melanie stared at her, stunned. All this time they'd thought Chase the threat. But it had been Rhonda, playing them all.

"Did you hurt her?"

"No more than I had to. She's in there." The gun jerked toward a dark doorway. "That's where you're going. Move it."

Melanie stepped into the room. She felt the gun trained on her back like the tip of an icepick poking her. Her senses were primed for a shot that would send a bullet ripping through her body. Cold as it was, sweat trickled down her spine.

In the dim light, she swept the flashlight beam across a broken desk and an overturned chair, then landed on Donna. She sat slumped against the wall, zip ties binding her wrists and ankles, a filthy rag gagging her mouth. Her eyes were wide and scared.

Ignoring the hissed threat to stop, Melanie rushed forward and tugged the gag free. Donna licked her lips.

"Are you hurt?" Melanie whispered.

"No." Her gaze darted over Melanie's shoulder. "But I don't know how we're getting out of this."

She rose slowly to her feet. Rhonda stood about five feet away.

Melanie forced her breathing to slow and tried to think clearly. She couldn't let fear keep her from acting, from doing what was needed to save her mom and herself. She wished Gage were there. His steady presence anchored her, helped calm her fears so she could function. If she was with him, they could take on any challenge.

"Get on the floor," Rhonda ordered. "Once I've got you tied up, we wait."

Melanie inched forward. She needed to close the distance.

"You don't want to do this. You haven't shot anyone." She gestured with her hand, hoping to draw Rhonda's focus. "There's still time to make a different choice."

Without any change in expression, Rhonda pulled the trigger. The gunshot pierced the air.

Donna screamed and Melanie lurched back, the flashlight flying from her hand and clattering across the floor.

She patted her chest, frantically feeling for an entry wound. No blood. No pain. She hadn't been hit.

She dropped next to her mother. "Are you hurt?"

"No, no. I'm not hurt," Donna breathed.

A click, then light flared from a camping lantern perched on a filing cabinet.

Rhonda voice was frigid. "Next shot won't be a warning. I'd prefer if this went according to plan, but either way, you'll end up dead. Now sit. Back to the wall."

Thunder boomed outside, echoing the gunshot. Melanie couldn't see any way to avoid it, so she sat.

Zip ties were cinched tight, biting into ankles and wrists. Beside her, Donna shifted like she was trying to find a comfortable position.

"If I'm ending up dead anyway," Melanie said, steeling her voice, "at least tell me the truth. Why, Rhonda?"

"Because I have no choice," Rhonda snapped. "Because you won't stop digging. I'm done being afraid."

She no longer looked like the polished banking official. Her eyes glittered with cold disdain, but also desperation.

Had Gage read the message Melanie'd sent? Once he did, she was sure he'd follow her into the mountains, but who knew when that would be?

Hope wavered. It could be hours before help arrived. She'd do what she could to buy time and trust they'd get a break and find some way to escape.

Donna moved again, her elbow bumping Melanie's.

For now, she'd keep Rhonda talking. She was beginning to think her mom was up to something.

Eyes on the gun pointed at her, Melanie asked, "Does this have to do with your son?"

Rhonda gave her a startled look. "You must have talked to Greg. He'll keep his mouth shut if he knows what's good for him."

Melanie's eyes narrowed. "That voicemail, it wasn't my mom, was it?"

Rhonda smirked. "Dylan, my brilliant son, showed me how to do it. He recorded his teacher's voice, then used an AI app to make the voice say whatever he wanted."

Melanie's stomach turned. "How did you record Mom's voice?"

"I went to the bank to open a CD account for Addy," Donna muttered. "The message I got about the dogs being dumped out here must have been fake too."

"Clever, aren't I? And it's surprisingly easy to send a call straight to voicemail without the phone ever ringing. Tech is such a blessing." Rhonda's voice dripped with false cheer. "In fact, I'll play a little snippet for you."

She produced her phone and hit play. A voice eerily like Melanie's told Chase she had new information and to meet her at the mill.

"He won't be able to ignore that. Now we wait for him to get here."

"You plan to kill him too," Melanie said, realization dawning. "He knows Dylan isn't Josh's son."

The other woman shrugged. "He saw me and Greg together that night, and later Greg told him about the baby. But I saw something too. I saw him next to your car, siphoning gas. He left right after you did."

"You kept each other's secrets." Melanie seethed, fury building like a wildfire racing through her veins. Rhonda's disclosure meant Chase Bradford had raped her, an attack that had altered the trajectory of her life. Rhonda had known he'd done it and said nothing. And by not coming forward, Walker McGrath had been wrongfully imprisoned. "You're as contemptible as he is."

Her ire was matched by the force of the gale sweeping down from the mountain. The building groaned with the force of the wind. Water dripped nearby.

"It wasn't personal."

"It sure as hell feels personal to me."

"Everything was working until you came back and started stirring things up. Now Chase has the FBI breathing down his neck at the bank and I'm afraid they'll screw up the financing to build our resort. He's freaking out and drinking too much, and when he drinks, he talks." Rhonda's tone reflected her disgust. "Everything is your fault. If you expose him as your attacker, he's got no reason to keep my secret." Rhonda gestured with the gun. "That's why you're a problem for me."

"You'll be charged for withholding evidence."

"No, I won't. I'm fixing things. All I ever wanted is for my son to have the benefits of the Lockwood name. With Chase out of the way, the FBI won't have a case, and once you're gone, I won't have anything to worry about." She glanced at Donna. "Your mom's merely collateral damage."

"You'll never get away with this." Melanie wanted to believe it. If Gage got her text, they had a chance. She wished she'd taken the time to give him more information.

"Oh, I will. I'll tell you how I'm solving all my problems." Rhonda seemed pleased with herself and wanted to share her plans. She drew a gas can from behind the desk. "Once Chase is in here with you ladies, I'll splash this gas around. Toss a match, and it's done. A little hike to where my car is hidden, and I'm out of here. It could be months before anyone realizes this place burned. Eventually, your cars will be discovered, and your bodies. There'll be an investigation, but it won't go anywhere. There nothing to tie it to me." She looked smug. "I'll be another shocked resident of Sisters, horrified about what happened to those poor people."

Melanie's fantasy of knocking Rhonda to the ground and punching her in the throat was shut down when footsteps echoed from the space outside.

"Melanie? I'm here. What the fuck do you want?" Anger threaded Chase's voice.

"Showtime," Rhonda said in a quiet voice as she moved to the door.

The second she was out of sight Donna spoke in a rush of whispered words. "I've got my pocketknife. I got the blade open but the angle's wrong and I can't cut the ties."

"Oh, my god, Mom. You're amazing." Unexpected hope surged.

Rhonda had bound their hands in front of them. Melanie grasped the knife and cut through the plastic binding Donna's wrists. She grimaced when the ties released. She took the knife and did the same for Melanie and in seconds they were both free.

"Melanie, you go. Get out of here and get help. I did something to my knee, and it hurts bad. I don't think I can walk."

"I'm not leaving you."

"You have to. I'll slow you down. I'll do what I can to protect myself, but you have to go."

"Mom."

"No, you've got Addy. You have to save yourself."

"No." Melanie brushed away a tear.

"Go, Mellie. Addy needs you."

Hating her decision, Melanie forced back tears and handed back the pocketknife. "Okay. But I'm helping you to your feet. Get to the doorway. If Rhonda gets past me, stab her in the neck when she walks in."

With Donna standing, Melanie retrieved her flashlight and crept to peer around the doorway.

Chase stood inside the bay opening. As she watched, Rhonda stepped into the light. He caught sight of her and stumbled back.

"What the hell, Rhonda? What are you doing here? Put that gun down."

Rhonda's laughter hinged on derangement. "You're not running this show, Chase. Not anymore. I'm done taking orders from you."

"Where's Melanie? What's going on?"

Rhonda's back was to her and with Chase's attention focused on the gun, Melanie crept out of the room. Staying low, she followed the wall, using the shadows as cover.

"Melanie's in here. She knows it was you, that you're the rapist."

"Fuck! You told her?" he snarled. "You bitch. I'll destroy whatever reputation you think you have. You think Josh won't divorce you once he knows you lied to him? He'll disown Dylan, and your kid will be left with nothing."

"That won't happen because you won't get the chance to tell him." Rhonda motioned with the gun. "Into that room."

"Fuck no. I'm not going anywhere with you."

Melanie darted behind a large piece of machinery. There had to be a back exit. She tried to remember her walk around the building. Had there been a door at the far end?

A strong gust of wind shook the building. A section of the metal roof lifted before tearing loose and disappearing.

Chase and Rhonda appeared poised in a frozen tableau with rain pelting through the opening. Chase lunged forward and gripped Rhonda's arm. They crashed into the log conveyor, both struggling for the gun. Melanie sucked in a breath as Chase forced Rhonda back toward the teeth of a giant saw blade.

Rhonda twisted and a gunshot rang out. The gun clattered across the floor. Chase and Rhonda both scrambled for it. When they rose, Chase held the gun. Blood ran from a graze across his forehead.

"This changes things, doesn't it, bitch?" he sneered, blood and rain running down his face like tears.

Rhonda bolted up the stairs.

Chase ran to follow her, then faltered when he spied Melanie.

"*You!* This is all because of you." He raised the pistol slowly. "Rhonda was on to something. Better this ends now. I'll take care of you first, then her."

Melanie stepped forward. Anger overcame her fear. "No, Chase. This is all because of *you*. You will rot in hell for what you did to me. You are a despicable excuse for a human being." Words bottled inside for fifteen years tumbled out. "Now everyone will know. No matter what happens here today, it will come out. People will know the deeply reprehensible and shameful thing you did to me, and how you let an innocent man go to prison for your crime. You're a monster."

"That was a long time ago. You deserved what you got for rejecting me. But you should have left it alone, moved on with your life like I did. Now I'm fixing this, and no one will know. I'll get rid of you and Rhonda. I'm a Bradford and people respect that. They'll believe anything I tell them."

"Are you so sure about that?" she asked coolly. "Are you really a Bradford?

Confusion flickered across Chase's face. "What the fuck are you talking about?"

"I got an email this morning from Neil Grafton. Did you know he had an affair with your mother?"

"I don't believe you."

"Believe it," she said, voice low and fierce. "We have a witness. Someone who overheard your mother telling Neil she was pregnant, and that it'd be easy to convince her husband the baby was his."

He shook his head in denial. "You're lying. Even *if* it happened, it doesn't matter."

"It matters, Chase, because she and George were having fertility issues. They were unable to conceive. He probably saw the pregnancy as a miracle. But it wasn't a miracle, was it?"

"You're making this up," he snapped. "I'm a Bradford."

"Then explain why Grafton swapped your name with Walker's as the DNA match. He did it because you're his son. He admitted it in the email."

"You're lying," he roared, fury blazing in his eyes.

Movement near the bay door made them both freeze.

Melanie blinked against a sudden gust of wind, and there he was.

Gage stood silhouetted in the open doorway, the storm roiling behind him. Legs braced, gaze laser focused, he leveled his gun on Chase.

"Drop the weapon, Bradford, or you're a dead man." Gage's voice cracked through the storm like a rifle shot, lethal and unflinching. Rain drenched his coat.

Relief crashed over Melanie in a dizzying wave. Her knees wobbled, but she forced herself to stay upright.

Chase's bravado collapsed. The gun trembled in his grip. Then his expression hardened and she braced herself.

A blur of motion and Shane Keller came in hard, taking Chase to the ground. The gun skittered across the floor. Gage surged forward and retrieved it as Shane wrenched Chase's hands behind his back.

Gage threw him handcuffs. He moved to Melanie as his gaze surveyed the scene.

"Gage, Rhonda is here," Melanie spoke urgently. "She ran up the stairs when Chase got the gun."

Donna, who'd hobbled to the doorway, shouted a warning that drew their attention up.

Rhonda stood on a narrow metal catwalk, hands wrapped around a massive industrial claw suspended by a rusted cable. Her expression was wild with desperation as she fought to move the heavy steel.

"Leave it, Rhonda," Gage shouted. "Come down. It's over."

"Rhonda, think of Dylan." Melanie raised her voice to be heard over the crashing storm. "Please. Come down. Your son needs you."

"I'm protecting my son." Her voice cracked with rage. "I'm doing what I have to."

With a wrenching cry, Rhonda released the heavy claw and let it drop.

It swung in a deadly arc bearing directly toward them.

Shane flattened on the floor beside Chase. Gage grabbed Melanie and pushed them both against the wall as the claw swung perilously close.

Like a massive pendulum, the weight swung back toward the catwalk.

Melanie's heart stopped. Rhonda realized her mistake and tried to scramble back. But it was too late.

The claw crashed into the catwalk, making the entire structure shudder. Rhonda lost her footing and grabbed for a railing that gave under her weight. Her scream echoed through the mill as she toppled over the edge.

Her cry died the instant she was impaled on a jagged saw blade.

CHAPTER NINETEEN

Mel burrowed deep into Gage's arms. They sat curled together on the couch, the soft rhythm of his breathing grounding her. After the fear and chaos of the day, the quiet wrapped around her like a blanket, slowly uncoiling the tightness in her chest.

They'd picked up Addy from Olivia's that evening, offering Ashley and Nick a brief rundown of the day's events. Addy, oblivious to the danger they'd survived, had been excited about the brown eggs she'd gathered from the chicken coop and got to take home.

Someday she'd know the full story, but not yet. Certainly not tonight.

After returning home, Melanie snuggled on the couch with Addy to watch a video while Gage made spaghetti. Not fancy, but it was warm and familiar. Comfort food. After dinner, Addy took her bath, then Gage read her bedtime books. Pancake snored on the soft bed Addy'd made for her, guarding her girl.

Melanie closed her eyes, letting her weight sink into Gage's. They were safe. Together. And for the first time in a long, long while, she could begin to imagine what forever might look like.

"You good?" Gage's arms tightened around her.

"I don't know. It's going to take time before those images fade."

"For me too. I heard that gunshot and I thought I'd lost you." He brought her hand to his mouth and rubbed warm lips over her knuckles. "But you're safe. That's what matters."

Chase had been arrested. After all these years, he would finally face justice. Satisfaction was overshadowed by the shock of Rhonda's death, her role in the cover-up a twist Melanie hadn't seen coming.

"I still can't believe Neil Grafton confessed," she muttered. "That he admitted he was Chase's father and tampered with the DNA results."

"The man's dying," Gage said quietly. "The warden told Sawyer he's only got weeks. Grafton wanted to clear his conscience before the end. Your email pushed him to do that."

She shook her head. "Maybe. I'll never understand how he could justify doing what he did."

Gage exhaled. "He knew what he'd done was wrong. But in his own twisted way, he was principled." He laced his fingers with hers and rested them on his chest. "Sawyer says Franklin and Boner admitted Bradford hired them. Their job was harassment. To scare you into leaving. Good thing you don't scare easy."

Melanie thought she'd been plenty scared. "We figured they were working for someone. Did Chase make the child abuse complaint?"

"He's not admitting anything, but the DA is digging in. I think they'll find the proof." Gage kissed her temple. "Bradford will be in prison a long time. For what he did to you, and for any federal banking charges the FBI might bring."

She shifted to look up at him. "I wonder what will happen with Dylan."

Gage shook his head. "Josh Lockwood came into the station after you left. He's gutted by Rhonda's death. Said he always suspected Dylan wasn't biologically his."

"The signs were there, but it must've hurt."

"Yeah. But he said he didn't care. He loved Rhonda and says Dylan is his son, no matter what. It'll be rough, but they'll get through it." He paused. "It's over, Mel."

She was quiet for a beat. Then, "Yeah, it's really over."

Melanie turned to face him fully, emotion rising in her chest. "Coming back to Sisters…was about hope. I wanted Addy to have a real home. I wanted peace. But I never let go of what happened. Not really. Now that the truth's out it's like I can finally breathe."

Gage brushed her hair from her face, his eyes steady on hers.

"Thank you," she whispered. "For fighting for the truth. For standing with me. For not giving up on me."

"I'd do it all over again," he said, voice rough. "Because you and Addy? You're everything."

Gage's tone changed. Brows drawn together, he stared intently at their entwined fingers. If he wasn't usually so sure of himself, she'd think he was nervous.

"So... Which house do you prefer? Yours or mine?"

She blinked. "What do you mean?"

"If you had to pick one to live in, which would it be?"

Her heart thudded. "Are you suggesting we move in together?"

"I was thinking of something more permanent?"

Permanent? Her eyes widened. "Um, yours is nicer."

He smiled faintly. "We could live here if you and Addy want, but I agree. My place has more room. For dogs. And kids."

Kids? As in plural kids?

She'd held on to her independence with dogged determination, feeling like she'd give up an important part of herself if she let anyone in.

But with Gage, she didn't feel like she was giving up anything. He was protective but not overbearing. They were better together. Stronger.

A smile tugged at her lips. "Mine has a barn with a chicken coop. And a fenced garden."

He chuckled. "True, but those are solvable problems. I've got room across the creek for anything you want to build. If you and Addy wanted to live there. With me."

She met his look, breath stalling. "Gage Landry, did you just ask me to marry you?"

His gaze held hers, deep as the forest at twilight. The air between them pulsed. "I love you, Melanie Brennan. I love Addy. I want to marry you. I want the life we can build together. Think you can love me back?"

There was a flicker of hesitation in his expression betraying his vulnerability.

"I already do." Her voice was soft but sure. "I love you, Gage."

He leaned in, his lips catching hers in a kiss that felt like a promise. She saw it in her mind's eye: quiet Sunday mornings with sleepy toddlers, shouted laughter around a campfire, birthdays and school projects. Growing old together.

"Addy wants us to get married," he murmured, brushing his lips along her jaw. "She brought it up when I tucked her in. Said she and Pancake want us to be a family."

"She loves you."

"The feeling's mutual." He rested his forehead on hers, his voice rough. "I love you so damn much. I want the life we can have together."

Melanie marveled at how much had changed in a few short weeks.

"I love you, Gage. And I'm all in."

***

Gage woke early, the sky outside the windows lightening to gray. He tightened his hold on the woman curled into his side. They'd needed each other during the night, needed the physical release of their love after the nightmare of the day.

Melanie stirred, rubbing her cheek against his chest. "Good morning." She pressed warm lips to the ridge of his pectorals, then his neck.

He let his fingers roam over her bare back as desire stirred. "How early does Addy wake up?"

"Not this early. Why do you ask?" she purred, even as her hand drifted along his ribs, then lower. "How about that? Someone is happy to see me this morning."

"I'm always happy to see you."

He rolled her under him, pushing up her top to take her nipple in his mouth. Her hands threaded through his hair. He gave the same attention to the other breast before he lifted his head and smiled.

"Hello, beautiful."

"Hello, handsome." She stretched languorously beneath his touch.

They made loved slowly, quietly, desire building until both were breathless. He explored with his lips—her chin, the hollow of her throat, the soft skin below her ear, groaning when she wrapped her hand around him, stroking lightly, then with more urgency.

When he slipped inside her, she was wet and ready for him. Her eyes grew heavy as she took him into her body, then they were moving together, slow at first, then more forcefully as control strained against its limits. She broke first, coming with a long, languid moan. He followed, his orgasm making him feel he'd been shot from a bow in a heady rush, arcing free through the air.

He rolled again, this time bringing her on top of him. She laid her head on his chest and Gage held her close to his heart. Over the past weeks, the restlessness and loneliness that had dogged him had evaporated, a contentment like he'd never felt taking their place.

***

With Pancake on a leash, Gage wandered the school carnival. Kids darted by in costume, chasing prizes and sugar highs. Melanie had her eye on a Kalua chocolate cake and dragged Esme to the cake walk. Kids and adults walked away from Antonia's face painting booth with flowers and peace symbols on their cheeks.

When Esme arrived that morning, Melanie had grabbed his arm and said, "This is Gage, my fiancé." Esme whooped, tackled Gage in a hug, then pulled back to wag a finger at him. "Mel's the best person I know. Break her heart and you answer to me."

In the crowd, he heard snippets of conversation about "something big" happening out at the Lockwood mill and news of Rhonda's death and Chase's arrest being passed around. The events of the day before would be big news anywhere, but in a little town like Sisters it reverberated through the community. Rhonda's deceit was over. Chase wouldn't be hurting anyone else.

Gage's relief was bone-deep. Donna had come out of it with a torn meniscus but a good prognosis. Melanie, somehow, was smiling again. And Addy? That little girl was sunshine wrapped in sparkles and grit.

That morning, they'd stopped by Donna and Paul's house to give their engagement news in person. His future mother-in-law had been thrilled, while Paul's reaction was more measured. Gage figured, like Esme, Paul would take him out if he hurt Melanie.

Addy and Isla ran to him, hands clasped. They both shone with princess costumes and glittery cheeks.

"Gage, can we play the ping-pong ball game over there?"

"Sure." They looked at him expectantly. Catching on, he asked, "Do you have tickets?"

"No, but you can get us more." Addy gave him her dimpled smile and Isla clasped her hands under her chin and batted her eyelashes. Gage blinked. Where did girls learn to do that?

"You're dangerous," he muttered, handing them a ten-dollar bill. He was so screwed but in the best way possible.

The girls shouted their thanks and raced off.

"Rookie mistake." Melanie joined him, grinning, her dimples flashing.

"They're con artists," Gage growled. "Tiny, sparkly grifters."

Esme laughed. "Welcome to parenthood."

He glanced between the two women. "Where's the cake?"

"We can pick it up when we leave," Melanie said.

The girls ran back, triumphant, each cradling a plastic bag filled with sloshing water and darting goldfish.

"We got goldfish." Addy beamed. "They're alive and everything. The man felt sorry for us because we're bad throwers and kept missing. He gave us extra."

"You've got to be kidding," Esme groaned. "A fish requires a tank and food and upkeep. How can they give kids fish at a carnival?"

"The man said we had to ask an adult first and Gage said we could," Addy said helpfully.

"What? I didn't—" Gage sputtered, and Melanie patted his arm.

"You've got a lot to learn," she said, amused. "Always read the fine print."

A woman approached, one hand resting firmly on a boy's shoulder.

"That's Liam," Addy whispered. She gripped Pancake's collar.

The kid looked normal, not like a miniature serial killer.

"Hi, I'm Kerry, Liam's mom. I'm sorry for the upset my son has caused your family." She nudged her boy forward. "Liam has something to say."

Liam scuffed the toe of his sneaker in the grass, then looked up at Addy, cheeks red. "I'm sorry for being mean. I won't do it anymore."

Addy studied him. "Why were you mean?"

"I dunno."

Addy nodded. "Okay. Do you want to pet Pancake? Being mean makes your heart sick. Pancake makes it better."

Gage's chest tightened. That kid didn't know it, but Addy had given him a lifeline. He dropped to his knees, and Pancake leaned into him. A moment later, Liam's face was buried in her soft fur. Pancake rolled to her back, and Isla and Addy joined in, rubbing the dog's belly while his dog soaked up every ounce of attention.

Kerry turned to Melanie. 'We're getting him into counseling. I just... I'm sorry."

Melanie's voice was soft. "It means a lot that you brought him. That couldn't have been easy."

She glanced at Esme, who nodded. "Would Liam like to go trick-or-treating with us tonight? We're going around with the neighbor kids and you're both welcome."

Kerry blinked, surprised. "I'll ask Liam if he wants to. Thank you."

They exchanged numbers, gave hugs, and Liam and his mom walked away. How did women forgive and forget so easily? Gage guessed that's where Addy's big heart came from.

"Time to go, girls."

There were groans of protest. Gage tugged on the leash, but Pancake didn't budge. "C'mon, Pancake. Let's go."

Pancake ignored him and seemed to relax farther into the grass. Addy handed him the fish and took the leash. "Here, Dad. I'll handle Pancake."

Gage froze. Dad? He liked the sound of that.

She whispered in Pancake's ear. The dog rolled to her feet like she'd been given a command from royalty.

Melanie reached up and kissed Gage's cheek, eyes shining. "We're already a family," she whispered.

They were.

And life couldn't be sweeter.

EPILOGUE

Melanie bumped the car door with her hip, her hands weighed down with heavy bags. Gage opened the back door to let out Pancake and then Addy from her car seat before taking the bags from Melanie.

Donna and Paul pulled up behind them to add to the vehicles lining the gravel driveway cf the big house at Cider Mill Farm. Paul retrieved a bowl covered in foil from the backseat while Donna caught up to Melanie, her limp barely noticeable.

She beamed and gave her daughter a hug. "Congratulations, my girl."

"Thanks, Mom." Melanie met Gage's warm gaze. "We're happy. We haven't said anything yet. I hope everyone won't be upset we didn't have a big wedding."

"You'll make your announcement when you're ready, and don't worry about folks. You did what's right for you."

Donna pulled Gage into a hug, then Addy. "I'm so happy for you all."

"Look, Nana." Addy held up a rose gold charm in the shape of a sun on a dainty chain around her neck. "Dad gave this to me when we got familied."

"How beautiful." Donna beamed at Gage before returning her attention to her granddaughter. "You'll have to explain 'familied.'"

"Mom and Dad got married and we all got familied. Even Pancake was there 'cause she's a part of our family." Barking dogs drew her attention. "Pancake found Shiloh and Bud," she exclaimed and raced off to play with the dogs.

"'Familied.' If that don't beat all." Paul shook his head. "That girl is all heart."

Smiling, Melanie said, "Let's go. I've got all this food for the charcuterie, and I want to put it out so people can start nibbling."

They trooped up the porch steps. Sawyer opened the front door with JT on his hip, and they walked into a house that smelled gloriously of Thanksgiving.

***

Melanie sat beside Gage at the crowded table, their shoulders bumping, Addy on her other side. So much had changed for her and Addy over the past year. Returning to Sisters had been an act of hope that she and her daughter could find the home and community missing from their lives. That promise had been fulfilled beyond her wildest dreams.

Her husband cherished her, their daughter was thriving, and they'd been absorbed into a big, sprawling family.

Everyone had brought something for the feast. Roast turkey on an heirloom platter, sweet potatoes in a cast-iron pot, baskets of golden rolls next to pies cooling on wooden boards. Candles glowed in Mason jars as the sky deepened to indigo outside the kitchen window.

They were all there, seated around the table. The sisters and their husbands, Delaney with Walker, Emery and Shane, Cam and Sawyer. Their children in high chairs, all born during a wild storm a year before.

Clara looked serene as she bent her head, listening as Walker murmured to her. Melanie thought Clara must feel utterly contented that her endeavor to unite her granddaughters had succeeded so beautifully.

Owen's arm draped across Keeley's back, her hand resting on the swell of her belly.

Sawyer tapped his glass and the conversation quieted. "Delaney's got something to say."

Delaney rose and cleared her throat. She fanned her face with her hands. "I promised myself I wouldn't cry, so here goes." She breathed deep and when she began, her voice strengthened as she spoke. "Thank you all for coming here for Thanksgiving," she sniffled. "Some of us are related by blood, some by bonds of friendship that run as deep as blood. We've been through so much these past few years, but those trials only strengthened us and brought us together to this place where we all belong."

Addy grinned, and Violet banged on her high chair tray.

"Thanksgiving means more than appreciating the plentiful food in front of us, and boy is there a lot of food. Y'all better eat up." That drew a few chuckles. "It means being grateful for each other. I'm so happy our whole family is gathered here on this day."

Walker rose to stand beside her. He held up his glass. "I propose a toast to us."

A chorus of voices responded, "To us."

Around the table, glasses were raised and clinked together.

Gage took Melanie's hand in his and cleared his throat. "I have something to add. We... Mel, Addy, me, Pancake, we took a few days in Reno and now it's official, we're married. Or as Addy says—"

"We're familied," Addy crowed.

With congratulations echoing around the table, Gage bent to kiss Melanie.

Platters and bowls were passed hand to hand, pitchers tipped to fill glasses, conversation ebbed and flowed. Fussy babies were moved to laps, spilled milk was mopped up, and the love of family glowed with the promise of life.

Dear Readers,

Thank you for joining me on the journey through Payback Mountain. *Forbidden Secrets* brings the sisters' stories full circle, and I'm so grateful you came along for every twist, turn, and happily-ever-after. I'd love to keep sharing new adventures with you – please join my newsletter so you don't miss what's next.

Not quite ready to leave Payback Mountain? Join my newsletter and you'll receive a *free Forbidden Secrets* bonus epilogue. **Bonus Epilogue with Newsletter Signup**

Already part of my reader family? Click here to read the bonus epilogue – no signup needed. **Bonus Epilogue for Subscribers**

Discover the full backstory on all your favorite Payback Mountain characters by starting at the beginning with *Dangerous Secrets*.

Looking for more of my protector romances? Want to explore my backlist? Check out my website, sign up for my newsletter, and follow me on social media and you'll get all the news about new releases as well as backlist sales.

But best of all, these are all ways I can connect with you. Go ahead and click a link—I can't wait to hear from you.

Check out my Website

I'd love for you to follow me:

Instagram
TikTok
Facebook
BookBub
Goodreads

About the Author

Murderer? Stalker? Mayhem? Are bad guys coming to get her? Nope, Diane is just a retired schoolteacher with a laptop. She's been married for decades. Decades! She walks Finn every morning (mostly). She FaceTimes with her grandkids. The most excitement she's had lately is a bumpy ride on a plane, and that's not the fun kind of excitement. But her heroines? They have all the thrills. Scary things happen to them. Hot, compelling men find them fascinating. And they always find their HEA.

An avid reader for as long as she can remember, Diane has always favored stories with strong female characters who go on adventures and can think themselves out of the most dangerous situations. It's no surprise that those are the kinds of books she enjoys writing.

Diane's love of the outdoors is reflected in her books. She was born and raised in Southern California, and family vacations meant camping in locations ranging from Big Sur to Death Valley to Zion. Two of her series are set in fictional towns in her happy place, California's Sierra Nevada Mountains.

Her love of travel took her to Sweden as an exchange student when she was sixteen and backpacking around Great Britain (after a week in Paris) while in college. She and her husband have enjoyed pulling their little trailer to the National Parks, including Yosemite, Yellowstone, and Pinnacles.

USA Today Bestselling author, and winner of the National Readers' Choice Award in Romantic Suspense, Diane retired from a career teaching high school history. She now has all the time in the world for writing, gardening, and travel. That's the theory, anyway. She is a member of the Orange County Romance Writers.

***Note to readers: Looking for High Sierras, Book 4? *Burnover*, High Sierras Book 4, is a novella you can find included with *Already Gone,* Book 3.

What Readers Are Saying About
USA TODAY BESTSELLING AUTHOR
DIANE BENEFIEL'S STORIES

Solitary Man

NATIONAL READERS' CHOICE AWARD
WINNING NOVEL

"I am in love with this story. I devoured this book and didn't want it to end. The chemistry between the characters and the plot kept me wanting to read late into the night. This is my first read from Diane Benefiel but definitely not my last. I can't wait to read more from this amazing author. Thank you, Diane Benefiel, for getting me hooked on your books!" ~ CJ's Book Corner

PAYBACK MOUNTAIN SERIES

Dangerous Secrets

"I couldn't resist this compelling tale of a wrongly convicted man and the woman who never stopped loving him." ~ Sue's Reviews

Honest Secrets

"I really enjoyed this book and the chemistry between Emery and Shane is phenomenal. Would love to see more of these books, to bring the other couples in Sisters together." ~Kathy Bateman

Secret Lies

"The book was excellent. Just the right amount of suspense and angst between the two characters. I loved the book and while it was

the first time I've read this author, I am now sold on her books. I'll
read all of her books." ~PR

Guarded Secrets

*"Guarded Secrets is a fantastic book! Keeley and Owen have
incredible chemistry, and their dynamic made for a fun read. I
enjoyed the blend of romance, humor, and a touch of mystery
throughout the story. The descriptions of the town and surrounding
areas bring the book to life. Diane Benefiel is one of my favorite
authors because of her talent for developing compelling characters
and engaging storylines. Her writing style is truly wonderful. I'm
always excited to start one of her books, and Guarded Secrets didn't
disappoint."* ~Kara W.

THE JAMESONS U.S. MARSHALS SERIES

Hidden Betrayal

*"An exciting, romantic read with a sexy hero and a determined
heroine who is hell-bent on doing things her own way. The romance
heats up as the plot thickens. Linc and Mikayla need to work
together to survive, but along the way, the sparks start flying. You
need to read this!"* ~Danube Eichinger

Hidden Judgment

*"Don't buy this book if you want to get anything done!! I couldn't
put it down! I laughed, I cried, I felt all the emotions that a
brilliantly written romance novel brings. I am anxiously awaiting the
third novel in the series!"* ~Sandy Morris

Hidden Loyalty

*"5 EXPLOSIVE STARS!! This book was explosive and had me
flipping pages. I love law enforcement and this one was perfect...*

Seth was hot and bossy, Bella kept him on his toes. This was my first book by this author and it will not be my last." ~Rhonda

HIGH SIERRAS SERIES

Flash Point

"Diane Benefiel takes us on a story filled with mystery, suspense, and action as we try to solve what is going on in the small town of Hangman's Loss. Flash Point is a story that will have you flipping the pages and wondering who is behind the attacks against Hangman's newest resident and why." ~ Sarah Reads

Dead Giveaway

*"I loved this second book in the High Sierras series. This is a story of two people who are attracted to each other, but reconnecting under the worst of circumstances. I discovered Ms. Benefiel's books and have loved the careful way she draws you into the story with characters that make you feel as if you are reading about friends. I am really looking forward to the next High Sierras book, **Already Gone**."* ~paytonpuppy

Already Gone

"This series has only gotten better and better! Seriously, there's something that really speaks to my heart about Maddy and Logan, and Hangman's Loss FEELS like a small California town tucked away in the Sierras. They're such a power couple! I read this book in just a couple of days—totally sucked me in. It's that perfect blend of fun, sizzle, and suspense! I just want to live in Maddy's life forever but since I can't—I can't wait for the next book!" ~Katharine Montgomery

Burnover in Rescued Anthology

"Sweet, sexy stories featuring furbabies and helping to save lives, it's a win win for all." ~Kara's Books

Deadly Purpose

"This book took me by surprise. I didn't expect to get so caught up in this book that my whole day was spent captured in its pages. It has been a long time since I couldn't put a book down but Deadly Purpose did this to me. I loved every page." ~WildfireJane

Clear Intent

"I'd been waiting on this one awhile!! I truly loved the story! I laughed, cried and got so frustrated I couldn't see straight! I'm now hoping there will be more from Hangman's Loss, I don't want to see this series end! Thank you for a very wonderful getaway!! I highly recommend this complete series!!!! Wow! Just Wow!!" ~Linda Helms

Break Away

"Oh man did I love this book. It was well written and has a great storyline. It's emotional and has a nice amount of suspense. I really need to go back and read the first six books in the series. Now saying that, this book definitely reads as a standalone. I haven't read the first six books, but I never felt lost or like I am missing anything with this story. You will obviously have some small spoilers since the books are all connected." ~CrazyBookLover

www.BOROUGHSPUBLISHINGGROUP.com

If you enjoyed this book, please write a review. Our authors appreciate the feedback, and it helps future readers find books they love. We welcome your comments and invite you to send them to info@boroughspublishinggroup.com.

Follow us on TikTok and Instagram, and be sure to sign up for our newsletter for surprises and new releases from your favorite authors.

Are you an aspiring writer? Check out www.boroughspublishinggroup.com/submit and see if we can help you make your dreams come true.

Love podcasts? Enjoy ours at
https://boroughspublishinggroup.com/podcast

www.ingramcontent.com/pod-product-compliance
Lightning Source LLC
Chambersburg PA
CBHW031958190626
46808CB00018B/1884